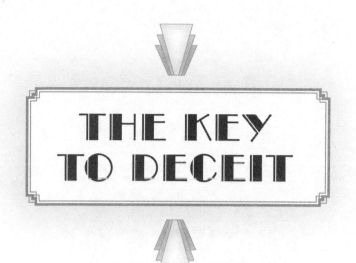

THE KEY
TO DECEIT

ALSO BY ASHLEY WEAVER

THE ELECTRA McDONNELL NOVELS

A Peculiar Combination

THE AMORY AMES MYSTERIES

Murder at the Brightwell

Death Wears a Mask

A Most Novel Revenge

Intrigue in Capri (ebook short)

The Essence of Malice

An Act of Villainy

A Dangerous Engagement

A Deception at Thornecrest

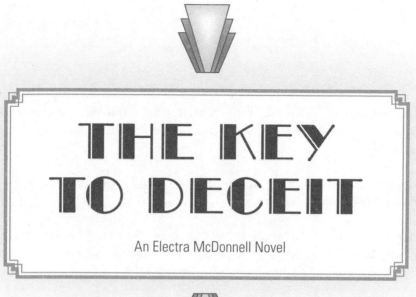

THE KEY
TO DECEIT

An Electra McDonnell Novel

ASHLEY WEAVER

MINOTAUR
BOOKS
NEW YORK

First published in the United States by Minotaur Books, an imprint of St. Martin's Publishing Group

THE KEY TO DECEIT. Copyright © 2022 by Ashley Weaver. All rights reserved. Printed in the United States of America. For information, address St. Martin's Publishing Group, 120 Broadway, New York, NY 10271.

www.minotaurbooks.com

Designed by Omar Chapa

Library of Congress Cataloging-in-Publication Data

Names: Weaver, Ashley, author.
Title: The key to deceit / Ashley Weaver.
Description: First Edition. | New York : Minotaur Books, 2022. |
    Series: Electra McDonnell series ; 2
Identifiers: LCCN 2022000894 | ISBN 9781250780508 (hardcover) |
    ISBN 9781250780515 (ebook)
Subjects: LCGFT: Novellas.
Classification: LCC PS3623.E3828 K49 2022 | DDC 813/.6—dc23
LC record available at https://lccn.loc.gov/2022000894

Our books may be purchased in bulk for promotional, educational, or business use. Please contact your local bookseller or the Macmillan Corporate and Premium Sales Department at 1-800-221-7945, extension 5442, or by email at MacmillanSpecialMarkets@macmillan.com.

First Edition: 2022

10   9   8   7   6   5   4   3   2   1

For my nephew, Anders Wilder Lea.
Auntie loves you, Binky!

THE KEY TO DECEIT

CHAPTER ONE

LONDON
31 AUGUST 1940

It's often a man's mouth that breaks his nose, my uncle Mick was fond of saying, and the bloke in front of me was doing his best to test the theory. His mouth was just about thirty seconds from earning him a fist to the conk.

"War or no war," he was saying, "I don't want a woman mucking things up."

I was trying hard to keep my temper down. After all, I was here on behalf of my uncle, a well-respected locksmith. He was out of town on another job, and he wouldn't be best pleased to return home and find that I'd walloped a paying customer. Though, in my defense, this fellow didn't seem at all likely to pay.

Things had seemed simple enough when I took the telephone call that morning. It was an unchallenging task—changing a few locks on the doors at Atkinson's Automobile Garage—and with the war on, we needed all the work we could get. I'd accepted the job, but when I'd turned up, tool kit in hand, Atkinson, the burly bounder in stained coveralls standing before me, had bridled at leaving his precious locks in the hands of a woman. We'd been going round in circles for ten minutes at this point, and my patience was wearing thin.

"Do you want these locks changed or don't you?" I asked tersely.

"Not by a bit of skirt, love," he said, gesturing toward the door to the office and the storage room that adjoined it. "I've got confidential records and expensive, hard-to-get parts in there that need to be kept safe. I can't take a chance on an improperly installed lock."

He was already taking a chance; the locks on both the office door and the storage room were flimsy pin-tumbler locks. For a moment I allowed myself the luxury of imagining returning to this garage in the dead of night. It wouldn't take more than a pick, a tension tool, and thirty seconds to open these doors. I could be in and out in a few minutes with his precious hard-to-get parts . . .

"You won't find better locksmiths in London than the McDonnells," I said, repressing my criminal instincts. Though, to tell the truth, a perfectly mediocre locksmith could have done just as well. It would be a simple task to remove the old locks and replace them with more secure Yale locks. I could have had a good start on the job by now if he hadn't been giving me a lot of poppycock.

Atkinson crossed his brawny arms over his chest. "I asked for Mick McDonnell, and I'll have Mick McDonnell or take my business elsewhere."

A lesser locksmith, a locksmith who didn't have stubborn McDonnell blood coursing through the veins, might have given up at this point. But if Uncle Mick had taught me anything it was that sometimes a fist was the answer, but, more often than not, charm, wits, and skill worked better.

I smoothed my expression and made my voice calm and reasonable. "Well, you've got Ellie McDonnell, and I'm perfectly capable of doing this job. I know as much about locks as you do about that Phantom." I nodded toward the Rolls-Royce parked inside one of the open garage doors.

He glanced over his shoulder. "So you think you know cars, then, too, do you?"

"A bit." My cousin Colm had always tinkered with machines growing up. He was a mechanic for the RAF now, but, in the years before the war, many was the hour I'd sat by his side as he mended and rebuilt various engines. I'd absorbed quite a bit of information in those sessions.

Atkinson snorted, and my ire rose once again.

I couldn't stop myself from giving him a haughty glare. "Contrary to what you believe, it is possible for women to know about things outside of the kitchen."

His eyes narrowed at my sarcasm. "Right. Tell you what, girlie. If you can name me even one part inside that engine, I'll let you change my locks."

"Do I have your word on that?"

"Sure," he said with a smirk, clearly not considering it much of a risk.

I looked at the car, recalling the things Colm had gone on about as he'd discussed the mechanics of luxury cars we'd never be able to afford.

"It's a Phantom III?" I asked.

I saw the surprise flash across his face before he covered it and gave a short nod. "A 'thirty-eight."

Luckily for me, the Phantom III was one of the cars Colm had talked about endlessly. It was that recognition that had drawn my attention to the beauty in the garage in the first place. Even more luckily, I had a memory like a sponge.

"Then it has a V-12, pushrod engine," I said. "A dual ignition system, and coil spring front suspension."

Atkinson was staring at me, his mouth hanging open just a bit.

"And there's an overdrive gearbox in the 'thirty-eight," I added for good measure.

His face went dark red, and I wondered if he was going to

renege on his promise to give me the job and send me off with a few choice words. Then, to my surprise, he laughed, a deep, chortling laugh, straight from his stomach.

"You didn't learn that in a kitchen," he said at last, pulling an oil-stained handkerchief from his pocket and rubbing it across his face.

"No, and I didn't learn locksmithing there either. I know what I'm doing."

He scratched his blond head and gave a short nod. "You can start on the office door," he said, jerking his thumb in that direction.

I gave an equally short nod in return and moved past him to get to work.

He'd made two miscalculations this morning. The first thing to know about the McDonnells was that there was always more to us than met the eye; the second was that you should never bet against us.

I arrived home a few hours later, disheveled and dirty. I'd pinned my black hair up atop my head, a kerchief tied around it to keep stray strands out of my face, but a few of my natural curls had begun to escape and spring out in places. I was dusty and oily from the garage. There were dark streaks on my clothes, my hands, and, I was sure, my face.

So I was not at what you might call peak appearance as I entered my uncle's house.

"Nacy!" I called. "I'm back."

Nacy Dean, the woman who had raised me and looked over the McDonnell brood like a mother hen since we were children, was still a live-in housekeeper to my uncle. While I now had a small flat of my own behind the house, I usually gave her an account of my comings and goings, as I had since I was an adolescent.

I was especially eager to tell her how I'd put the mechanic in his place. By the time I'd left the garage, Atkinson had been as pleased as punch with the new locks, and there had been no more mention of how a woman couldn't do a proper locksmithing job. I'd even been given a firm handshake at the close of the deal.

It had been almost as satisfying as walloping him on the nose might have been.

There was no answering call from Nacy, and I thought she might be in the kitchen. I went in that direction, through the sitting room off the small entrance hall, and stopped short when I saw the figure standing there.

"Good afternoon, Miss McDonnell," he said.

"Major Ramsey," I replied. My hand moved automatically to push a stray curl behind my ear in a completely useless attempt to tidy myself up a bit.

The major, who worked in the intelligence service in a capacity that had yet to be fully explained, had recruited my uncle and me, so to speak, earlier that month. We had been caught breaking into a safe, and the major had given us the choice between jail or doing a bit of safecracking for king and country. The decision had been an easy one, and it had led to an adventure that had been on my mind constantly over the past few weeks, one I would be unlikely to forget for the rest of my life.

Though the major had said he might be in need of our services in the future, I hadn't really expected to see him again so soon. And I certainly had not expected him to show up in the parlor unannounced when I was covered in grime from a job. Then again, the major had the charming habit of catching me at my worst.

He, meanwhile, was standing there, formal and elegant in his spotless uniform, his service cap tucked under one arm. It seemed to me that he had grown even more starched in the weeks since I had seen him; his general bearing would not have been amiss in the King's Guard. Which made my disheveled appearance all the more marked in contrast.

"I've come looking for your uncle," he said, politely ignoring my general disarray. "Mrs. Dean told me he was out but that I might wait here to speak to you."

I noticed the empty teacup on the table beside the chair the major had obviously just vacated.

Nacy had a sweet spot for the major. I was sure she had been only too glad to see him show up on her doorstep and to provide him with a cup of tea and a bit of company while he waited for me to return.

"Where is Nacy?" I asked, half expecting her to suddenly appear with a plateful of fresh scones.

"I believe she went to the market."

Of course. The local grocer put out fresh deliveries this time of day, and Nacy was always sure to make the most of our ration coupons.

Not only that, she'd have wanted me to find the major here alone. She had the ridiculous notion that I might be romantically interested in him. Which I certainly was not. Pretty is as pretty does, and the major never did things prettily.

I pushed these thoughts from my mind and focused on trying not to smooth out my clothes or check the mirror on the wall across the room to see how dirty my face was.

Instead, I gave him a polite smile. "What can I do for you, Major?"

"I have a matter I wish to discuss with you. Do you have a moment?"

"Of course."

There was no special warmth in his tone, no hint of fond remembrance of the adventure we had been through together. He was as cool and formal as if we hadn't just worked together to save the country from Nazi spies.

Well, what had I expected? The major wasn't the sentimental sort. He certainly hadn't sought me out because he missed me. If there was one thing I knew about Major Ramsey, it was that he was a man who was very devoted to his work. It was this superior devotion that made him such an asset to his country.

He was, in fact, annoyingly superior in so many ways. Superior intelligence, superior skills, superior good looks. It was a trial, at times, to put up with the man.

"Please, sit down," I said, motioning to the seat behind him.

He hesitated. I realized he didn't know if I would sit in my dirty clothes, and he was far too gently bred to take a seat while I stood.

To ease his mind, I lowered myself onto the edge of a wooden chair that would be easy enough to clean. I crossed the cleaner of my trousered legs over the dirtier one and folded my hands on my lap in such a way that the oil-stained nails weren't as noticeable.

I studied him while he resumed his seat. He looked well, though I had seen firsthand that he worked at rather a breakneck pace and often seemed to forgo rest. Perhaps things had been less hectic since the time we had worked together, but I very much doubted it.

The tan he'd had when I'd last seen him, a remnant from his time stationed in North Africa before our adventure, had faded. Other than that, there was little difference. He was very tall and solidly built, filling out his uniform with the sort of straight-backed perfection that a tin soldier might aspire to. His blond hair was cut short, and his eyes, an unusual shade of twilight blue, were cool and assessing as they settled on me.

"You've been staying out of trouble." It wasn't a question. The major hadn't been above having me watched before, so I wouldn't be surprised to know he'd had someone checking up on me. Of course, I couldn't really blame him. I didn't suppose his superiors would look kindly on us running amok after we'd aligned ourselves with their operation.

"We've been trying to keep ourselves busy."

"I'm glad to hear it," he said, then promptly brought the subject

back around to the purpose of his visit. "As I said, I came here looking for your uncle."

"Yes, he's gone up to Yorkshire," I said lightly. "He had a job
there, converting some uppity lord's country house cellar into a
place to safely stash the goods he evacuated from Mayfair."

I remembered halfway through the sentence that Major Ramsey's uncle was an earl, but it didn't stop me from finishing the
thought.

Major Ramsey chose to ignore my slight on the nobility. "Is there
any way you might get in touch with him?"

I didn't know why, but I felt both disappointed and annoyed
that he'd wanted to speak with me only as a means to get to Uncle
Mick.

"I don't know that I can," I said honestly. "The place is very
remote, and he said it wasn't likely we'd hear anything from him
until the beginning of next week."

I could tell at once this wasn't the news he'd been hoping to
hear. It was never easy to know what Major Ramsey was feeling,
except for those rare instances when his temper was rising, but he
didn't take much care concealing the expression of impatience that
crossed his features.

"There's something rather urgent that's come up." He looked
at me as though he expected me to do something about it. He was
used to people hopping to whenever he snapped his fingers, and he
always seemed to forget that I wasn't much of a hopper.

I raised my eyebrows slightly. "I suppose you could drive up to
Yorkshire and make the round of country houses searching for him
if you're desperate."

His eyes narrowed ever so slightly at my flippancy. But, really, I
didn't know the particulars of where Uncle Mick was, so there was
no use in pretending I did.

The major appeared to consider something for a moment; I
waited. I knew him well enough to know that he was reformulating

his plans based on new information, moving on to some less desirable Plan B. I also knew he was probably trying to decide whether or not I might be part of this plan.

At last, he made up his mind, though he didn't appear in the least bit happy about it. "Perhaps you may be able to help me instead."

"Oh?" I said sweetly in the face of his unenthusiasm. "I'm all ears."

"I was alerted last night that a young woman's body was found floating in the Thames."

That was unfortunate, of course, but I wondered in what way Uncle Mick or I could possibly be of help in this situation. Bodies were dragged out of the Thames all the time for any number of reasons.

His next words, however, caught my attention.

"There is a . . . device locked on her wrist. A bracelet. Of sorts."

"And you need it removed."

"Yes."

"Can't it be broken off?" I asked.

"It could, as a last resort. But I was hoping to have it remain intact, with as little damage as possible. We've tried already to remove it without success."

"I see." I considered this for a moment. "And are you certain that this 'device,' as you call it, is something . . . relevant to your work? It might just be a young woman who died under strange circumstances that have nothing whatsoever to do with the war."

"That's possible," he said. "But unlikely."

Yes, it did seem unlikely. Anything odd that happened these days was likely to hold some significance. What was more, I had a feeling that whatever this mysterious device was, the major recognized that significance.

"Where was the body found?" I asked.

He didn't answer immediately. He was always careful to

consider before he spoke, making sure whatever he had to say would not reveal more than he intended. It was, no doubt, a useful trait in a man in the intelligence service, but, personally, I found it very irritating.

Finally, he spoke. "In the East End, though we haven't been able to determine yet if that's where she was killed."

The careful answer made it clear there was something he wasn't willing to tell me at present, so I moved on to my next question. "Do you know who she is?"

"No. She wasn't carrying any documents. Or, if she was, they are somewhere in the Thames."

"What about fingerprints?"

"We have people working on that now and have also been canvassing the area in case anyone saw something, but thus far we haven't had any success along either of those lines. The cuff is our only lead at present. I realize this isn't the most pleasant of tasks, which was one of the reasons I was seeking your uncle. But it seems to me that we don't have much choice." He fastened me in his lavender gaze. "Do you suppose that you could have a look at the lock, Miss McDonnell?"

I spoke the words before I could think better of it. "Yes, of course."

CHAPTER TWO

There would be plenty of time to regret my decision on the way to the mortuary. I wasn't entirely sure why I had agreed to do what would certainly be an unpleasant task. I couldn't be the only locksmith in London capable of removing a bracelet from the dead woman's wrist.

Deep down, however, I knew the reason. Two reasons, really.

The first was that, like most Londoners, I was willing to do whatever I could to help the British cause. My two cousins, who had been raised practically as my brothers, were away doing their bit, Colm in the RAF and Toby in the army. We hadn't heard from Toby since the Battle of Dunkirk, nor had there been any official word of what had happened to him. At this point, the best we could hope for was that he was in a German stalag somewhere, waiting to come home to us.

If my cousins were risking their lives in this war, the least I could do was remove this bracelet, or whatever it was, if the major thought it might provide some sort of important information.

There was also the second, less noble motivation. I had to admit that a part of me had reveled in the excitement and danger of our previous mission. I had missed that feeling during the past few weeks of dull locksmithing jobs. Thieving had had its own kind of thrill, but there was something even more exhilarating in doing a dangerous job for a noble cause.

I would die before I admitted it to him, but the truth was some part of me had been hoping the major would turn up with a need for our services. This wasn't exactly what I'd had in mind, but I would take what I could get.

"Will you give me five minutes to clean up?" I asked the major.

He ran his eyes over me—probably thinking it would take more than five minutes for me to make myself presentable—and gave a short nod. "I'll be in the car."

I hurried to my flat, where I scrubbed my face and hands and changed into a fresh blouse and a tweed skirt. Then I pulled the kerchief and pins from my hair, running a comb through it until it was halfway under control.

In less than five minutes, I joined Major Ramsey in the big government car parked in front of the house.

I was greeted warmly by Jakub, the major's driver. We'd become acquainted during my last adventure with the major. Jakub and his wife had fled Poland before the Nazi invasion, and their son, a soldier in the Polish army, had been missing in action.

"Any word of your son?" I asked him.

He shook his head. "Not yet, miss. But soon. I think we shall hear very soon."

"Yes, of course. There's no word of my cousin either. But we are still hoping for the best."

There wasn't much more to be said of the matter. This war was quickly teaching me that sometimes the best one could do was carry on and hope for the best.

We rode along in silence after that. The major was a taciturn sort of man in the best of conditions, and today he was positively grim.

I was certain there was more to all of this than he was telling me. A dead woman, wearing a mysterious bracelet or not, would

THE KEY TO DECEIT

not ordinarily be enough to call in military intelligence. So what was it that had caught his attention about this woman's death? I wondered if I would discover it upon seeing the body.

We arrived at the hospital, entering through a side door, and I followed the major along a long hall, down a flight of stairs, and through a set of double doors into the mortuary. It was a large room with rows of steel tables, an oversize sink, and cupboards and shelves filled with bottles and medical instruments. It was brightly lit and cool. There was the unpleasant scent of death and chemicals in the still air, and I fought the urge to shudder.

I followed the major farther into the room, toward where a figure was standing, his back to us, in an even brighter circle of light that was shining down from an overhead light onto the table before him.

"Dr. Barker," the major said.

A man turned. I realized with a start that there was a body lying on the table near him. The sheet covering the body was pulled back to the waist, a large, white arm poking out, nautical tattoos visible against the stark skin. This was a man, not a woman, so it was not the body we had come to see. It was, nevertheless, a bleak reminder of what this place was.

"Ah. Ramsey," the doctor said. He didn't sound particularly pleased to see the major. This didn't entirely surprise me, because Major Ramsey was the sort of chap who went around bending people to his will without caring a jot if they liked him or not as long as they did what he said.

"I've brought along the locksmith," the major replied in an equally cool tone. It seemed he wasn't any fonder of the doctor than the doctor was of him.

The doctor glanced at me, his steely gray eyes sweeping over me in an assessing way. I did the same to him. He was a tall, thin man with the vague air of a scientist. I'd seen it before; Dr. Specs O'Malley, a professor friend of my uncle's, often had the same distracted manner, as though half his brain was always occupied with calculations and could not be bothered with anything else.

Dr. Barker gave me a short nod, apparently deeming me good enough for the task. I felt vaguely gratified that he had not commented on my being a woman in a man's profession as the garage mechanic had this morning.

"This way," he said brusquely.

He led us to another table, a little bit farther into the room, past two other large steel tables that were mercifully unoccupied. It took an effort to keep from slowing my steps as we moved closer to the task at hand. I fancied myself capable of adapting to most situations, but the morgue isn't the type of place a girl wants to adapt to.

At last, Dr. Barker stopped in front of a table and reached up to turn on the light above it.

There was a form lying on the table, draped with a sheet, and I felt a growing sense of dread. My hands were cold.

I had seen dead bodies, of course. The last time had been a few weeks before on a beach outside of Torquay at the culmination of my previous adventure with the major. But there was something cold about this place, bodies lined up to be examined like scientific specimens; the grim, sterile atmosphere was enough to give me the creeps. We Irish are no strangers to the laying out of the dead, but this was very different. I didn't like the way this room felt.

The major glanced at me, and I forced myself to look him in the eye without blinking. He was making sure I was up to the task without asking me, and I wanted him to know that, unpleasant though it may be, I was perfectly capable of doing this.

All the same, I would be glad to be out of this place and back in the sunlight.

The doctor moved forward and pulled back the sheet.

There was a woman lying on the table. She had been undressed as a prelude to her postmortem, but someone, probably in preparation for my arrival, had covered her torso with a towel to preserve her modesty. Above the towel, her arms and shoulders were bare, and I saw the metal cuff that encircled her wrist. It was a bracelet, but a strange one.

Before I focused on the object, however, I looked more closely at her face. I felt I owed her that much, somehow. She was pale, her skin like cold porcelain, white and very smooth. Her expression was peaceful, oddly enough. There was something a bit comforting about that.

Pushing away more sentimental thoughts, I tried to gather what information I could. The woman had dark hair and looked like she was about my age, maybe a bit younger. What I could see of her body showed no obvious signs of violence. There were no large cuts or bruises, though I saw a few abrasions that were probably from her time spent in the Thames, encountering the various debris that was always floating in the river.

When I spoke, I was afraid my voice wouldn't come out, but it sounded almost normal. "How . . . how did she die?"

"We haven't determined that yet," the major said.

"We'll conduct the postmortem once we've taken the bracelet off," the doctor said. "Though it would have been better to start it sooner."

This last bit was clearly aimed at the major. The doctor was miffed, it seemed, that the major had given the order to wait. Major Ramsey wasn't at all concerned about the doctor's ire, of course. He wanted this matter attended to before anything else, and that's the way it would be.

I redirected my focus to the cuff, away from the dead woman who wore it.

It was a thick gold cuff that was a bit too large for her thin white wrist. It was hinged at one side and opened at the other. Unlike traditional cuff bracelets, however, this one had a small lock that kept it from opening without a key.

Even more unusual was the piece that adorned the cuff. It was a large, thick cameo, about the size of a man's pocket watch. It appeared to be a locket of some sort, for there was a tiny keyhole at the side of it as well. The cameo was peach with a delicately carved Grecian woman holding an urn. The piece looked both old-fashioned and off somehow, like a poor imitation of something that might have been worn by a Victorian woman. It was oversize and clunky on her small arm, not the sort of thing a modern woman would wear.

"I've never seen anything like this," I said as I completed my examination. I still had not touched it. I would not be able to do so without coming into contact with the woman's cold hand, bloodred nails contrasting startlingly against the white fingers, and that gave me pause.

"What can you tell me about it?" the major asked.

I wasn't a jeweler, of course, but we both knew I'd had more than my fair share of experience with the acquisition and sale of jewelry.

"I think it's high-quality gold," I said. "It looks Victorian, almost in the style of a mourning brooch that might have held a lock of a deceased loved one's hair, but I haven't seen one this large or one that locks." I gave him a weak smile. "Not much call to lock up a dead person's hair."

"Then you think it's English?" He asked this casually, but there was something in his tone that caught my attention.

I pulled my eyes from the bracelet to look up at him. He was watching me, his expression steady and unreadable.

I looked back at the cuff. "Probably," I said at last. "Though I have the feeling this piece has been cobbled together. It's unlike any antique bracelet I've ever seen. I think it's been made out of older pieces to create something new."

The major looked across the woman's body to the doctor, who had moved to the other side of the table. "And you have drawn no conclusions about her nationality?"

"I'm not Sherlock Holmes," the doctor said irritably. "Or

Dr. Watson either. There's no way to tell that sort of thing from a corpse. You can't look at her fingernails and determine she was from Switzerland or any such nonsense."

I glanced down at her hand. "You can tell she was probably well-off or at least associated with someone who could pay for luxuries."

The doctor looked over at me. "What do you know about it?" he asked. I couldn't help but feel there was a bit of curiosity along with his irritation.

"I don't know much about it," I admitted. "But her manicure is fresh and well maintained. She clearly hasn't been doing any menial labor or working too hard with her hands."

"Very good," the major said. "Anything else?"

I glanced again at the woman's face. "Her ears are pierced for earrings," I said. "Was she wearing any?"

"No."

"Any jewelry other than the bracelet?"

"None."

I had hoped for a ring of some sort, perhaps with an inscription in it. That would, of course, have been too much to hope for. And even a male investigator would have been likely enough to notice something like that.

"What about her clothes?" I asked.

"We've had someone look them over," the major replied. "She was dressed in a blue dress and a fur coat. Standard underclothes. Nothing particularly unusual."

Standard underclothes. He was such a prig sometimes.

"Did you have a woman look at her clothes?" I asked.

He glanced at me. "Why?"

"Because a woman is more likely than a man to notice the details of women's clothes, don't you think?"

"Are you volunteering for the job?"

I hadn't been, actually. Clothes weren't really my forte. As a criminal, one likes to blend in as well as possible, draw no attention. High fashion has the opposite aim and, as such, was never much something I ascribed to. Really, I had never much cared what I wore as long as it was comfortable and serviceable.

Nevertheless, I thought I could probably do a better job of it than whatever police sergeant he had tossing the clothes around.

"I might as well, while I'm here," I said.

Honestly, I was a bit glad to have a moment to step away from the body. As professionally detached as I was trying to be, it was unnerving to see this lovely young woman lying cold and dead before me.

Major Ramsey led me across the room to a table. There were several items laid out on it, most of them items of clothing.

I looked at the dress, which had been laid flat on the table. It was nearly dry now. I reached out and touched the sleeve. "This is an expensive dress," I said.

"How do you know?"

"The quality of it. It's a department store dress, not hand-tailored for her, but it's expensive nonetheless. She'd have money."

"Perhaps it's an old dress."

I shook my head. "The style is fairly modern."

I had the feeling that he had already known that. He was from a wealthy family. He would know the difference between an expensive dress and a cheap one, whether or not he admitted it. Was this meant to be some kind of test?

Well, that was fine with me. I had come here to do a job, and I was ready to do it to the best of my ability. So instead of challenging him on the point, I continued to look at the dress to see what else I could determine. I wanted to find something that would genuinely surprise him.

I set the dress down and moved along the table.

There was a pair of silk stockings, a pair of lace drawers, and a satin slip. The major said nothing as I looked at them. It was a bit uncomfortable, to be honest, studying a dead woman's underclothes in company with a man. But he didn't seem in the least ruffled by it, and I decided not to be either. This was a clinical examination. We were looking into a potentially criminal matter. Or perhaps something even more serious than that.

"Silk stockings," I said. "These aren't easy to come by."

"Yes," he answered.

I rubbed my fingers over them and then looked at them a bit more closely. This was something.

"Laddered at the knees. Both knees. Symmetrical. As though she fell." It might have happened at any time, of course. The dress would be a bit longer than the knees, and she might have kept the stockings since it was difficult to get them. They didn't look as though she had attempted to mend them or keep the ladders from spreading, however.

He leaned over my shoulder to look at them but said nothing.

I glanced at the drawers next. Despite the major's comment that they had been "standard," these underclothes were expensive. Satin and lace.

I moved along, looking next at the slip. It had been white once but was stained by river water. Other than that, it was in pristine condition.

"Good quality underthings and all very new," I said. "Between these and the dress, it seems she purchased a new wardrobe recently."

I cast my eyes over the garments again, looking for anything else that might be useful. "There's no blood on the clothes," I noted.

"No. And no marks on the body to indicate that she was shot or stabbed. If she was murdered, it's possible she was strangled. It's a clean way to kill."

He said these things in such a bland way; it sometimes took me

by surprise until I reminded myself that he was both a soldier and
an intelligence officer. Even then, it was hard to get used to.

A lot of people might think I'd be hardened to such things,
having lived, for lack of a better term, a life of crime. But we'd
always been the sort of criminals that avoided violence, avoided
people altogether. We'd slip in, do the job, and slip out, our marks
none the wiser. Before meeting the major, I'd never encountered
cold-blooded murder.

I looked at the last item on the table, a fur coat. I let out a little
whistle like Uncle Mick did when he was impressed.

"Sable," I said, stepping closer but almost afraid to touch it. It
was matted and a bit crusty from its time in the Thames, but there
was no disguising the quality of it.

The major had said there was nothing particularly unusual about
the woman's clothing. In his world, this was the type of thing women
wore. But I was looking at these items from a different perspective.

"Never bought a woman a fur coat, Major?" I asked cheekily.

"No," he replied.

I wondered briefly what sort of presents the major would give
a woman he was courting. Nothing sentimental, that much was
certain.

"This would cost a working woman a year's salary," I said,
rubbing my hand along the luxuriant fur. "Maybe more. I'd start
here, if I were you."

"What do you mean?"

"There can't have been that many coats of this quality sold in
London over the past year. Perhaps you can run down who made
the purchase."

He nodded.

It was a pity that this lovely thing would probably end up in
police custody somewhere, languishing away. It should be used and
appreciated. Or at least sold. Even in secondhand condition, it was
worth a great deal.

"She might even run in your circles, Major," I said. "I'm surprised you don't recognize her."

"So what we've established is that this woman was well-to-do," he said, ignoring my comment about his social status.

"Yes, I think so," I said, though there was something about all of this that seemed off, something I couldn't quite put my finger on. "Everything about her indicates she had money. Her clothes, her nails, even her hair."

He looked at me. "What can you tell about her hair?"

"It's been freshly cut."

"How do you know that? She's been floating in the Thames for hours."

I blinked. Perhaps I would never grow used to the major's cold military air.

"I can just tell," I said, trying to summon that same sort of detachment. "Her hair is cared for, the ends are very even, showing they've been recently cut. No matter the damage done to her coiffure by the water, it's still apparent that she's been to the hairdresser fairly recently."

"Anything else?"

This meant, then, that he was at least listening to what I had to say. Despite myself, I couldn't help but feel gratified that the major was taking my observations to heart. Usually, he was imperious and high-handed. It would be too much to say that he was condescending, but he occasionally treaded the line.

I didn't answer him right away. Instead, I considered all the pieces as a whole, the picture they presented from a woman's perspective. And then I realized what had been bothering me about all of this.

"I don't think she had a wealthy background," I said. "I think she came by a good deal of money only recently. The clothes are all new and expensive, her hair and nails freshly done. And there's the sable. My guess is she had a windfall of some sort and was making the most of it."

His eyes settled on me for a moment as he absorbed this information, and then he gave a short nod. "Thank you, Miss McDonnell," he said. "You've been very thorough."

I knew what he was going to say next, and I braced myself for it.

"Now it's time to remove the bracelet."

CHAPTER THREE

We returned to the table, and I took out a small tool kit that I carried in my pocket. It was a leather pouch with small leather loops in which were placed a few necessary tools. It was an easy lock on the bracelet, not the sort of thing any mildly competent locksmith couldn't have opened. It wouldn't have taken Uncle Mick's superior skill—or even mine—to make quick work of it.

I stepped toward the table. Ignoring the two men who were watching me intently was easy enough; ignoring the fact that the bracelet was worn by a dead woman was a bit more difficult to forget. Her white hand lay cold and still on the table, waiting for me to release it from the cuff.

I decided to set to working first on the cuff's lock before opening the cameo locket atop it. Slipping a tiny pick out of my case, I reached out with my free hand to hold the cuff still. The side of my palm brushed the dead woman's hand, and I said an old Irish prayer in my head that she would be granted peace.

Then, mustering all my focus, I set to work.

Inserting the pick into the lock, I began to maneuver around the inner mechanism. The lock on this cuff was similar to—though not as sturdy as—an old-fashioned handcuff that might have been used by the police. We'd had several sets in Uncle Mick's workshop that the boys and I had played with as children. More than once, Colm and Toby had "arrested" me and left me somewhere to free myself. I had them to thank for the fact that I could unlock this particular cuff with my hands literally behind my back.

After only a moment, I felt the slight click of the mechanism releasing. This was not a lock that had been made to provide any sort of serious security. It seemed more a safeguard than anything, a way to keep it from being lost or stolen.

The cuff fell open, and I slipped it from the woman's wrist.

I looked up at the major for further instruction.

"Now the locket, if you please. You can work here." He gestured toward an empty table.

"Will you hold the cuff?" I asked as I set it, faceup, on the table.

He came and gripped the cuff, holding it steady while I again inserted my pick, this time into the little lock of the cameo locket. The Grecian lady with her urn seemed to look up at me from the cameo, her face solemn as I prepared to reveal her secrets.

The major's hand, in marked contrast to the dead woman's, was warm when mine brushed against it.

This lock, too, was simple—simpler, even, than the cuff had been—and gave easily beneath the tool. If the major and his men had not been concerned about damaging the piece, they might have opened it with the slightest bit of force.

I set the pick down and reached to open the locket. It was second nature, to open what I had unlocked, but the major stopped me before I could even begin.

"That's very good," he said, his hand on the bracelet, moving it out of reach. "Thank you."

He didn't want me to see whatever was inside the locket, then. I felt a moment of indignation, but then I had to acknowledge this was fair enough. If there was something sensitive in the locket, the fewer people who saw it the better. That didn't stop me from being curious, of course, but I was learning that sometimes, in this business, it was better not to know.

I nodded in response to his thanks. "Is . . . is there anything else?"

"No. I'll walk you out."

Without opening the cameo locket, he slipped the cuff into his pocket.

I turned to Dr. Barker to say goodbye, but he had already moved away, farther into the room. I wondered, for just a moment, how many other bodies were at rest in cold storage, waiting to be laid out on tables in this place, but I decided it was best not to think about it.

Instead, as Major Ramsey indicated that I should precede him, I walked out the way we had come, glad to leave the place behind me.

Even as we walked up the stairs and back into the comparatively cheery hallway of the building, my mind was still on the woman on the table.

"Do you suppose she was dead before she went into the water?" I asked, breaking the silence.

"Perhaps. Though I think it could also be possible that she was fleeing something and ended up in the water either by accident or to evade capture." I was a bit surprised that he would share this much of his thought process with me.

"That would tally with the tears in the knees of her stockings."

My thoughts returned to the dead woman. She hadn't worn a wedding ring. Was there someone waiting for her anyway? Did she have a sweetheart somewhere who was frantically searching for her?

It didn't do any good to think these kinds of thoughts, of course. There was nothing I could do to change what had happened to her. Nevertheless, I couldn't help but think how very hard it would be for her family to wonder where she was.

"Are you all right?" the major asked suddenly as we stepped outside.

I realized that I had closed my eyes, taking a deep breath of the fresh air.

I turned to look up at him. "Yes. It's just . . . sad."

"Yes, I suppose it is," he said vaguely.

I knew that it wasn't the sort of thing the major would think much about. He'd already been hardened to matters that would weigh heavily on the rest of us.

Even in the time I had known him, he had been forced to do things that would have broken lesser men. I thought of the old quote, about some men being born great and some having greatness thrust upon them. It was much the same with strength of character. The major must always have had a good deal of that in him. It was clear that he was, by nature, intelligent and extremely competent. But the army had added an edge to those natural gifts. It had formed an impressive amalgam of resilience and fortitude.

I wondered, though, if there wasn't some softer part of him that he kept hidden from the world—maybe even from himself.

Of course, if there was a softer side to Major Ramsey, he wasn't going to show it to me.

We walked the rest of the way to the car in silence.

"Jakub will drive you home," he said, opening the back door of the car. "I'll be in touch, Miss McDonnell."

Before I could make any reply to this, he had closed the door and gone striding off down the street, the cuff in tow.

He was always dismissing me without so much as a by-your-leave. Just when I felt that we might be getting somewhere in our professional association, he would demonstrate that I wasn't much more than a useful tool to be pulled from the toolbox whenever I might prove helpful and tossed back in again just as quickly.

It was infuriating to be so summarily dismissed and even more infuriating to be left with the beginnings of a tantalizing mystery, the solution to which I might never be privy.

I leaned back against the seat and let out a breath that was half sigh and half huff of displeasure. War was vexing in so many ways.

I had Jakub drop me off not far from Hendon Central. Nacy had asked over breakfast if I would stop at the shops for a few things when my job for the day was done, and there was still plenty of time before they closed. We liked to divide and conquer where the shops were concerned. Nacy made her rounds and I made mine, both of us trying to outdo the other in terms of what our allotted ration coupons would get us.

I went down the busy street, going over in my mind all that had happened today even as I made a mental list of what I needed at the market. It was a strange juxtaposition, living in wartime. One always had to balance the mundane with the shocking, stand in a queue for bread while knowing there were spies and killers trying to bring England to its knees.

As I walked, I stopped to look at a poster that was plastered on the side of the building.

The illustration was of a woman holding a letter to her chest, gazing sadly into the distance: GET A WAR JOB. HELP BRING HIM HOME. I didn't know if it would bring Toby back, but I'd got a war job, all right. And it was a good deal more than I'd bargained for.

I reached the shop and stood in the queue to get butter with my ration coupons and then in another to get a bit of beef. I also managed to get two good-size potatoes and a few early apples. It was odd to me how much things had changed since the war started, that we queued for food we'd had heaps of a few months ago. It was almost as though we lived in a different world.

Fitting, since I was a different person.

I'd been a thief a month ago. Sometimes I still thought of myself as one, like today when I'd briefly cased that mechanic's garage. But sometimes it seemed hard to believe that it had been me, that it had been my family's way of life for so long.

Oh, we had done all the usual things to rationalize it. We were robbing the rich to feed ourselves; they had more than they needed; they deserved to be taken down a peg or two. But now that we had turned over a new leaf with the help of the major, things had changed. War was changing all of our lives, for better and for worse.

Only a week ago, several bombs had been dropped on London. Though we'd long been told to expect it, it had still come as something of a surprise. After months of waiting, after so many Londoners had fled to the countryside and then cautiously returned, people had begun to believe that it might be all right, that the Germans might not come. Then those bombs had fallen, and we had remembered that the war wasn't over but just beginning.

We all knew, deep down, that it was probably only a matter of time before things got worse. They'd invaded Poland, Belgium, and France. They had been occupying the Bailiwicks of Jersey and Guernsey since June. It seemed probable enough that our island would be next in their sights.

There was a sense of dread, knowing what was likely to come. Could our city survive it? But, of course, it could. London had seen fire and famine, plague and pestilence. And there'd been wars aplenty before now. We could see this one through and be all the stronger for it.

I was confident of what the end would be. It was only getting there that was going to be difficult.

I arrived home a short while later with my sack of provisions.

"Nacy, are you home?" I called upon entering the house for the second time that day.

"I'm in the kitchen, love!"

I ought to have known, since a delicious scent was wafting from that direction.

I followed the aroma and found her washing dishes at the sink.

"Something smells wonderful," I said, setting my bounty, such as it was, on the table.

"I found a recipe for trench cake from the last go-round with the Germans," she said. "I doctored it up a bit, and I think it's going to turn out well."

"I'm sure it will," I said, brushing a kiss across her cheek. I was of the firm belief that Nacy could make a delicious soup from grass and twigs. If ever a woman was born to beat rationing, it was Nacy Dean.

"I was a bit late getting to the market, and this was all I could get," I said. "I had a job to do for Major Ramsey."

She looked at me, her brows raising and a sly smile spreading across her face. "Did you indeed? Well, I can't be cross with you for that, can I? I'd spend any time I could with that man, were I you."

Nacy had taken an instant liking to the major, based solely on his looks, which, I'd grant her, left a favorable impression. She wasn't usually one to have her head turned by a pretty face, but she had made an exception for the major.

"It wasn't a lark," I said. "I . . . There was a dead body in the Thames."

"Oh, how unpleasant," she said, drying her hands on a dish towel.

I nodded.

"I won't press you on the details, Ellie, since I know the sort of work you do for the major is hush-hush. But I do hope you won't have to do anything too upsetting."

She waited a moment in respectful silence before she continued. "And the major? How is he?"

"Fine," I replied.

"No doubt he's been missing you," she said as she came over to the table to inspect my goods.

I smiled. Nacy was the closest thing I'd had to a mother, and she had many of the feelings toward me that a mother might have: pride in my accomplishments and the conviction that any eligible men I might meet must automatically be in love with me.

The fact that the major and I couldn't spend five minutes in each other's company without becoming snappish did nothing to dim her confidence that he fancied me.

"I don't think so," I said. "I did the job, and he dismissed me."

"He'll be back around," she said with assurance.

I didn't bother to argue with her. Instead, I told her about my trip to the grocer and the butcher, and we agreed that the potatoes would best be used in a stew and the apples in an apple cake that we could all enjoy several slices of.

As we settled down to dinner a short while later, however, I couldn't seem to get the dead woman out of my mind. Who had she been? Not knowing gave me more sympathy for her and what she must have been through.

Whether she'd been murdered or simply drowned, it must have been awful to have died that way, all alone.

I remembered the ladders in the knees of her stockings. Had she been running from someone, as the major surmised? But even if she had stumbled and then, in her haste, ended up in the water, would she have drowned? Surely she would have been close enough to shore to make it out of the water, even if she couldn't swim.

It was no good speculating, but I'd never been a girl who was happy with the unknown. We were a family who thrived on unlocking things. That extended beyond locks.

I wondered how Uncle Mick was faring up in Yorkshire. I hoped he was making quick work of it and that he would return home soon. I was eager to discuss this matter with him.

CHAPTER FOUR

Two days passed without me hearing anything from either Uncle Mick or the major.

I had another simple locksmithing job, which was good both for the business and for keeping my thoughts occupied. My evenings were a bit harder to fill. Aside from knitting socks for soldiers while listening to the wireless, there was not much I could do to feel useful, and my thoughts repeatedly returned to the death of the mysterious woman. Even my much-loved mythology books couldn't seem to distract me.

I kept finding myself pondering ways in which I might aid in discovering the dead woman's identity. Was the bracelet a potentially useful clue? In our line of work, we'd naturally forged several valuable connections in the jewelry world. If I didn't hear from the major soon, perhaps I might be able to work up a sketch of the bracelet and begin asking around. It wasn't likely to lead to anything, of course, but it would be better than waiting for a call that might never come.

On the second night, however, my telephone rang. My hand was on the receiver within one ring, but I waited until the third to answer it so, if it was the major, he wouldn't think I'd been sitting by the phone. "Hello?"

"Hello, Ellie. It's Felix."

"Oh," I said, careful to keep my voice cheerful, despite the traitorous feeling of disappointment. "It's good to hear from you, Felix. How is Scotland?"

Felix Lacey was a longtime friend of my cousins who had become a friend—and perhaps something more—to me, as well.

He had been discharged from the navy after losing the lower part of his left leg during a battle. Now that he was back in London, there was something a bit different between us, the feeling that things were moving in a direction that went past friendship. He had become entangled in my adventure with Major Ramsey, and in the days afterward, we had spent a good deal of time together.

Then one day, a week ago, he had rung me up to say he was going to Scotland on business of some sort. This was the first I had heard from him since.

"It's been swell. Listen, Ellie, I've a train to catch, but I wanted to see if you would meet me for dinner tomorrow night. I have some news. I got a letter from Billy Norris."

I froze. I knew instantly what the letter was in reference to. It had something to do with my mother.

"What . . ." I began.

"I'm sorry, love, but the train's just pulled in. I just wanted to call ahead and make sure you're not busy. Tomorrow night at Antoine's at eight o'clock?"

"Yes," I said. "All right."

"Wonderful. See you tomorrow, sweet."

He rang off then and I set the receiver down mechanically, thinking about what he might have learned. Felix had recently told me about a contact he had who might be able to shed some light on my mother's dark past.

But now was not the time to dwell on that. It would do me no good to think about it until I spoke to Felix. There was no use counting chickens before they hatched.

I let out an exasperated sigh. I knew he meant well, but I was a bit cross with Felix for ringing me up this way and then leaving me in suspense. At least it would be for only one day. The major would probably leave me in suspense about the dead woman's case indefinitely.

Everywhere I turned there seemed to be more questions and very few answers.

With a feeling of resignation, I made a cup of tea and then grudgingly picked up my knitting. It might not be an adequate distraction, but at least another soldier would have warm feet.

It was early the next morning when my telephone rang again.

My first thought was that it was probably another call from Felix, though I didn't know why he would be calling me before breakfast.

"Hello?"

"Miss McDonnell, please?" said a cheery voice on the other end of the line. It was vaguely familiar, though I couldn't place it.

"This is she," I answered cautiously.

"I'm calling with a message from Major Ramsey."

I remembered now who the voice belonged to: Constance Brown, the major's new secretary. I had met her once at the end of my last assignment with Major Ramsey.

Though I'd been waiting to hear from the major, I found I was surprised. He had said he would be in touch, but I had begun to believe it was likely just a form of speech, the sort of thing one says when one wants to be rid of someone with a hasty goodbye. It had seemed unlikely that he would contact me, especially given how secretive he had been about the strange bracelet's contents.

"Yes?"

"He asks that you come to his office at ten o'clock this morning, if that is convenient." I was quite sure that Constance had added all the polite words to the major's message. He probably barked orders at her every morning and she was left to handle them with finesse. I didn't envy her the job.

"Very well," I agreed, trying not to sound too excited at the prospect of continued involvement in the case. "I'll be there."

I was having breakfast with Nacy in the dining room a short time later when we heard the sound of the front door opening and a familiar voice calling out, "Top of the morning, lasses!"

"Uncle Mick!" I said, as he appeared in the doorway. I was glad to see him; things were always so quiet when he was away.

"Good morning, Mick. I hope you wiped your feet; I've just mopped. I'll get you a plate," Nacy said, rising from the table and disappearing into the kitchen before Uncle Mick could protest. It wouldn't have done any good anyway. Nacy thrived on mothering the entire family. She had by turns coddled and scolded Uncle Mick just as much as my cousins and me for as long as I could remember.

"Wiped them twice!" he called after her, winking at me.

I heard her grunt of disbelief from the kitchen.

He laughed and made his way to my chair and leaned to brush a kiss on my cheek. "How are you this morning, Ellie girl?"

"I'm right as rain," I said, using one of his expressions. "How was Yorkshire?"

"Grand." Uncle Mick moved to his usual chair and sat down. "A good job, it was. I enjoyed it very much."

"And did you meet his lordship?"

"He stood over my shoulder nearly the entire time," my uncle said, his eyes twinkling. "I'm not entirely sure he trusted me."

"Then he had good instincts," I replied.

"He didn't have to worry about me, lass," he said with a grin. "Not now that we've turned over a new leaf."

We had agreed with the major not to do any more thieving while we were involved with the government. I was determined to keep to the deal and thought my uncle was, too, but I also suspected it would be a difficult habit for Uncle Mick to break. For him, the challenge and the thrill were more of a draw than whatever ill-gotten gains we acquired from our illegal endeavors.

But it appeared that this bit of legitimate business had been challenge enough to energize him. He looked well, though he usually gave the appearance of vitality and good health. My uncle was a man of average height, thin and wiry, his movements quick and sure. Hair that had once been as black as mine had gone mostly gray, but his green eyes were bright in a merry, good-humored countenance. I felt a rush of affection as I looked at him; I was glad he was home.

Nacy came back into the room with a plate and a teacup. Uncle Mick picked up the pot and poured himself a cup. He preferred coffee, but Nacy and I didn't drink it and so there was none brewed this morning.

We chatted for a while about Uncle Mick's job in Yorkshire and the two jobs I had done here.

"That fellow gave you trouble for being female, did he?" he said as I related my encounter with the garage mechanic. "I'm likely to go there and give him a piece of my mind."

"No need for that. I set him straight."

He nodded. "That's my girl. And everything else has been quiet?"

"Ellie has been seeing the major again," Nacy piped up.

Uncle Mick's fork stopped halfway to his mouth, and he turned his keen green eyes on me. "Is that so?"

I had intended to mention that detail to Uncle Mick in my own good time, but now I might as well come out with it.

"He needed my help with a lock," I said, wondering how much of this I should share without consulting the major. Our family had never kept secrets from one another and was as trustworthy as the Bank of England when it came to matters of national security, but I still knew I'd better consult the major before sharing the details.

"Really, he came here looking for you initially," I added.

"I'm sure it was my handsome face he wanted to see." Uncle Mick winked at Nacy.

I frowned at him. Much like Nacy, Uncle Mick had grand notions that some sort of romance might develop between Major Ramsey and me. While he'd never been any great admirer of the government, he liked the major's fortitude and the way he remained cool under pressure. He and Nacy would share knowing looks whenever I mentioned the major, which I found annoying in the extreme.

They both knew as well as I did that it was never going to happen. The major, as if a strict military background wasn't enough, was also the nephew of an earl. He was a toff through and through, and there wasn't the slightest likelihood that he would ever be interested in a romantic relationship with a woman of my background.

Not to mention the fact that he was terribly fond of laws, and our family had always been more than willing to break them.

No, he wasn't ever going to look twice at me, and, attractive though he may be, I couldn't even begin to picture him fitting into my ideas for my future. So it was no sense in either of them getting their hopes up.

Besides, there was Felix.

What would he have to tell me tonight? I wondered. Whatever it was, I would be glad to see him. It suddenly occurred to me that I had missed him while he was gone.

I realized Uncle Mick was watching me, and he seemed to realize the trail my mind had followed. He'd always been too clever by a half.

"Heard from Felix, Ellie?" he asked.

"Yes. As a matter of fact, he rang last night. He was on his way back from Scotland. We're to have dinner this evening."

"I hope you're not taking anything he says too seriously," Uncle Mick said. He liked Felix a great deal but didn't consider him a good enough match for me. Not that I was asking to be matched to anyone at the moment.

I sighed. This wasn't the conversation I had hoped to have at the breakfast table.

"You don't need to worry about Felix," I said. "I can manage him."

"You'd do better managing the major," Nacy put in.

I nearly laughed out loud. If Nacy had spent more than five minutes in the major's company she would have seen that he was not a man who could be managed.

"In any event," I went on, "I'm to meet with the major this morning to discuss the matter further. In fact, I'd better leave now if I want to get there on time. I'll tell him that you're home, Uncle Mick. I'm sure he'll want to involve you."

He flashed a grin. "If he wants to keep it between the two of you, I understand."

I rose from the table with a sigh. "If you two hens are done clucking, I'll be on my way."

I had just reached the front door when Nacy called after me. "You look lovely, dear, but perhaps you might want just a dab of lipstick."

I slammed the door behind me.

CHAPTER FIVE

I took the Tube to Knightsbridge, then walked the rest of the way to the major's office. "Office" was a technical term for what it really was: his private Belgravia residence, which had been converted into a headquarters for his operations. He hadn't intended to tell me that he owned the grand place. This was information I had gleaned in a roundabout way. Whatever his faults might be, he wasn't one to flaunt his wealth in the face of those less fortunate.

It was a lovely white stucco town house with a wrought iron balcony, the exterior sandbagged in preparation for the bombs we were all sure were soon to fall.

I went up the front steps and rapped on the door. It was opened almost immediately by a very pretty young woman with glossy blond hair, a friendly smile, and eyes that matched the dark blue suit she wore.

"Good morning, Miss McDonnell," she said, ushering me in. "It's nice to see you again."

"Good morning," I said. "It's nice to see you, too." I meant it. Constance's cheery presence was a pleasant prelude to a meeting with the major.

Major Ramsey was nearly always stiff and formal with me. Mainly, I supposed, because he disapproved of my past as a thief and, deep down, resented having to go to such lengths as partnering with criminals. He operated according to a very strict set of guidelines, and theft for profit was well beyond the pale.

In his defense, however, I had the impression that he was never overly cheerful, even on the best of days, and poor Constance probably had to put up with a good deal.

She seemed as though she was managing well, however. Her natural warmth was offset by a sense of crisp efficiency, and she struck me as more than capable of handling this demanding job. "The major is expecting you. He said to send you back whenever you arrive."

"Thank you."

I knew the way to the major's office quite well. In fact, I knew a great deal about the layout of the ground floor of the house, as I had been imprisoned here for a short time when Major Ramsey was coercing Uncle Mick and me into working for him.

But some things were better off forgotten.

I reached the major's office and knocked smartly on the solid door.

"Come in."

I opened the door and stepped inside. He was seated behind the desk but rose to greet me.

"Good morning, Miss McDonnell," he said.

"Good morning, Major." I could detect nothing from his expression about why he might have called me here.

He indicated that I should take a seat and then took his.

"Thank you for coming at such short notice." He was on his best behavior, and I was growing suspicious.

"Always glad to help," I answered.

His lavender-blue eyes met mine in a direct gaze. "I'm glad to hear it; there is a matter with which I think you might be able to assist me."

I waited. I didn't intend to pepper him with questions as though

I was extremely flattered that he'd asked for my help. I knew my own worth; I also knew he wouldn't have asked for my help if he could have found some other way to do what needed doing.

"I've heard from Dr. Barker. The cause of the woman's death was not drowning," he said. "There was no water in her lungs; she was dead when she went in. Or, at least, not breathing."

That was a cryptic statement if ever I heard one. "What does that mean?"

"She was injected with some sort of toxin," he said. "Dr. Barker thinks it may have been a paralyzing agent that caused the lungs to stop working."

I gasped. "How horrible. Then she may have been alive when she was pushed in . . ."

"Not for long, at any rate," he said, as though this was supposed to be a comforting thought.

"But . . . you said there were no marks on the body." I knew I was grasping at straws, not wanting to believe that the young woman had suffered such an ugly death.

"There was a small puncture mark slightly below her ear that wasn't immediately visible, as it was covered by her hair."

I felt vaguely sick. "Then . . . isn't this a matter for the police?"

"No. This isn't a simple murder."

I tried to process everything that he was telling me. Before, it had seemed possible, if unlikely, that this woman had been going about on some secretive yet harmless errand of her own and had died an unfortunate but purely accidental death. This new revelation meant that we were definitely dealing with something more sinister.

The major was quiet for a moment, apparently considering what he was about to say, and then he shifted tacks. "I had considered asking you the question I'm about to ask without giving you context, but I realized it would be highly unlikely you would cooperate without being taken into my confidence, at least to a certain extent."

If he had been Colm or Toby, and if I hadn't still been reeling from the information he'd just dropped on me, I would have stuck my tongue out at him for this assessment.

Instead, I offered him my sweetest smile. "I'm glad you understand me so well, Major."

"After leaving you at the mortuary yesterday, I brought the cuff here and conferred with an associate on its contents," he said. "In combination with the results of the postmortem, it's obvious that the dead woman was involved in espionage."

Its contents, he had said. Then there was something in the bracelet's locket. He had stopped me before I could open it, but it seemed he had come to the conclusion that I could be of assistance. It must've been important. Major Ramsey wasn't about to involve the likes of me unless it was absolutely necessary.

"The cuff bracelet was a camera," he said.

I was surprised. I'd never seen a camera that small. I knew, however, that a lot of ingenious things were dreamt up during wartime.

"It was cleverly made, the elements fitting into each other so that it could be extended from the bracelet to take pictures and then retracted to conceal it. There are, from what I understand, similar cameras that have been put in pocket watches in the last few decades. This was a variation on that type of device."

"May I see it?" I asked, curious.

"I don't have it at the moment. I have someone more familiar with technology examining it, but we're fairly certain that it was manufactured in Germany and placed inside English jewelry."

This should not have been a surprise, but I still felt a jolt. Even now, it was sometimes difficult for me to believe that we were engaged in a war, that there was a nation actively plotting against us, willing to do whatever they could to bring about our downfall. Even worse, there were people right here, in England, who were acting as agents of our attempted destruction. It wasn't that I was naïve; it was just that I had never imagined I would live to see something like this. Then again, who does?

I realized, of course, the implications of a German agent taking photographs in the East End. The area was home to docks, factories, and warehouses. The Germans would clearly be interested in knowing what was going on in that area of town.

"We're also attempting to recover the photographs," he went on. "Obviously, the locket was not watertight, and the film spent a good deal of time in the Thames. One of our men has had some previous experience with developing photographs. We've set up a darkroom, and he's going to attempt to salvage the film to see if we can determine what sort of pictures are on it."

There was nothing I could do to help with the development of the waterlogged camera film, and he knew it. So there must be something more.

It didn't take me long to find out what it was.

"We did a more thorough going-over of her clothing," he said. "I have someone making inquiries at furriers, as you suggested. We also found something sewn into the lining of her jacket."

I chided myself for being so awed by the sable that I hadn't been the one to discover whatever had been found.

He opened his top desk drawer and pulled out something, setting it on the desk between us. At first glance, it was surprisingly unglamorous. It was a small, misshapen, soggy leather pouch.

"What is that?" I asked.

"Open it."

I leaned forward and picked up the pouch. It was still damp to the touch and smelled faintly of wet leather and the less pleasant odor of the Thames.

There was a drawstring at the top of the bag, and I pulled it loose, glancing inside the bag.

Then I looked up at the major. He was watching me carefully for a reaction.

"Go ahead and dump them out," he said.

I turned the bag over and carefully shook the pouch. There was a faint clinking sound as about a dozen small gemstones spilled out onto the desktop. Dazzling white, fire red, brilliant blue, forest green.

I looked down at them. "These are real jewels."

"How do you know?" he asked.

I looked up at him, a wry smile pulling at the corners of my mouth. "I make a living taking things like this from safes, Major. I know paste gems from real ones when I see them."

"You *made* a living," he corrected me.

I waved a hand at this technicality. "Whatever the case, these are real diamonds. Real sapphires. Real emeralds."

I scooped a few of the gemstones into my palm and shifted them slightly under the lamplight, watching as the jewels picked up the light and refracted it into thousands of dancing prisms. None of the jewels was overly large, but they were all beautifully cut with exceptional clarity.

"These are worth a good deal of money."

"That is no doubt why she had them so carefully concealed on her person," he replied. "But those were not the reason I've brought you here. At least, not entirely."

I looked up at him. "No?"

"No."

He held out his hand across the desk.

Reluctantly, I dropped the gemstones into his outstretched palm.

He glanced down at them before his eyes came back up to mine. "And the diamond."

I dropped the diamond I had artfully pilfered into his hand with a mischievous smile. "Just testing you."

He met my gaze with that stone-faced expression that did not deign to acknowledge my teasing before dropping the gems in his hand and those that remained on the desk back into the leather pouch.

"While I think these gems certainly play a part in the overall scheme of things, it's not my main focus at the moment."

My brows rose ever so slightly in question.

"There was one other thing that was in that pouch."

Stuffy and proper as he pretended to be, the major had a bit of the theatrical in him. He liked to save the big reveals for last.

He reached again into his drawer, and I waited with bated breath to see what could be of more interest than a sackful of jewels.

He held up the item, and I stared at it, wondering if he was now teasing me.

When I found my voice, I couldn't keep the surprise and disappointment from it. "A clock key?"

CHAPTER SIX

"What can you tell me about it?" He set it on the desk and pushed it across to me. I reached over, picked it up, and examined it, though I really didn't think there could be much more to it than met the eye.

It was a little brass key of the type used to wind up clocks. It had a flat bow with two rings that looked almost like the head of a pair of tiny scissors. There were no markings on it that I could see. "It looks antique," I said. "By the size, I would guess maybe a mantel clock."

"That's it?"

I looked up at him. "I'm not a clockmaker."

"This is a key, isn't it?"

"Of a sort," I said with exaggerated patience. "But it's really only used to wind clocks, which have different mechanisms than locks."

"Then you're saying you can't be of any assistance where that key is concerned."

I felt my left brow lift as my patience ebbed. I hated it when he took that superior tone. "There's not a lot of call for locksmiths to break into clocks, Major. Maybe you'll have to blackmail a clock-maker into service this time around."

We frowned at each other.

"All the same," I added, "I don't know that a clockmaker could tell you much more than I have. Certainly not to which specific clock it belongs, if that's what you're thinking. Clock keys are not unique. There are a few different sizes, but they're not like door locks. This size key would fit thousands of clocks. A unique key to an old Austrian cuckoo clock with secret Nazi documents inside would make a wonderful start to a mystery novel, but I'm afraid this key won't prove much of a useful clue in real life."

He sat back in his chair with ill-disguised bad humor. "Well, we shall pursue other avenues with that. The real reason that I've asked you to come here is that I need to know the names of some of the less-reputable fences in this city that you've sold your stolen jewelry to over the years."

This was, no doubt, the question he had been meaning to put to me at the beginning of all this, the one he had said he knew I wouldn't answer without more information. So everything had been leading up to this.

It had already occurred to me that I might be able to put some of our contacts to use, but this was not what I'd had in mind. What the major was asking was outrageous.

It was my turn to sit back in my chair. "I don't think so."

His frown deepened. "What do you mean, you don't think so?"

"You just expect me to make you a list?" I said, as surprised he had asked this of me as he was surprised I had refused him. No, perhaps not *quite* as surprised. Major Ramsey usually snapped his fingers and got what he wanted, so it had probably not occurred to him that I would refuse him.

"A list would be very convenient," he said, his voice taking on an edge.

I gave a little laugh. "I'm sure it would be, but that's a negative, Major. It's all well and good that you've ruined my uncle's and my operation with this law-and-order business. We're glad to do our part. But I'm not sure I should turn you on to others who are living on the outskirts of the law."

"This is not a time for flippancy, Miss McDonnell."

I felt the flash in my eyes. "I'm not being flippant, Major Ramsey. I'm entirely serious. I'm happy to use my criminal skills in service of king and country, but that doesn't include ratting out my acquaintances to the government."

Major Ramsey leaned forward again, his eyes boring into mine. "I can find out all I need to about these people with or without your help."

I crossed my arms. "Excellent. That would solve both our problems, wouldn't it?"

We looked at each other, neither of us willing to budge. The major was used to using that lavender glare of his to intimidate people, but I wasn't the least bit sorry for my sarcasm. It was he who was behaving boorishly. Besides, lavender was one of the least intimidating colors, as far as I was concerned.

"We have, of course, a list of men who have been arrested or suspected of such crimes in the past," he said. "It will be easy enough to find men who are, as you phrased it, on the outskirts of the law, so there's no need for you to go on shielding your associates. But if you're determined to be difficult, then there's nothing else for us to discuss."

It was a bluff. I knew that well enough. Despite his claims that he could do it on his own, he needed me. He could attempt to find out the bare minimum about the people who dealt in jewelry in our world, but he wouldn't be able to approach them for information. Any of the men we had worked with in the past would smell a government man a mile away.

If that's the way he wanted to play it, though, he could be my guest.

I stood up from my chair. "All right. If that's the way you feel about it."

His eyes met mine, and I offered him a small smile. "I hope you find what you're looking for, Major."

I turned then and began walking toward the door.

"I sometimes forget that blood will out," he said just as I reached for the handle.

I turned on my heel to glare at him, anger surging through me. "What is that supposed to mean?"

"That Irish stubbornness. Doesn't matter that you've been born and bred in London at all, does it?"

He hadn't meant, then, what I'd assumed: a reference to my mother. He was one of a few people who knew my past, and it was a relief that he hadn't thrown it in my face. But I was still angry with him.

"I don't like to be browbeaten. You've no call to be high-handed with me. Not when you need my help."

He looked very annoyed as I pointed this out, proving my point. He wouldn't get far along these lines without me. This was my world, not his.

"And, another thing," I went on. "You can't just dangle tidbits of information like a worm on a line and expect me to bite. Either I'm in this, or I'm out of it."

There was a brief moment when we stared each other down. I could see he was weighing his options. He didn't like giving in any more than I did, but he needed me, and we both knew it.

Then he pointed to the chair I had left. "Will you sit down, and we'll begin again?" While the terse gesture left something to be desired, at least his tone was pretending to be polite.

I didn't move. I wasn't going to be ordered around like one of his subordinates. I might technically work under him, but that didn't mean I was one of his little soldiers to do as commanded. He needed to remember that fact.

He gave a short sigh. "I'm sorry, Miss McDonnell," he said, his gaze still holding mine. "You're right. It isn't fair for me to ask you for help without telling you why I need it."

Every so often he would offer an apology that would catch me completely off guard. I suspected it was part of his arsenal for bringing people around to his way of thinking, but I would take what I could get.

I moved back to my chair and sat down. But just on the edge, in case I needed to march out again.

"I can't give you full details at present," he said, "but I will tell you what I can."

I nodded; that was good enough for now.

"We've been asking discreet questions since the discovery of the body. The dead woman matched the description of a woman who was noticed in the vicinity of several East End factories. Her presence was conspicuous enough that a few people in the area remembered seeing her, though we could find no one who knew who she was."

"She wasn't a very good spy if she called attention to herself," I said.

"She wasn't a professional, no. I think she was a civilian recruited by the Germans. She was probably an Englishwoman in that case, or could pass for one. She was likely approached by someone who paid her to take photographs in key areas. Probably been offered more payment than she could refuse. As you mentioned, her hair and nails were recently done, and the clothes and coat were expensive. She'd been paid handsomely for the service."

"But why would they pay her in jewels?" I asked. "Wouldn't that only call more attention to her?"

"Perhaps they couldn't come up with that much money in pounds sterling," he said. "Jewels have no noticeable currency and are fairly easily converted into money. Perhaps not as much as before the war, but enough to buy some pretty new things."

"And that's why you want the names of some less reputable jewelers," I said, the vague ideas I'd had at the beginning of this clicking neatly into place. "You think she might have sold something to one of them before—which she used to buy the fur, among other things—and whoever she sold it to would be able to give you some information?"

"I think there's a good chance one of them might know something."

I considered this for a moment. "But what you haven't really explained, Major, is why you're so interested in catching the woman's killer. Granted, it's a shame for anyone to die so young, but if she was indeed a German spy, it could be viewed that her killer did you a favor."

"Succinctly put, Miss McDonnell," he said, something like dry amusement in his eyes.

It probably sounded heartless put that way, but it was true enough; I didn't see why British intelligence should be so interested in finding this woman's murderer.

"I believe she was killed by her German contact," he said. "The toxin used to murder her is not a common way to kill someone, and it doesn't appear that anything—with the possible exception of her identification papers—was taken from her before she was dumped in the Thames."

"But why would someone murder her if she was getting information for them?"

"That's what we'd like to know."

"Wouldn't they have taken the bracelet when they killed her if they knew there was film in it?"

"It was locked on her wrist," he reminded me.

"Yes, but still," I said. "One would think that they would have found a way if it was worth killing over."

"That's why I don't think they killed her for the information," he said. He didn't elaborate, and I could tell he wasn't going to. There was more to all of this than he was telling me, but I supposed

I couldn't expect him to lay all his cards on the table at once. At least he hadn't tried to pawn me off with half-truths.

"Now, Miss McDonnell," he said, "I've been as open with you as I can. It's time for you to share a bit with me."

He fixed me in his steady gaze. It was my turn to give him a bit of information, and I still felt wary about doing it.

"You're not going to arrest these people?" I said. "I'll deny it all if you do."

He let out a short breath. "I don't have any interest in rounding up London's criminals. I'm not the police. I'm concerned with matters of national security. I need not remind you that the fate of our country may be at stake."

He tended to pontificate a bit when he was feeling like I wasn't being cooperative enough, so I wasn't entirely impressed with this little speech. But what he said was true enough.

I would just have to trust him.

"The first person I would go to is Pascal LaFleur," I said. It felt a bit like a betrayal saying it, but Monsieur LaFleur was the sort of man who would want to see the Germans foiled. And while his connections ran deep, he was excellent at covering his tracks. Should the government decide it wanted to look at him later, it would be difficult to prove anything.

"He's a pawnbroker?" the major asked.

"No, a jeweler. Or was, once upon a time. He owns an antiques shop now. There are a lot of different items that go through his shop, but he buys and sells a lot of jewelry. Legitimately, I mean."

"But there is a criminal side to his business?" he asked.

"Well, there are elements that are . . . crime adjacent, you might say."

I could tell he was watching me, but I didn't meet his gaze. "Would you care to elaborate?"

I sighed. "We . . . have sold a few things to him in the past."

To his credit, the major took this in stride and didn't press for details. "And he makes questionable acquisitions frequently."

"Occasionally. His real sideline is in paste jewelry. He's very good at paste replicas. He has, in the past, been known to make copies of jewelry on the sly. Gentlemen with gambling debts who don't want their wives to know they're selling jewelry, that sort of thing. Monsieur LaFleur would often buy the jewelry and make copies for the husbands to return to their wives' jewelry boxes. Then the genuine jewels would be put into different settings and sold in his shop."

"So you think his name is known in certain circles as a place where jewels may be bartered under the table."

I nodded. "It's why I said I would go to him first. He's fairly well known in our circle as someone who is both clever and discreet. He's not a shifty character. He's a good man who just isn't too concerned with the provenance of the things that pass through his shop."

"Do you think he would have been willing to buy these jewels even if he knew where they were coming from, a German spy?"

"No," I said immediately. "That's not what I meant. He just doesn't ask many questions when jewelry comes his way, that's all. But he would never willingly do anything to help the German cause."

"How can you be sure of that?"

I paused to consider the reasons behind the certainty in my gut. Major Ramsey wasn't likely to accept that as proof.

"He's lived in London for the past twenty or thirty years, at least. He isn't the closest of my connections, but he and Uncle Mick go back a long way."

Monsieur LaFleur and my Uncle Mick had been friends for years. Their encounters were not limited to the buying and selling of jewelry; as a child, I would often accompany my uncle to the antiques shop. They would smoke their pipes and drink while swapping outlandish tales. I had loved to listen to them talk while I wandered Monsieur LaFleur's shop, looking at all the beautiful baubles.

Uncle Mick and I had sold pieces to him several times. And once my uncle had had paste replicas of jewelry made to be placed in safes he was stealing jewelry from. It was a rare case, one in which he knew the exact dimensions of the pieces he was after before he went in. Monsieur LaFleur had made the replicas for him, and they had split the proceeds that were gained by the sale of the real jewels. No one had been the wiser.

So far as I knew, there was a woman somewhere wearing a necklace she had no idea was not made of real diamonds.

No need to burden the major with this bit of knowledge, of course.

"Your uncle's staunch loyalties to this country aren't proof of Monsieur LaFleur's," the major said.

And then I remembered suddenly a conversation I had overheard between him and Uncle Mick once, the two of them talking in somber voices so unlike the normally cheerful tones that came naturally to both of them.

"He lost three brothers at Verdun," I said. "He was the only one who survived. He'd never lift a finger to help the Germans."

Loyalty to a country could be bought, perhaps, but not by the country that had taken all a man's siblings.

The major said nothing for a moment, then gave a short nod. "Then he sounds like a good place to start."

There was a brief pause, as though he was trying to make up his mind about something. And then he came out with it. "Do you suppose you might make the introduction?"

I knew he wasn't pleased to have to ask, so I didn't show how pleased I was that he had to.

"Yes," I said. "When?"

"Now."

I wasn't surprised; the major wasn't one to sit still when there was a job to be done. It was still early, and I had no pressing plans. If there was a German spy to catch, the sooner we began the better.

I nodded. "All right. Let's go."

CHAPTER SEVEN

Monsieur LaFleur's antiques shop was located in Marylebone. The major had Jakub drop us off a short distance away, and we walked from there so we wouldn't draw too much attention to ourselves.

He hadn't said much on the way there, probably focused on the questions he would like to ask Monsieur LaFleur once we arrived. I, meanwhile, was focused on whom I would point him to next if this lead didn't take us anywhere.

I still wasn't entirely comfortable with giving up our connections. It wasn't that I really thought the major would turn us over to the police. Even when the war was over, he would have more important things to occupy him. Nevertheless, it was disconcerting to share the secrets of our trade with an outsider.

I wished now that I had brought Uncle Mick with me. I would have to tell the major that we needed to bring Uncle Mick into this now that he was back from Yorkshire.

"This is it," I told the major, coming back to the matter at hand as we stopped in front of a little store tucked between a tea shop and a bookstore. LAFLEUR'S ANTIQUES, the sign read in gold letters against glossy black paint.

The storefront looked just the same as it always had, the brick exterior a bit faded but always tidy, the windows gleaming even

on cloudy days. Behind the glass, an array of interesting objects
sat on display: china dolls, a silver tea service on a wooden side
table, a painting of a ship on a stormy sea, and an enormous gold
harp.

The major pulled open the door. I entered and he followed,
closing the door behind us. I felt a sense of nostalgia as the scent
of the place hit me: old paper, silver, the comforting smell of warm
dust, like an attic room in the sunshine.

For just a moment, I stopped in the doorway and took it all
in, just as I had when I was younger. Unlike some of the grander
antiques shops in the city, brightly lit with glittering glass cases,
LaFleur's was small and cramped, the shelves and cases crowded
with a variety of objects, everything illuminated by an array of
colorful glass lamps that hung from the ceiling.

As a child, it had been one of my favorite places to visit with
Uncle Mick. I had always felt like I was stepping into Aladdin's
cave, the riches piled up around me in every direction. There was
a jewelry case on display toward the front where cheap costume
pieces lay among Victorian brooches, rings, and bracelets. Silver
and gold, enamel and Bakelite, all mixed together without any great
care in their arrangement. Somehow, it only made the display more
appealing.

Now, with a somewhat more practiced eye, I could see that
there was not a great deal of high-quality jewelry in the shop. At
least, not out where the customers could see it.

I knew, however, that there was also a room in the back, behind a locked door, where there were pieces that weren't as welcome to scrutiny as the wares that lay behind the glass cases.

Major Ramsey hung back a bit, looking around him, as I
moved farther into the shop. It was his custom, probably in his
training, to take in his surroundings and gain his bearings in whatever place he entered.

I glanced over my shoulder at him. He and his large frame

seemed out of place in the crowded confines of the store, rather like a bull in a china shop. If the bull wore a spotless uniform and moved with graceful purpose.

Making my way around the tables and shelves, I went to the little desk in the corner where I knew Monsieur LaFleur would be sitting, tinkering with one of his projects.

"Bonjour, Monsieur LaFleur," I called as I approached. He was wearing a loupe and leaned over something that lay on a green velvet cloth on the counter.

He looked up at me, taking the loupe from his eye. "Ah! Mademoiselle Ellie," he said with a smile. "It has been a long time."

He stood and came around the desk, took my hand in his, and leaned over it in a courtly manner that was better suited to the previous century than this one.

"You look lovely, *chérie*," he said. "More beautiful than ever."

I smiled. Decades in this country had not affected his French charm at all, though I sometimes suspected he amplified it for the benefit of the ladies. He was short and thin, his shoulders a bit stooped from years of bending over jewelry. His hair, though gone white, was still thick and matched the bushy eyebrows over sharp-yet-warm brown eyes.

"I'm glad to see you, Monsieur LaFleur," I said, squeezing his hand. "It's been far too long."

"Yes, yes. Your Uncle Mick owes me a visit. I lost to him at our last game of cards, and it is time for me to win my money back."

"I'll tell him to come and see you," I promised with a smile.

"Yes, very good." His eyes, over my shoulder, noticed the major approaching. "And who is this?"

"I've brought a friend with me today," I said. Friend was, perhaps, being overgenerous, but it was the easiest term to use.

Monsieur LaFleur turned to the major, looking him up and down appraisingly before turning back to me. "Come to pick out an engagement ring, *ma chérie*?" he asked, with a twinkle in his eyes. "I have something that would do very well. And I will give your young man an excellent price."

"No," I said quickly, before he could disappear into the back room and emerge with a tray of engagement rings. I didn't dare glance at the major. He would be, I was sure, appalled at the idea that Monsieur LaFleur might think we were planning to be married. Plus I was fairly certain that I was blushing, and I didn't want the major to see.

"He . . . he is on the hunt for someone who may have been working with the Germans," I said. The major and I had agreed that I could give the bare minimum of information to Monsieur La-Fleur in order to gain his trust and cooperation. Monsieur LaFleur was my friend, but he guarded the secrets of his associates closely, as we all did. Nothing less than the true importance of our mission was going to convince him to tell us what we needed to know.

The jeweler's face darkened, both anger and sadness evident in a flash across his face at the mention of our enemies.

"We want to know if a young woman has been in recently trying to sell anything very valuable. Perhaps some high-quality gems," I said. "Someone who wanted to do it quietly?"

Monsieur LaFleur looked from me to the major and then back to me. He was wondering, I was sure, if the nature of our less-reputable work was all right to discuss in front of the major.

"It's all right," I said. "Major Ramsey knows about some of our dealings."

I was sure the major didn't miss my use of the word "some," but I was also sure he didn't expect me to confess all of my sins to him. The ones he knew about were already enough.

"We think the person who sold them was paid to work for the Germans, and we are trying to track them." I offered him a small smile. "You see, I am working for the government this time; you know I wouldn't do that if it was not important."

I didn't look at the major as I said this, but I knew he wouldn't miss the little dig. It appeared that Monsieur LaFleur was considering something. Then he said, "If you will wait here just a moment?"

"Of course."

He turned then, removing a key from his waistcoat pocket and unlocking the door at the corner of the room, disappearing behind it.

"He trusts you alone with the merchandise, I see," the major said, nodding to the piece Monsieur LaFleur had been working on when we'd arrived. It was a diamond bracelet he'd left unattended on the green cloth, the jewels glittering in the bright light from the lamp at his desk.

As usual, I bristled at the major's casual reference to my past wrongs. "I'm not a common thief," I said defensively.

"No. I would never call you common, Miss McDonnell."

I wasn't sure if this was a compliment or not, but I was still irritated that he thought I might try to lift something from Monsieur LaFleur's desk. It wasn't as though I went about London grabbing things and sticking them in my pockets. Even thieves had standards.

Besides, Monsieur LaFleur was a friend. I wouldn't do that to a friend.

I didn't know why the major's comments bothered me. It shouldn't matter what he thought of me. But somehow it did. Whatever camaraderie had developed between us by the close of our last mission seemed to have faded, and he was keeping me at arm's length as he had when we'd first met and he hadn't quite trusted me. It stung in a way I couldn't quite name.

Thankfully, I didn't have long to dwell on this before Monsieur LaFleur reemerged from the back room. He came to his desk and motioned us forward.

"You are looking for something like these?" he asked, gently dropping the contents of his hand onto the green cloth. Three gemstones sparkled up at us.

I felt my heartbeat increase. Could it be that we had found a lead so easily?

The major stepped forward.

"Would you be able to compare them to these?" He surprised me by removing the leather pouch from his pocket. I hadn't realized that he'd been carrying the jewels around with him. It made sense, of course, that he'd brought them for comparison, but I wouldn't have thought he'd tote them around like so many coins in his pocket.

Monsieur LaFleur took the pouch and emptied the contents beside the others. He gave an excited murmur in French and picked up his loupe.

Taking his seat at the desk, he began examining the jewels. I glanced at the major and found him looking at me. I gave him the faintest of smiles. It was just possible that we might be about to have some very significant answers to our questions.

Monsieur LaFleur examined the major's gemstones carefully before picking up the three from his back room and examining them in turn. It didn't take all that long, but it seemed like forever. Maybe because I was practically holding my breath in anticipation.

At last, he looked up, removing the loupe. "These all have a very similar cut. I believe they were removed from the same piece of jewelry."

I looked excitedly at the major, but his intent expression was fastened on Monsieur LaFleur. "How sure are you of this?"

"Fairly certain, Major," he said. "I cannot, of course, be positive, but they are all of the same cut and similar size. I think they were removed from a piece of jewelry, a necklace, perhaps. It would have been a very fine necklace indeed. All of these gems are of excellent quality."

"Any ideas as to its provenance?" the major asked.

"If I had to guess, I would say France. They are French cut, though, of course, that does not mean they necessarily hail from there. The style has been popular in past decades."

All the same, France would make sense. With the Germans occupying France, they'd no doubt "acquired" several fine pieces left behind by those who had fled or, more likely, those who had been detained. Perhaps one of those pieces had been disassembled to pay a British spy.

"And can you give us a description of the person who sold these to you?" the major asked.

He shook his head. "I'm afraid I cannot."

"Why not?" Major Ramsey's tone had grown clipped as it did when he was impatient, and this was not the impression I wished to leave with Monsieur LaFleur, so I stepped forward.

"Monsieur LaFleur, can you tell us where you got them?" I asked. "The major is not concerned with the . . . technicalities of legality. We only wish to find out more about the woman who we believe had them in her possession."

"I understand, *chérie,* and I will happily tell you all I know. But I did not do business with the seller. I purchased them from Monsieur Smythe."

I let out a little breath of disappointment. I knew Smythe, and things had just become more difficult.

"He approached me perhaps two weeks ago," Monsieur LaFleur went on. "He says he has acquired some new pieces. Very fine pieces. Not the sort of thing he usually sells. He told me he had gotten them for a good price and wanted to sell them to me, since most of his customers do not have the money to pay for them."

I nodded. It wasn't the complete answer we had been hoping for, but it was valuable information nonetheless.

Monsieur LaFleur picked up the gemstones that the major had brought and gently dropped them back into the leather pouch.

"These are worth quite a lot," he said. "You should be careful with them."

"I will," the major replied, putting the pouch back into his pocket. "Oh, and one more thing. Can you tell me anything about this?"

He pulled something out of the pocket where he had just

deposited the leather pouch and set it on the table. It was the clock key.

Monsieur LaFleur looked at it and then back at the major. "A clock key?"

I felt triumphant; that was the exact same reaction I'd had.

"Is there anything you can tell from looking at it?" the major asked.

Monsieur LaFleur picked it up and studied it. "It is an older clock, I would say from the condition of the key. I cannot give you a year or even a type of clock, though I should not think it was much larger than a mantel clock."

The major nodded, his features unreadable.

"Thank you," I said to Monsieur LaFleur. "You won't tell anyone that we have been here asking about this?" I said before the major could say the same thing in a less polite way.

"No, no. Of course not." He made a locking motion with the clock key. "I will not even make the *cuckoo*."

I smiled. "Thank you so much for your help, Monsieur LaFleur," I said. "It was lovely to see you again."

"Yes, yes. It was lovely to see you, too, *chérie*. Good luck with your searching."

"Yes, thank you," the major added. "You've been most helpful."

Monsieur LaFleur handed the clock key back to him. "I am happy to be of help in any way I can." A sly expression crossed his face. "Don't forget to come back to me if you do happen to need an engagement ring, Major." Then he winked.

"I shall remember that," the major said.

I managed a smile before I turned and walked stiffly from the shop, the major behind me.

To my relief, the major made no comment about Monsieur LaFleur's trying to sell him engagement rings once we were outside.

"Now on to see this Smythe?" he asked. Of course. The major was not one to be diverted from his task by trivialities.

THE KEY TO DECEIT

I tried to decide the best way to break the news to the major and, in the end, just came out with it.

"You're not going to be able to go there," I said. "You're not going to be able to walk into Sooty Smythe's shop and get any information out of him."

"'Sooty'?"

"That's what he goes by. He worked for a chimney sweep when he was young and was always covered in soot. I don't suppose he's answered to anything else for fifty years."

"You know him well, then?"

I shrugged. "We're acquainted. I haven't had many dealings with him myself, but I know him well enough to know that you're not going to get anywhere with him."

He looked at me with the expression one would expect him to have when faced with opposition. "Why do you say that?"

"He's something of an anarchist. He hates coppers, the government, the military, any sort of authority."

"And what makes you think he'll associate me with any of those groups?"

I gave a little laugh. "Everything about you." I waved a hand to encompass his whole person. "You'd stick out like a fish out of water in a place like that. Even if you weren't in your uniform, you march everywhere you go."

"I most certainly do not."

"He'd have you pegged as a government type the moment you step inside the door," I insisted.

"Thank you, Miss McDonnell, but I've learned to fit in when necessary."

I crossed my arms. "It's not going to work, Major. He's savvy; he'll see through you."

"Miss McDonnell . . ."

I shook my head. He could argue as much as he liked, but I was going to stand my ground on this one. Because it was important.

Normally I wouldn't have pushed so hard on an issue, but I felt very strongly about this. I had no doubt that the major was extremely competent. He might be able to pass himself off as a great many things, but he was not going to fool Sooty Smythe.

The major seemed to realize that I wasn't backing down, and, to his credit, he gave it due consideration.

"Do you have an alternate suggestion?"

"You're not going to like it," I said.

"No," he agreed. "I assumed as much."

"I'll have to bring Felix."

"No."

I wasn't surprised at this reaction; he and Felix had not been exactly chummy the last time we'd worked together. But Felix's skill had been a large part of our last mission's success, and I thought the major was being unfair.

"Felix and Sooty have worked together before," I said. "He trusts Felix. He likes him, and Sooty Smythe likes very few people."

It was an interesting part of Felix's personality that he was very debonair and polished when he wanted to be, but he also had the ability to blend into less reputable circles. Like my cousins, he had run with a rough lot as a boy. He knew when to smile and when to let the threat of something darker lurk in his eyes.

"If you know Smythe so well, why do you need Lacey?" the major said, still fighting against the idea.

"Because I haven't seen Sooty in years. It'll be better if I bring Felix. They have an understanding of sorts." I wasn't going to volunteer that Felix had used his forging skills to create fake authenticity documents for several pieces for Sooty over the years. No sense burdening the major with that information.

He let out a short breath and looked away, apparently considering the matter. Then he glanced at his wristwatch. "Can we pick him up now?"

As usual, once the major changed course, he was full speed ahead.

"No," I said. "But I'm having dinner with him tonight, and I'll discuss it with him. We can go and see Sooty tomorrow."

The major looked annoyed. "I do hate to interfere with your social life, Miss McDonnell, but I must remind you that this matter is of the utmost importance."

I glanced at my own watch. "He was taking the train back from Scotland last night. I don't know what time he'll be arriving. I don't have any way to contact him before we meet tonight."

We looked at each other for a long moment. He was calculating behind those pale blue eyes, and at last he decided that he wasn't going to win this one.

"Fine," he said, then turned and strode in the direction of the street where Jakub and the car waited for us.

I followed after him with a roll of my eyes. He could stalk about all he wanted, but that didn't change the facts. He would just have to accept that not everything could be done on his terms.

CHAPTER EIGHT

As it was, I was nearly late to meet Felix for dinner.

It wasn't a date. We were meeting so he could tell me his news. On the surface, we were friends who had known each other for years. That there was more beneath the surface that neither of us was quite ready to acknowledge was something I didn't ponder at the moment.

All the same, I'd done my best to pretty myself up a bit after my long day chasing down leads with the major. I'd put on a green dress that matched my eyes, managed to get my hair under control, and even daubed on a bit of makeup and a spritz of the expensive Parisian perfume Felix had given me for Christmas the year before.

When I arrived at the restaurant where we were going to have dinner, Felix was already there.

"Hello, lovely," he said, rising to greet me. "You look wonderful, as always."

He leaned forward to brush a kiss across my cheek, and I could smell the familiar scent of his aftershave and tobacco. It was difficult to explain how Felix could both make me feel so comfortable and give me a strange, uneasy sensation like butterflies in my stomach at the same time.

He helped me off with my coat and then we settled into our seats.

I saw a slight flicker of discomfort on Felix's face as he sat, and I wondered if his leg was troubling him after the long train ride from Scotland. I opened my mouth to ask him about it and then closed it again. Felix didn't like to be fussed over, and anytime I had mentioned his leg in the past he had brushed it off and changed the subject.

He was getting on very well with his prosthetic limb, but I knew there was a part of him that was determined to prove to himself that he could do everything he did before his injury. I worried that he would push himself too hard, but Felix had never been the kind of man who shared his difficulties, and he wasn't likely to do so now.

All the same, this change must be hard for him to adapt to. He had breezed through life up until the war, everything falling into place for him, his good looks and charming personality paving an easy road.

To face battle and loss of a limb after so effortlessly pleasant a life must have been quite a shock, and there was the occasional shadow that crossed his eyes that let me know I was right. I supposed the war had done that to a lot of people.

"I've missed that pretty face of yours," Felix said as we picked up our menus. "I was pining for you the entire trip."

I laughed. "I don't believe you thought of me once in the entire week, Felix Lacey."

He feigned indignation. "I thought of nothing else, I assure you. You haunted my dreams."

Felix was always full of charm and blarney, as Uncle Mick would say. But the knowledge that half of what he said was bald flattery didn't make him any less appealing. Felix was the sort of man who made you happy to be charmed.

And it wasn't only his charisma that made him attractive. He had matinee idol good looks to match: a tall, elegant figure with dark hair and eyes and a mustache like Douglas Fairbanks, Jr.

Women liked the way he looked, and they liked the things he said to them. Felix had made the girls' hearts flutter for as long as I'd known him.

But he had always treated me a bit different than he did the other women he had wooed. For one thing, Colm and Toby would have boxed his ears if he'd ever treated me too cavalierly. Maybe that's why things were different between us now. We had been friends and confidants long before we'd thought of becoming anything else.

Even now, with the definition of our relationship hazier than ever, I knew that I could trust Felix and rely on him. Despite his cheery flirtations, there was something real and steady at the foundation of our friendship, and I cherished it.

"How was your trip?" I asked.

"Successful," he said with a brief smile.

"You never told me why you were going to Scotland."

"No, and if you ask me, I shall instantly change the subject."

I knew what that meant. He was hiding something from me. My first silly thought was that he might have a girlfriend there. But I didn't think that was the sort of thing he would conceal. He had no reason to.

But the second possibility wasn't comforting either. He had been there on a job. Most likely an unlawful one.

"Felix . . ." I began.

He held up a hand. "Better not ask anything you don't want to know the answer to, Ellie."

I felt suddenly worried. Like my family, Felix had never been one to quibble about which side of the law he landed on. His skills as a forger had earned him money in several less-than-scrupulous situations. But, also like my family, he had never been one to play for stakes that were too high.

Until it had been necessary.

Then we had all worked for extremely high stakes on the side of right. It had felt good, I realized, having virtue backing us up. It had changed the way I looked at myself, whether I wanted to admit it or not. I felt different, better, knowing that I was working for the people of my country rather than against them.

I didn't know what would happen when the war was over or what my life would return to. But none of us did, did we? We could only go on doing the best we could and trust that the future would work itself out.

I had assumed Felix felt the same way, that having done his service in the navy and for the government, he might be inclined to move toward a career inside the law. Now his evasiveness about what he'd been up to in Scotland made me wonder.

Felix, after all, had not agreed to work under Major Ramsey in any future capacity. He'd assisted us in our first endeavor because we needed him. Because he was loyal to his country. But he didn't appear to see what we had done as the opportunity to turn over a new leaf.

It made me hesitant to bring up the matter of the new mission with him, so I decided to wait until the time was right. Perhaps a drink or two would make him more inclined toward helping me talk to Sooty.

The waitress came to take our order then, diverting the conversation for the time being. She left our table giggling and blushing after Felix's interactions with her. I watched, somewhere between amused and exasperated.

Then he turned his attention back to me. "What have you been doing while I was gone, Ellie?"

"More of the same," I said. I told him about Uncle Mick's job in Yorkshire and my own locksmithing experiences.

"But back to your trip to Scotland," I said, trying to shift the subject around. "Felix, you know the major can get you work if you need it. You don't have to . . ."

"I don't need Ramsey to get me a job, Ellie." He said it gently enough, but there was a firmness beneath the words that let me know that there was no use arguing. It was no surprise that Felix wasn't exactly keen on the idea.

I decided that I might as well have out with it now and let the chips fall where they may.

"Felix . . ." I said. "I . . . well, speaking of the major, I need to ask you something."

"Oh?" he asked in a tone that gave nothing away.

"Yes. You see, I'm working with Major Ramsey again."

His features hardened almost imperceptibly. I don't think anyone but me would have noticed the change that came over them, the slight glint in his eye as he waited for me to continue.

I briefly related to him the matter of the dead woman in the Thames, the miniature camera strapped to her wrist, and the major's belief that she had been murdered by her German handler. I then told him we needed to see if we could get any information from Sooty Smythe.

The waitress brought our food then, and we broke off the conversation for a moment as our plates were set before us.

"Sooty Smythe, eh?" Felix said when the waitress had left, disappointed that she no longer held his attention. "I haven't seen the old devil in years. I wasn't even sure he was still alive."

"He's the sort of fellow who will outlive us all," I said.

Felix said nothing. I could tell he was thinking things over, and I didn't want to give him too long to come up with excuses.

"Will you go with me?" I asked.

"Oh, certainly," he replied. "I wouldn't allow you to go alone to a place like that. Sooty isn't known for his chivalry."

"I don't think he'd do me any harm," I said. "All the same, I'll be glad of your company."

I considered myself savvy as far as the criminal underworld went, but Felix had an even keener eye than I did. He was able to read people on a level I had never seen in anyone else, and he knew how to play them. It was a useful skill.

We agreed to go first thing in the morning and changed the subject after that.

Felix spoke in a vague way about his time in Scotland. About the smoky pubs where he had spent his evenings, the whiskey and haggis and tatties. He was a wonderful storyteller, and I was easily diverted from any of the things we had come here to discuss.

Once our plates had been pushed away, however, I knew that it was time to find out what his news was.

"You said you had word from Billy Norris," I said. I realized my heart had set to racing.

"Yes." He fixed me in his steady gaze. "I rang my landlady to tell her I'd be coming home, and she told me about the mail that had been piling up while I'd been gone. She mentioned the letter, so I rang you up before I got on the train."

Billy Norris had been a shipmate of Felix's in the navy. One night, in a drunken bout of conversation on their ship, he had related to Felix that his mother had been, for a time, an inmate at Holloway and that she had befriended a famous murderess.

At last, it had come out that this famous murderess was Margo McDonnell. My mother.

It was the family secret that no one ever talked about, the one few people besides Felix even knew: my mother had been convicted of my father's murder and sentenced to death before I was born.

It wasn't an unusual or even particularly interesting story, as far as murders went, yet it had gained a lot of notoriety at the time. We weren't a rich or connected family or one who would normally have caused any sort of sensation.

But my mother had been beautiful, and the crime had been brutal. It made selling newspapers easy, and the press had eaten it up. In a way, I ought to have been thankful for that, because almost everything I had learned about the case had been from newspapers.

There had been a highly publicized trial and the expected conviction. She'd escaped the gallows, however. After discovering that she was with child, she'd been reprieved, her sentence commuted to life in prison. She'd given birth to me at Holloway and died there of the Spanish flu just after my second birthday.

I didn't remember her at all, of course. Uncle Mick, who was my father's brother, and Nacy had raised me from the time I was months old. They, along with Colm and Toby, were the only family I had ever known.

They had brought me up in a warm, loving household with music and laughter and stories. I had never wanted for anything.

Yet a part of me still missed the mother I had never known. Perhaps she would have died from influenza whether or not she had been in prison. That had occurred to me. Millions had, after all. Perhaps it was not so very noteworthy a death just because of the location where it had happened. All the same, it hung over my life like a shadow.

And a part of me had always believed in her innocence.

In every article I had read about the whole affair, in every public statement she had given, she declared that she had loved my father and would never have killed him.

The jury hadn't believed her. Nor had the public. They couldn't be blamed, I supposed, for killers often protest their innocence.

Until the day she died, however, she had maintained that it had not been her. And my belief in her was deep, not in the wishful way of someone who believes a lie. It was like an instinct, a feeling in my gut that I couldn't shake no matter how hard I tried to put the past behind me.

It wasn't something I had ever discussed with Uncle Mick. He had been close to his brother, my father, and I knew his feelings about my mother would be complicated.

And then Felix had told me about Billy's story.

Billy's mother had said most of the women in Holloway proclaimed their innocence. But she had believed my mother and had said there was something my mother had told her that seemed to add weight to her story. Billy hadn't remembered what it was. He'd been too drunk for that.

But Felix hadn't forgotten.

He'd debated on telling me about it, but, in the end, he had realized I deserved to know. We'd agreed that it wouldn't hurt to find out more about the matter, to see if Billy's mother might have something important to share.

So he'd written Billy and asked him if his mother still lived in London and if she'd be willing to talk to me. We'd been waiting for the answer for several weeks, but I'd put it in the back of my mind.

And now here was the letter.

"What does he say?" I asked. My voice sounded much steadier than I felt.

"I haven't opened it yet," Felix said. "I thought I should wait until I was with you."

That was just like Felix, so considerate of my feelings that he hadn't taken the opportunity to learn something before I did.

"Shall we open it now?" I asked.

"Of course."

He tore open the envelope and slid the letter out. I leaned closer to see it. It was written on cheap stationery, the ink a bit smeared in places as though it had been left carelessly on a desk and completed in bursts between drinks and card games.

I'd received several letters like that from Felix while he was away. He was terrible about remembering to write, and his letters had always given me the impression that he was in a great hurry to complete them.

Felix's letters, however, had not contained this same abundance of expletives and misspelled words as his comrade greeted him warmly and inquired after his health and how life was treating him now that he'd left the navy behind.

Finally, he got around to the part that interested me. It was almost an afterthought to the letter.

"My mum says she'd be pleased to see your friend. Is it the girl whose photo you showed me? The black-haired one with the bedroom eyes? I hope she gave you an appropriate welcome when you returned home."

I glanced at Felix, who cleared his throat. "Don't pay attention to that. Sailors talk rather roughly sometimes."

"But was it my picture?" I asked, unable to keep from smiling at his uncharacteristic discomfort.

"Well, yes. You gave me your photograph to take with me, you remember? It was rather a boon to my reputation to be able to show it to the fellows. Not a one of them had a prettier girl."

I gave him my best imitation of a sultry look. "And do I have bedroom eyes?"

"That's neither here nor there," he said, moving the letter away before I could read any more. That was probably for the best.

All the same, I was secretly pleased that he had shown my photo to his shipmates. It let me know that he had been thinking of me and seemed yet another indication that there was something more than just friendship between us.

I didn't know why things always had to be so complicated between men and women. Why was it impossible to say what we wanted to say and ask the questions we needed answers to?

"Wait," I said. "Does it give her address?"

He looked down at the letter. I reached for it, but he pulled it out of my reach. Whatever Billy had said at the conclusion of the letter was something he clearly didn't want me to see.

"Here," he said, tearing a scrap off the bottom of the letter and handing it to me.

In the postscript he had added his mother's name, Helen Norris, and her address.

Suddenly, the levity of the moment seemed to fade, and I felt the impact of what I was holding. I stared at it for a long time, those few words offering me a doorway into the past.

It was something I'd wanted for a long time, but now that it stared me in the face, I was a bit afraid of it. Because once I walked through that door there would be no looking back.

"Are you going to see her?" he asked.

"Yes," I replied at once. There wasn't really a question, was there?

"Do you want me to go with you?"

I considered this. Felix knew more about my past than anyone else. I had entrusted him with my darkest secret, and he had been my only confidant about it for years. Even so, I felt that it was something I should pursue on my own.

"I appreciate that, Felix," I said. "But this is something I need to do alone."

Felix accompanied me home. I was comfortable traveling London alone at night. I'd been raised to look after myself, and I knew the safest routes and what to watch for. What was more, I knew most of the people in our neighborhood, and they knew Uncle Mick and my cousins. There were few men in Hendon who would give me any trouble.

All the same, it was sweet of Felix to walk me home. It was different now that things were dark with the blackouts, and I was glad of the company. Besides, I didn't want to argue with him for fear he would think I was worried about his leg.

So we walked along at a pace that was comfortable for him. I slipped my arm through his, both for the enjoyment of being near him and hoping that it might ease a bit of the weight on his injured limb.

We reached Uncle Mick's house and walked along the little path through the kitchen garden to my flat. It was very dark in the shadow of the house, and I moved a little closer to his side.

At the door to my flat, I let go of his arm and moved to insert the key and open the door.

"Thank you again for dinner," I said, turning back to him. "It was delicious."

"Let me take you to a nightclub soon. I've been wanting to dance with you again."

"That sounds lovely." I paused. "Do you want to come in for a cup of tea?"

He hesitated. "I . . . suppose I'd better not," he said. "It's rather late."

I raised my brows. "Worried I might ruin your reputation?"

He grinned. "Something like that."

"Is it my bedroom eyes?" I asked, recalling the line from his shipmate's letter.

His eyes caught mine, and I felt the shift immediately. The humor in his gaze had been replaced by something warmer, something more intent.

It seemed as though time stood still as we looked at each other, both of us aware that something was happening and both of us wondering how we should proceed.

Then he stepped a bit closer, and I felt a flutter in my stomach. Anxiety, excitement. Desire. My eyes were still on his, though I had to tip my head back ever so slightly now that he was closer.

I saw his eyes flutter to my lips, and I knew that he was going to kiss me.

We had kissed once before, the previous year on a night like this—fragrant and moonlit—perhaps just to see what it would be like after so many years of friendship. It had been wonderful, heady with the strangely uncomplicated passion of youth, and free of expectation.

The next day we'd gone back to business as usual. We'd never discussed it, but I'd thought of it often since. I wondered if Felix had. If he had told his shipmate about the kisses we had shared one summer night under a starry sky when all had been right with the world.

He moved almost imperceptibly closer, so close I could feel the warmth of him through the cool night air.

And that's when I heard Uncle Mick's voice cut through the darkness. "Ah, Ellie. You're home."

CHAPTER NINE

We moved quickly apart. Or, to be more accurate, I did. Felix had very little reaction to Uncle Mick's sudden appearance. Though he shifted back ever so slightly, he wasn't one to be embarrassed in situations such as these.

I didn't know why I was, precisely. I was a grown woman and could do as I pleased with whomever I pleased. All the same, one didn't exactly like being caught almost kissing a man by one's uncle.

"Oh, Felix," Uncle Mick said guilelessly as he approached us out of the shadows. "You're here, too."

"Good evening, Mick," Felix said with a smile that showed he knew exactly what Uncle Mick was about.

My uncle had interrupted us for a reason, and the reason was Felix. If it had been Major Ramsey standing at my door, I was fairly certain Uncle Mick would have silently retreated.

"Ellie tells me you were away in Scotland," he said affably.

"Yes. Had some business to tend to."

Uncle Mick nodded. "I was up in Yorkshire. Just got home this morning."

We all stood there for a moment.

"Well, I'll be off," Felix said, bringing an end to the awkwardness. He turned to me. "I'll pick you up in the morning?"

I nodded.

He leaned and brushed a kiss across my cheek before turning to my uncle. "Good night, Mick."

"Good night, Felix."

Felix left unhurriedly, and, once he was out of sight, Uncle Mick turned to me. "Didn't mean to interrupt."

My brows rose. "Didn't you? Your timing was certainly uncanny."

"I was just on my way to my shop," Uncle Mick said innocently. "Do you want to come and visit awhile?"

I was still a bit miffed that he'd ruined my evening's romance, but I could never resist spending time with him in his shop.

We walked along the well-worn path in the yard that led to his workshop. Stepping inside, I was greeted with the familiar scent of old metal that always gave me a feeling of nostalgia.

This was one of my favorite places in the world, a magician's lair and an artist's atelier. This place was as much a home to me as the big house had been throughout my childhood, as my flat was now. There was a sense of comfort and security within these walls, memories that had been made in every corner.

I walked to the wall that held rows of pegs on which keys of all descriptions were hung. As I had since I was a child, I ran my hand along them, the bows tinkling in an eerie sort of music as they bumped against one another. Then I took my usual place in the desk chair as Uncle Mick settled down at his worktable, which dominated the space in the front part of the shop.

"Your dinner with Felix went well, then?" he asked as he picked up a mechanism he had been tinkering with before he had gone to Yorkshire.

So we were going to discuss this, were we?

"Yes, we had a very nice evening," I said, purposefully vague. As I should have expected, this had no effect on Uncle Mick.

"And what are his intentions, do you suppose?" My uncle was many things, but he wasn't exactly subtle.

I couldn't help but give an exasperated chuckle. "You didn't give me a chance to find out."

He looked up at me, his expression uncharacteristically serious. "I know you're a grown woman, Ellie," he said. "But that doesn't mean I don't want to look out for you. As I said this morning, I like Felix. But you know as well as I do he's never been exactly consistent where women are concerned."

I couldn't decide if I was touched or offended by his meddling in my romantic life. Then again, I ought to have been used to it. He and my cousins had been chasing away any boys who so much as looked in my direction for years.

"I don't know what's going to happen with Felix," I said gently. "But I do know that I care about him, and I'd like to see if there's anything more to it than that."

He nodded. "Fair enough, my girl. I won't pester you about the matter, but you know I'm here if you need to talk."

I nodded, touched by the fatherly affection. "Thank you."

"Now hand me that pick, will you, lass? This lock keeps sticking."

Felix picked me up early the next morning. All things considered, we decided not to have breakfast with Uncle Mick and Nacy and got a cup of tea and some toast and jam at a little café near the Tube station.

Then we took the Tube from Hendon to Whitechapel.

Sooty's shop was tucked into an alley between a tobacconist and a chemist that sold remedies of dubious origin.

The building looked as though it had been there for hundreds of years, the bricks worn smooth by time and grimy with the soot of earlier eras. I was glad to see that the front door was propped open by an iron dog's head. That meant Sooty was in.

He didn't hire employees, as he didn't trust anyone. If there was some reason he couldn't be there, the door was closed. But he was nearly always there. He lived in a flat above the store and spent all of his time in the dark, crowded confines of the pawnshop.

I looked at Felix.

"Ready, love?" he asked.

I nodded, and we entered the building.

The pawnshop was like something from a Dickens novel. It was crowded, dusty, and dim inside, the only light coming through the grimy windows. There were shelves upon sagging shelves crammed with every sort of bric-a-brac imaginable. Most of it was old and worn, the sort of thing that would be of little use to anyone who could afford better.

The only clean place in the entire establishment was one glass display case, front and center, behind which Sooty held court like a king, as though if he wandered away from it for a moment he would be relieved of his valuables.

If the shop was Dickensian, that went double for Sooty. He would have slipped easily into that world, and he would have thrived in it. There was something dark and shadowy about him, a sense that he belonged in another era entirely. Or that he had been living for long enough to remember a time when all the tarnished objects in his shop had been shiny and new with promise.

He looked up as we came in, his eyes moving from me to Felix and back to me again. There was something of the old lecher in his face. He was thin and stooped with sharp, dark eyes and grayish-white hair that hung long and unkempt to his shoulders. His skin, despite his age, was surprisingly smooth, probably because he rarely went outdoors.

"What can I do for you?" he asked, his tone not particularly trustful.

"Hello, Sooty. It's me, Felix Lacey," Felix said.

His grim expression eased ever so slightly as he peered at Felix. Then: "Lacey, my boy." A grin split his face, exposing dark, crooked teeth. "It's been an age."

"It has indeed."

"They haven't caught up with you yet, eh?" he asked Felix. I knew what he meant. Felix hadn't been called up. A man like Sooty Smythe didn't believe in the military, and I expected he would've spit when he spoke of it if he didn't want to dirty the floor of his shop.

Not that it was all that clean.

"I've been discharged. Lost part of my leg in France," Felix said in that casual way he had of relating the details of his injury.

Sooty's face darkened. "Should've run out before they shipped you off. Might've gone to Ireland."

"I was happy enough to do my bit," Felix replied. He motioned toward me, changing the subject. "I don't know if you remember Ellie McDonnell?"

Sooty's gaze came back to me. He studied me for a moment. "Mick's girl?"

I nodded.

"Sure I remember you, though you were nothing but a little mite the last time I saw you. You've grown into a beauty."

"Thank you." There was something less lecherous in his demeanor now that he knew who I was. Everyone who knew Uncle Mick respected him, and those who didn't at least knew better than to cross him.

"How is old Mick?"

"He's doing well," I said.

"But you didn't come here just to visit," Sooty said, his gaze growing sharp. "So why are you here?"

That was direct enough.

I stepped forward. This was the part that was going to be tricky. We couldn't let on that we'd gotten too chummy with the government. If we did, he wouldn't lift a finger to help us.

"I saw Monsieur LaFleur yesterday," I said. "He told me that you'd sold him some gemstones recently."

Sooty said nothing; his expression didn't even change. I knew this meant he was on the alert.

"We're looking for the woman who sold them to you," Felix said easily. He knew as well as I did that we had to tread carefully, but he was pressing ahead nonetheless.

"How do you know it was a woman?" Sooty asked.

I didn't know if he was testing me, or if this was some new twist in the investigation.

"Wasn't it?" I asked.

Sooty's expression grew shrewd.

"Frenchy knows as well as you do that I've always been one to keep my mouth shut," he said.

It was true enough. Sooty was a lot of things, but he wasn't loose-lipped. He had a reputation for hoarding secrets like a miser, and that was one reason he'd been so successful throughout the years and why he often came across valuable objects that one wouldn't normally think to bring to a place like this. People who had objects that were too recognizable to off-load at more reputable shops knew that Sooty could be trusted to take them and keep quiet.

I wondered if the dead woman had been pointed in his direction or if she had merely stumbled upon him by chance. Either way, she'd picked a good person if she wanted to be secretive about her movements.

However, I figured that between Felix and me, we'd have enough charm to get Sooty to loosen up a bit.

"The thing is," Felix said smoothly, "she owes me money."

It would have been good for us to come up with a story before coming in here. I had, in fact, figured that we would tell him some version that was close to the truth. Felix had decided to improvise, so there was nothing I could do but go along with it.

Sooty gave a slight shrug. "That's not my problem, mate."

"No," Felix agreed readily. "But she's stolen our share of those jewels and is planning to donate the money to the government for the war effort. I only want my fair share."

I managed to keep my eyebrows down as Felix's story evolved and expanded, but it was a difficult task. I'd heard him spin some yarns in my time, but this was elaborate even for him.

Sooty's eyes moved to me. "And what part do you have in all of this?"

That was a good question, wasn't it?

Luckily, I'd always been good at thinking fast. "Felix and I were in on the deal together. We'd got some goods, and she was supposed to split the profits with us. Instead, she ran off with the money."

I watched his face carefully; I wasn't sure he was buying what we were selling. Felix was undeterred, however.

"I'm not asking you to pay up what she owes, Sooty. I'm only trying to find out where she might have gone."

"Don't you know where she lives?" Sooty asked.

"Come on, Sooty. What are you, the police? Stop asking questions and just tell me what I need to know."

Felix had the unique talent of always knowing precisely how to walk the line. He wasn't too eager nor was he too reticent. There was an easiness in everything he did that made you believe what he was saying. Because he seemed to believe it himself, it made you want to believe it, too.

Sooty, it seemed, was not immune to this quality. He was distrustful, but he had always liked Felix, and I could see that he wanted to help him.

"We won't tell her that we talked to you," I said. That part, at least, was true enough. The poor woman was beyond caring about such things now.

"There was a girl in here," he said at last. "And I bought a few jewels from her. I don't know that there was anything special about it."

We all knew that wasn't true. For one thing, the gems had been of exceptional quality, and she had no doubt parted with them for much less than they were worth.

"What can you tell us about her?" I asked.

Sooty considered. "She was a pretty woman. Dark-haired. Shapely."

"Did she give you a name?" Felix asked. "She's always using aliases."

Sooty gave him another crooked grin. "I don't bother too much with names. Not when they're selling instead of pawning, you understand."

I looked around the pawnshop again. I didn't imagine there was much here that people came back to claim. Sooty's real stock-in-trade was the sort of dealings he had done with the dead woman, under the table and no questions asked.

"And she didn't mention anything about where she might be living?" I asked.

"No."

I had the sinking feeling that, after everything, we weren't going to learn anything from Sooty Smythe. Felix, however, had not yet given up.

"What about any associates? Did she mention anyone?"

Sooty seemed to consider this for a minute. "She mentioned her 'benefactor.' Said it with kind of a laugh. I thought it must be some rich man gifting her his wife's jewels. She also mentioned a boyfriend who didn't seem to be the same person." He gave us a speculative smile.

"You can't give us anything else?" Felix asked.

"I've given you more than I should already," Sooty said, his eyes flashing.

I knew it was true. If I hadn't brought Felix with me, I wouldn't have gotten nearly as much information.

"Well, thank you," Felix said.

"I hope you get your money," Sooty said.

"Thank you," I repeated.

"Give my regards to Mick."

Felix took my arm and we turned toward the door.

"Oh, there was one other thing," Sooty said.

We looked back at him.

"It was strange. When she was in here selling the gems, she also bought an old clock."

CHAPTER TEN

It was difficult to conceal my excitement at these words, but I think I managed to keep from looking too thrilled.

"A clock?" I asked, with just the right amount of interest.

Sooty nodded. "A mantel clock," he said. "It didn't work very well. It was always losing time. But she wanted it anyway."

"Did she say why?" Felix asked in a slightly mocking tone that also kept from being too curious.

Sooty shook his head. "Just said she took a fancy to it."

"What did it look like?" I asked.

"A clunky wooden thing with curlicues. Had a pink face with gold filigree. Said she liked the pink face."

Felix made a noncommittal sound. "Well, we'll be seeing you, Sooty."

And then we exited the shop.

It was a bit disorienting, stepping out of the close darkness of the shop into the daylight. I was almost dazzled by the sunshine and fresh air.

"I always come away from this place feeling vaguely as though I could use a bath," Felix said.

I laughed, squeezing his arm. "You were wonderful."

He grinned. "I'm glad to hear you say so. I'm only sorry we didn't learn more. I wish he could have given you a name."

I nodded, thinking. "Chances are she wouldn't have given him her real name anyway. But what did she want with the clock? It's all so odd. She kept the clock key with the jewels, hidden away. That has to mean something, doesn't it?"

"One would assume so," Felix said. He had removed his cigarette case from his pocket and put one to his lips, bringing his lighter to the tip.

It had gone relatively well, all things told. Sooty had been in a genial mood, as his moods went. We had learned a good deal more than we would have if I had gone with the major, that much was sure.

I wondered, all the same, what the major would have thought of Sooty. He was certainly a character. They wouldn't have liked each other, but, given the chance, I think they both would have grudgingly appreciated qualities in the other.

Whatever the case, we needed to relate what we had learned to Major Ramsey as soon as possible.

"Let's go to see the major," I said.

Felix's stride slowed. "Perhaps you'd better go without me."

I turned to him, exasperated. "I don't know why you've taken such a disliking to him, Felix."

His eyes caught mine. "Don't you?"

I frowned at him. "Don't be ridiculous, Felix."

He shrugged, blowing out a stream of smoke. "I know I have no right to be territorial, Ellie. But all the same . . ."

I brushed this aside. Now was not the time for this sort of conversation.

"This is important," I said. "And he's going to want your account of it as well as mine."

"All right," he said with a sigh. "I've gotten involved this far, I might as well dive in the rest of the way."

* * *

We arrived at the major's office and Constance opened the door for us.

"Good morning," she said brightly, her eyes lingering with interest on Felix as she ushered us into the town house. She hadn't encountered him before, and I knew what a good first impression he always made on women.

"Is the major in?" I asked. "I believe he's expecting us."

"Yes, he is," she said, turning her attention back to me, "but he's in a meeting at the moment, if you would wait?"

"Certainly."

We took seats on the yellow silk sofa across from the desk in the parlor that had been converted into a makeshift office. Constance went back to her desk and resumed working at her typewriter, the clatter of keys a pleasant background sound to my thoughts.

I was curious who was meeting with the major this morning. In the time I had known him, I hadn't seen any other military officers in his office. Though, perhaps it wasn't entirely surprising; this was something of an unorthodox enterprise he was running here.

It wasn't much later when I heard the sound of a door opening and footsteps coming down the hall.

I recognized the man who appeared a moment later. It was Kimble, one of the major's associates who had been involved with us on our last caper. Kimble had been a former Scotland Yard man, let go for some sort of behavior that had been outside of the Yard's bounds. From all I had seen, it could have been anything up to and including outright murder. Kimble was a man of absolutely no expression who related everything from the weather to acts of startling violence in the exact same tone.

"Miss McDonnell, Lacey," he said, with a slight nod to us. Without stopping for any other pleasantries, he continued right out the front door.

The last time Kimble had been called in to assist, there had been a chance the plan would devolve into bloodshed. Was he here about the same case we were, or was it something else entirely? I was certain Major Ramsey would have several irons in the fire.

"I'll just see if the major is ready for you," Constance said, rising from the desk and disappearing down the hall.

"If Kimble's in on this, things can't be good," Felix said, voicing what I had been thinking.

"We don't know that he's in on anything," I replied. "Perhaps it was just a social call."

Felix scoffed at this, but I didn't have time to say anything else before Constance reappeared.

"The major will see you now," she said.

"Thank you," I replied, leading the way. Felix, after casting a parting smile at Constance, followed behind me like a reluctant shadow.

The door to the major's office was open, and we went in. He was standing behind the desk, every hair in place as usual. He looked up at us with an unreadable expression, his cool eyes settling first on me then on Felix.

"Good morning, Miss McDonnell, Lacey."

"Ramsey," Felix replied.

There was certainly no love lost between the two of them. They hadn't liked each other from the beginning. It was because they were entirely different kinds of men. Both of them were intelligent, decisive, and extremely competent. But while the major was stern and taciturn, Felix was charming and devil-may-care. And he had never given a fig for what the law said. Truth be told, it was something I had always enjoyed about Felix, the way he was as willing as the rest of my family to skirt the bounds of respectability.

But their differences made it difficult to find some sort of balance between the two men when I was with them. It left me feeling a bit in the middle, which was never a comfortable place to be.

Well, they would just have to get over their dislike for each other. They had worked together before with good results. Perhaps eventually they would learn that they made better allies than enemies.

"Sit down, will you?" the major said, indicating the two chairs before his desk.

I sat, and the men followed suit.

"We saw Kimble in the hall," I said.

The major didn't answer.

It was clear there would be no more information forthcoming on that score, so I decided to forge ahead with our reason for coming here. "We've been to see Sooty Smythe, as I said we would."

The major waited.

"He admitted to getting the jewels from the woman," I said. "But he didn't know her name."

"Or he was unwilling to tell it."

"No," Felix put in. "He would have told me if he did."

The major's eyes flicked to Felix, but his next question was directed at me.

"Were you able to get anything else from him?"

"He said that she bought an old mantel clock. One that didn't work very well. She insisted on taking it, though."

The major didn't look as excited by this news as I had been. But I supposed it wasn't any sort of importance in the grand scheme of things. We had a clock key, after all. It was apparent that she had had a clock somewhere that was of some significance. Until we knew where it was, however, this information would do little good.

"Anything else?" he asked.

"Sooty said she mentioned a benefactor, which I suppose could be the spymaster, and also a boyfriend, but that was all he . . ."

My words trailed off as the major opened his desk drawer and removed something from inside, setting it before us. I realized it was a stack of photographs.

Without asking, I reached forward to take them and began sorting through.

"The photographs in the bracelet camera have been developed. At least some of them survived with very little damage. A few were blurred, but it's clear enough what they are."

"Just as you thought," I said, noting that the first few photographs were of the docks and factories.

"Yes. As I surmised, they are pictures of the factories and other key locations. But it's worse than that. Look at the one at the bottom of the stack."

I sifted through quickly until I came to the one at the bottom. In contrast to the others, it wasn't a picture of a London locale. Instead, it was a photograph of a sheet of paper with something written across it. *G02A04—East End.*

I looked up at him. "I don't understand."

"She's labeled this film, documented who took it and where. If I had to guess, it would be group—*gruppe* in German, if you prefer—two and agent—*agentin*—four. We've seen similar identifications in past interceptions." The major leaned forward. "The point is, I believe that this woman, whoever she was, was not working alone. She was one of several individuals who have been taking photographs for the Germans."

I realized the implications of this. "You think there's a spy ring photographing London for the Germans, to give them a clearer picture of targets."

He nodded. "We know she had a handler who was probably the one who killed her. I assume there was some reason it became too risky to continue paying her for information. Perhaps her boyfriend found out what she had been doing and was going to go to the authorities. Perhaps she'd had a change of heart. Whatever the case, they realized that she was too much of a risk to them."

"But how do you know there are others involved? Perhaps she

was just one lone woman who'd somehow got ensnared in something."

The major sat back in his chair and took a moment to consider before answering. At last, he said, "We've received intelligence that there is a German operative on the way to London to collect something very important."

I frowned. "What sort of something?"

"From coded messages that have been intercepted, it seems that there is a cache of film that has been gathered by several spies. Photographs that could be potentially very dangerous to us in the coming months."

I realized what he meant. "You think the Germans are going to bomb us."

"In my opinion, it's a matter of weeks. If not days."

I ought to have been chilled by these words, but I felt a sudden burst of my Irish blood rush through me, and my chin went up a touch in defiance. "Let them try," I said.

Felix smiled. "That's my girl."

"We can't stop them from reaching London, obviously," the major said. "The barrage balloons and the RAF will only be able to ward off so many. But if they are able to get their hands on detailed information about key target sites in London and get that information back to Germany, it could cause a lot of problems for us."

I thought of the hundreds of giant balloons flying over London, holding steel cables aloft in hopes that they would retard dive bombers. Would we have to find out how well they worked? I prayed not.

"It's not only potential bombings we have to worry about, of course," the major continued. "Any information about our resources, distribution, supply lines, etcetera, could be detrimental in German hands."

Felix had been silent for most of this conversation, but now he leaned forward a bit, his gaze intent. "You say that they are attempting to find this cache of film the dead girl had been contributing to. Do you have any idea where it is?"

"No. Fortunately, I don't believe their operative has arrived in London yet."

"Then it's rather like a race to the finish line," I said.

The major nodded. "We need to get our hands on that film before the Germans do."

CHAPTER ELEVEN

We left shortly afterward, the major making it clear that he had no further use for us at present.

"I'll be in touch," he said, as he always did when he was trying to be rid of me.

Although it was a bit galling to be so summarily dismissed, the truth was there was nothing for Felix and I to do that could help, not now. We were starting considerably behind the Germans, and we needed to find a way to make up for lost time.

It was just a question of where to start. Major Ramsey was focused on that detail, no doubt, but I felt helpless not being able to do anything about it at the moment.

"Where to now, love?" Felix asked when we were outside. "Do you have any other spy missions for me on this fine afternoon?"

I looked up at him. My thoughts had begun to move along other lines. I had made up my mind that morning about what I wanted to do, provided the major didn't need us. Since there was nothing to be done at the moment, I would proceed as planned.

"I . . . I think I'm going to see Mrs. Norris," I said. I had been both looking forward to and dreading my conversation with the mother of Felix's shipmate, and it seemed to me that the best thing to do would be to get it done.

"You're sure you want to go alone?" he asked.

I nodded. "I . . . I need to do this by myself. You understand?"

"Of course, I do, Ellie," he said gently. "You'll ring me later?"

"Yes. I'll let you know what she says."

He took my hand and squeezed it. Then he turned and left me alone to do what I needed to do.

The address was easy enough to find, a small house in a quiet street in Fulham. There was a little fence around the property and tidy window boxes with a profusion of flowers. I don't know what I had been expecting exactly, but this little bit of perfect domesticity in the middle of the city was not in keeping with the scenario that had played out in my head.

It was an unfair prejudice, I realized. This woman had been in prison, and I hadn't thought she would have retired to this sort of life. I chided myself for thinking this way. If anyone should know that time in prison did not comprise the whole of a person's history, it should be me.

I felt unaccountably nervous as I walked up the front steps and used the heavy brass knocker to rap on the door.

All was quiet for a few moments, and I wondered if she wasn't home. Disappointment and relief played tug-of-war with my insides as I stood there. This could wait until another day. If she wasn't home, I would come again. But I still stood there.

Just as I had nearly made up my mind to leave, I heard the sound of a bolt being thrown and then the door opened.

A woman stood looking back at me. I was not sure how I had pictured her, knowing she had spent time at Holloway. But this woman looked like any other woman who would have answered a door on this street. She was older than my mother would have been now, white-haired and pink-skinned. It was only in her eyes, which were a pale blue, that there was a hint of some of the difficulties she had lived through.

"Yes?" she asked.

"Mrs. Norris?"

"Yes."

"My name is Ellie McDonnell."

Recognition came into her features and she stepped back from the door, motioning me to enter. Wordlessly, she shut the door behind me and turned and led me into a little parlor off the entryway.

The interior of her house was sparse and tidy. The furniture was older but in excellent condition, and the floors shone bright with beeswax polish. A vase of flowers sat on a table, and the curtains were lace. She hadn't boarded up her windows, and I wondered if it was because she didn't want to or because she had no one to help her do it.

She motioned toward an overstuffed chair in one corner, and I took a seat.

"Would you like some tea?" she offered.

"Oh, no. I don't want to trouble you. I've already imposed upon you, arriving unannounced as I have."

"It's no trouble. I was going to make it anyway," she said.

"Then I would love a cup. Thank you."

She went away to the kitchen, and it gave me a few moments to collect my thoughts.

I was not of a nervous disposition. I hadn't been raised that way, and it didn't seem that it was in my nature either, for there was little that really set me on edge. All the same, this was the first time I had met anyone who might be able to tell me something about my mother.

I had thought of questioning Nacy about her, but Nacy hadn't lived with the family before my mother was sent to prison. She had been living in the south and had come to London only when Uncle Mick took me in and, as a widower, had needed help raising three small children.

No doubt she had heard a good deal about the situation and about my mother, but it wasn't firsthand information.

The only other person who could give me that was Uncle Mick, and I had known for years it wasn't something he wanted to talk about. He couldn't be objective. Not when it was his brother who had been killed.

I knew he must have harbored anger toward my mother. He'd loved my father. They'd been best friends, just as Colm and Toby were. So it must have been unbearably hard for him to come home one evening to find his brother dead on the kitchen floor and realize that all evidence pointed to his sister-in-law.

And yet he never spoke a word against her to me. When he had told me of what happened, it had been only the bare facts. No anger, no judgment. I knew that I was just as much her daughter as I was my father's, but Uncle Mick had never showed any sign of bitterness that her blood ran in my veins.

But the silence that surrounded her was somehow almost as bad as anger or hatred might have been. That silence had left an empty space in my heart that couldn't be filled by anything else.

Worse was the fact that I had begun long ago to believe she was innocent. Until the end of her life, she had never wavered in her insistence that she hadn't killed my father. I knew that knowing the truth wouldn't change the past. But I felt, somehow, that knowing would make a difference to my future. That putting the pieces of my past into place would give me a better picture of who I was meant to be.

All of this passed through my mind in a whirl, and I was left to try to sort out my feelings as I waited for her to return.

A few moments later, we were settled with the tea tray before us. The tea was strong, though we were on rations now. I thought it was probably on my account and appreciated the gesture.

"I . . . I believe your son told you about me?" I said.

She nodded. "He said that you'd likely be here to see me. I told him I had no objection. I've never tried to hide my past."

I wondered what that was like, to embrace a past without any hint of shame. Of course, the past that bothered me wasn't mine; it was the one I had come here to discuss.

Our tea poured, she settled back into her chair. Though she couldn't be much past sixty, she moved slowly, as though her body ached. I wondered if prison life had been difficult on her, or if there was some other reason that she seemed frailer than her years.

"I knew your mother fairly well," she said, jumping into the topic without preamble. "A lot of the other prisoners steered clear of her. She wasn't friendly, as such. Of course, the whole thing had been a shock for her, and I believe she was still deeply mourning your father when she was sent to prison."

I found myself leaning forward. In that moment I felt the impact of how little I knew about my mother. This was the first account I had had of her from someone who had known her. Aside from the brief conversation I'd had with Uncle Mick when I was finally old enough to ask questions about my past, there had been only the newspaper accounts of the case I'd surreptitiously gathered and pored over like they were the map to some sort of grim buried treasure.

"But our cells were across from each other, and, in the way it sometimes goes, we struck up conversations here and there," she went on. "Eventually we got chummy, you might say, and began sharing about our lives with each other."

"What was she like?" I asked. I hadn't really planned to ask that question, but it came out on its own as though it had been sitting there waiting for years for the chance to be asked.

Mrs. Norris considered this for a minute.

"She was beautiful. You look a lot like her, you know."

I flushed at the compliment, not knowing how to process the warm feeling it gave me to be compared to the mother I had never known.

"A lot of people held that against her, thought she was using it to her advantage. But she couldn't help how she looked any more than she could change the other things about her. She was kind, bright, and funny. She cared about other people. Kindness is something that fades quickly in prison, but your mother was kind to the end. She would help others whenever she could, in small ways that wouldn't draw notice."

I felt the clench of emotion in my chest. I thought I'd been able to harden myself about the things that pertained to my mother, but this was something completely new.

"You'll find a lot of women in prison who claim they're innocent, but I never believed any of them but your mother. There was something in her eyes . . . We had a talk one night, and she told me that she had been thinking everything over, and that she believed she knew who had killed her husband. She said that there was proof of her innocence, but to reveal it would do more harm than good."

I was suddenly alert.

"What did she mean?" I asked, leaning forward in my seat.

Mrs. Norris shook her head. "I wanted to ask her more, but the guards came by then and hustled us off to our cells. The next morning, she didn't come into the yard, and I heard she'd gotten fever."

She didn't have to say the rest. My mother had died of the Spanish flu not long after.

"I didn't catch the flu," she said. "I don't know why. Sometimes it seemed as though there was no rhyme or reason to it. Much like many things in life."

I considered what she had told me. There had been some secret my mother had known, something that, if brought to light, would have been more catastrophic than her spending the rest of her life in prison. She had been sentenced to death and still had not revealed it. What could have been worth dying for?

I looked up to see Mrs. Norris watching me, her expression shrewd but kind. "You'll want more answers, I know. If you've come to me, you'll go to others."

"Are there others?" I asked.

"There are two people who may be able to tell you something more," she said. "The first was her barrister, Sir Roland Highgate."

I had heard the man's name many times throughout the years, in association with other big criminal cases. My mother's case had been one in a long line of sensational cases. It had occurred to me, of course, that I might one day want to talk to him, but I had always put it off. Perhaps because the McDonnells had always avoided associating with the law in any capacity.

"You think he might have something to tell me?" I asked.

"Your mother said that he knew more about her case than anyone else. That he had done all he could to investigate the matter. She said that he had truly believed in her innocence."

This was a valuable bit of information. I'd known who my mother's lawyer was, of course, but I hadn't really believed him to be an ally. It had always seemed to me that he must have taken her case for the publicity. It was good to know that he had truly wanted to help her.

I nodded. "Thank you. I'll try to go and see him."

"And the other is her friend, Clarice Maynard."

I frowned. This was a name I hadn't heard, not once in all the years I had been gleaning information on my mother's case.

"Who was she?" I asked.

"Your mother's closest friend, from what she said. They were always writing letters back and forth. Your mother said that she didn't know how she might have made it through the whole thing if it wasn't for her friendship with Clarice."

"Does she still live in London?" I asked.

"I don't know. Your mother didn't say."

I wondered what had become of this woman. Was she still alive? Why had she never come to visit me if she had been so close with my mother? I'd never so much as heard her name.

It seemed, then, that I had two very good avenues open to me.

There hadn't been any definitive answers, but there was much I had to consider.

"Thank you so much for your time, Mrs. Norris," I said. "You've been most helpful."

She gave a nod. "I wish I could tell you more. But if I think of anything else, I'll be sure to let you know."

We exchanged telephone numbers, and I thanked her again for her time and for the tea.

I turned to leave then, but her voice stopped me as I reached the door. "Ellie."

I looked back at her.

"She didn't get to keep you very long after you were born, but she loved every minute of it. She was proud of you, prouder than she was of anything else."

I think she knew how important this was to me, and I felt an overwhelming sense of gratitude to her.

"Thank you," I whispered.

She nodded. "I wish you luck."

CHAPTER TWELVE

As it turned out, there wasn't going to be any time for quiet reflection as I returned to the house. Major Ramsey was there waiting for me.

This time he wasn't having tea with Nacy in the parlor. He was standing at my door. He caught me by surprise as I rounded the house and walked toward my flat, since the big car was not parked out front. Apparently, he'd found an alternative method of travel.

"Hello," I said. "I didn't expect to see you again so soon. Have you been waiting long?"

"No." The terse answer and the tone in which it was uttered didn't exactly hide the fact that he was in a mood.

I sighed inwardly. I had been looking forward to a cup of tea and a gramophone recording to restore the sense of balance my visit with Mrs. Norris had thrown off-kilter. But it seemed that was not to be.

I opened the door to my flat, and he followed me inside. He removed his service cap and tucked it under one arm. He made no move to sit down. It didn't appear he would be staying long, then.

"Well, what's the matter?" I asked, as I closed the door behind him.

"We've identified the dead woman," he said. "We were able

to find her through a purchase record on the coat, just as you suggested. Her name, or at least the one she gave, was Myra Fields. Her
address is in Clapham."

This was a good thing, wasn't it? Then why did he look so grim?

His next words answered my question. "I'm afraid I'm going
to need you to accompany me."

There it was. He needed my help and, as usual, was loath to
ask for it.

"Oh?" I asked, as though I wasn't the least bit interested in
the assignment. In truth, of course, my heart had already started
beating faster.

"I think it will draw undo attention if I go alone. A man in
uniform asking questions is always deemed suspicious. If you're
with me, we might be able to play it off."

I suppressed a smile at the resigned way he said this. We'd
played the couple once before, at a fancy event where we'd needed
to get into a safe.

It was also at that event that I'd kissed the major. Or, to be
accurate, he had kissed me. It had been part of a ploy, meant to
distract a quarry from the fact we had been in a place we were not
meant to be, breaking into a safe. But it had been a proper kiss all
the same.

In the weeks since it had happened, I had tried not to give it
much thought, but my mind still drifted in that direction occasionally. Perfectly natural, given that the major was a good-looking man
in a city where eligible men were in short supply.

Natural or not, however, I realized that these thoughts weren't
in the least productive.

I looked up at him and our eyes caught for just a moment. I
had the ridiculous notion he might have been thinking about that
kiss as well, but I quickly brushed it aside. I doubted the major had
thought about it even once since it happened.

"All right," I said. "But the two of us going in there and asking questions is likely to draw suspicion in itself. I think you should let me go in alone."

"No."

I'd known, of course, that he would say that, but I forged ahead.

"People will be more likely to talk to me if I'm alone," I persisted. "I can pretend I'm a relative of Myra, that I've just been notified she's dead."

"No."

"Major . . ."

"It is out of the question." There was something in his tone that made me realize he wasn't going to back down. Not that he usually did. But it was clear that this time even listing all the reasons why it made sense was not going to change his mind.

"All right, then," I said. "What do you suggest?"

"We'll go in together, as I said. You can still pretend to be a relative."

"And you'll be my . . . what?"

"You're clever, Miss McDonnell. You decide." It was a challenge if I'd ever heard one.

"Fine. You'll be my husband."

I had said it to get a rise out of him, but his expression didn't change. "You're not wearing a wedding ring."

Leave it to him to think of that.

"I guess you'll just have to be my beau, then," I said.

I was enjoying his discomfort more than I should. But posing as a couple really was the easiest way for a man and a woman to go about asking questions together. Anything else might draw notice. So he would just have to learn to live with it.

We took the Tube, as the major hadn't wanted to draw any attention to our movements with his car.

On the walk from the station to Miss Fields's address, the major laid out the objectives of this particular mission. We were to gain access to Miss Fields's lodging house, get what information we could, and find a way to search her room, if possible.

"Are you certain you won't let me go in alone?" I asked as we slowed upon nearing the address. The lodging house was a large Victorian pile that had seen better days. All the same, it looked clean and respectable enough.

He didn't even glance at me. "I'm certain."

I sighed. "Fine. Then do try to act madly in love with me."

I hurried up the front steps of the lodging house before he could respond. I knocked on the door, and it was opened a few moments later by a fresh-faced young woman.

"Hello," I said, schooling my face into one of grim stoicism. "I need to speak to someone about Myra Fields."

"I don't know . . ." She opened the door a bit farther and got distracted by the major before she remembered me and finished her sentence. "I don't know any Myra Fields. I've just moved in. But if you want to come into the parlor, I'll get Mrs. Paine for you. She's the landlady."

"Thank you."

She held the door for us, then led us into a spacious parlor off the entryway. There was a young couple sitting on a sofa by the open window. The man, a young fellow in a navy uniform, rose as we entered.

"They need to speak to Mrs. P," the girl who had opened the door said. "Can you clear out, Suzy?" She turned and left the room, presumably in search of Mrs. Paine, before Suzy could answer.

"I do hate to put you out," I said, "but it's rather urgent."

"That's all right," she said, somewhat ungraciously.

She was annoyed, but the sailor gave us a nod and reached for her arm. "We'll go for a walk, Suze," he said. Whatever he felt about giving up their privacy in the parlor, he wasn't going to argue about it in front of an officer, whatever military branch he hailed from.

Suzy and her young man walked out just as another woman walked in.

She had platinum hair, the dark roots grown out, and makeup that was smudged around her eyes. She had a cigarette between two fingers and a harried, long-suffering expression on her face as she came into the room.

"You wanted to see me?" she said.

She caught sight of Major Ramsey then, and one hand went up to unconsciously smooth her hair. I knew quite well the impulse to straighten oneself up in his spotless presence.

"I'm afraid I don't take couples," she said. "Just single girls. Mrs. Tully, across the road, she takes couples, though only short term. It's really a small hotel, so that won't work if you're looking for something longer."

"We're not here for a room," I said. "My name is Elizabeth Donaldson. I'm here about Myra Fields."

A frown wrinkled the landlady's brow. "I'm afraid Myra's not here."

"I know," I said softly.

"Oh, do you know where she is? I haven't seen her in a few days. I was beginning to believe she might have run out on her rent."

I drew in a sad breath. "I'm afraid it's something much worse than that. Myra . . ." I paused to feign gathering my emotions and was startled when the major put a sympathetic hand on my back.

"It's all right, dear," he said to me. Then he turned to Mrs. Paine. "I'm afraid Myra Fields is dead."

Mrs. Paine gasped, a hand to her chest. "What do you mean?"

"She was drowned in the Thames," the major said, his hand still resting on the small of my back.

"I just can't believe it," she murmured. "Poor Myra. Whatever happened?"

"We don't know, as of yet," the major said. "We were hoping you might be able to tell us something."

Mrs. Paine drew in a steadying breath on her cigarette. "I don't know what I can tell you," she said. "I'm certainly very sorry to have lost one of my girls. I get to feel as though they're family."

"Had you known Myra long?" I asked.

"She'd been here about six months," Mrs. Paine said.

"We'd be happy to settle what she owes you for her rent and take her things," Major Ramsey said smoothly.

A slight frown wrinkled Mrs. Paine's brow. "Have you spoken to John?"

"Who is John?" I asked.

She looked at me, a hint of surprise on her features. "John Pritchard. Her young man."

"She wrote to me about him," I said. "About a young man she was involved with, I mean. But I'd never met him. I live in Kent, you see. We've just come up."

Mrs. Paine nodded. "Well, someone is going to have to tell John."

"Do you know where we can reach him?" the major asked.

She shook her head. "To be frank, there are a lot of men coming and going. Just in the parlor, mind. I don't let the girls have visitors anywhere but here. But, all the same, it's rather a busy place. Myra always called it Paddington Station."

She seemed to realize that she had been rambling and gave an apologetic smile before she returned to the matter at hand. "John usually comes on Wednesdays," she said. "If you'll leave a number where I can reach you, I'll ring you up when he comes."

"It would be better for us to tell him in person, I think," I said sadly. "Is . . . is there anyone else, one of her friends, perhaps, who might know how we could reach him?"

Mrs. Paine took another drag of her cigarette and seemed to consider. "You could talk to Cindy and Jane. They were her two closest friends here, thick as thieves the three of them."

"Are they here now?"

"Cindy may be. I don't think Jane has come back from her shift at the factory yet. I'll just go and see . . ."

"Thank you," I said.

She left the room, and I turned to the major. We shared a look, though we didn't say anything telling. If this was Paddington Station, it was important to carry on the ruse.

"I'm glad poor Myra had such a nice place to live until . . . until the end."

"Don't cry, dear," he replied automatically, though he was not even looking at me. Something else had caught his attention.

I followed the direction of his gaze to the other side of the room.

It was then I caught sight of the clock sitting on the mantel.

CHAPTER THIRTEEN

It was just as Sooty Smythe had described it, and I didn't see how there could be any mistake. It was a heavy wooden piece with ornate carving and an unusual pink-colored face. More interestingly, watching it for a minute convinced me that it still wasn't working right. In fact, it didn't seem to be working at all. There had to be some other reason it was displayed on the mantel.

I was about to go over to it when I heard approaching footsteps. A moment later Mrs. Paine came back in with a tall, sturdily built young woman with glossy red hair. I saw the young lady's gaze zero in on the major and decided to let him proceed with this one. I had the feeling he'd have better luck than I would.

"Good afternoon. My fiancée is a cousin of Miss Fields," the major said, gesturing to me, by way of introduction. I noticed that he didn't give her his name. "We're sad to say that Miss Fields is dead."

A look of shock flashed across Cindy's face. And then her eyes welled up with tears. "Are you sure?" she asked.

The major nodded. "I'm afraid so."

"Oh no!"

"There, there," Mrs. Paine said automatically. "Have a sit down, Cindy. I'll find you a handkerchief."

The major pulled one from his pocket and handed it to the weeping Cindy, who had sunk into a chair and began to dab at her eyes.

Then he came over to me and, to my surprise, took my hand. Then I felt the cold metal against my skin. He'd taken the clock key from the same pocket as his handkerchief. So the major wasn't above a bit of sleight of hand. He was learning.

I palmed the key and gave him an adoring look.

"I think, perhaps, we could do with a cup of tea," Mrs. Paine said. I had the impression she would just be glad to escape the room.

"Some tea would be lovely, if it's not too much trouble," I said.

"No, not at all. Be back in a flash."

She left the room, and we were left with only Cindy, who was still dabbing her eyes with the major's handkerchief.

"Get her out," I mouthed to the major.

He gave me a short nod.

"I know this has been a shock, Miss . . ."

"Prince," she said. "Cindy Prince."

"This has been difficult for all of us, knowing Myra as we did. I'm afraid my fiancée needs a moment to gather herself. If you would be so kind as to show me to Miss Fields's room while Mrs. Paine is preparing the tea, I can assess what might need to be done and then we can all have a nice cup together."

He smiled at her then. He so seldom smiled that I found myself a bit dazzled by it. And if it impressed me, there was no way Miss Prince was going to resist it.

"Yes," she said, sniffling a bit but composing herself. "Yes, I can show you her room." She looked suddenly much less bereft than she had a moment before.

She rose and began to lead the major from the room. "You'll be all right, darling?" he asked me over his shoulder.

"Yes, I'll be fine. I just need a moment to compose myself."

As soon as they cleared the door, I hurried over to the mantel. I examined the face to see if there was anything unusual about it, but nothing seemed out of the ordinary. Except the fact that the clock wasn't working.

I opened the glass case covering the face and inserted the winding key the major had slipped me into the clock. I turned it, and there was a slight click. I knew that feeling well enough: it was a mechanism releasing.

Gently, I turned the clock around and saw that the back had popped open slightly. I pulled it open the rest of the way and saw a roll of film inside.

Glancing over my shoulder, I slipped it out and examined it. There was no note or anything significant attached. I wondered if I should remove the film. But no, probably better to leave it where it was.

As I replaced the film roll, closed the back of the clock, and resecured it with the winding key, I wondered who it had been left for. Myra, perhaps? And who had left it? Mrs. Paine had mentioned that there were people coming in and out all the time. How difficult would it be for someone to slip in and put film there? No more difficult than it had been for me.

I heard footsteps in the hallway and moved back to the sofa, taking a seat there.

Mrs. Paine returned carrying a tray with the tea-things on it. She glanced around.

"Has Cindy run off with your young man?"

"She's gone to show him Myra's room," I said. "I needed a moment to collect myself."

She nodded. "Thoughtful of them. All the same, I'd watch out for that one. She's a fast worker, if you know what I mean."

I gave a small laugh. "I'm not worried."

Mrs. Paine gave a shrug, as though she thought I would just have to learn the hard way. Then she carried the tray to the table.

"How do you take your tea, dear?"

"Might I have just a bit of sugar?" I asked. I normally took my tea as sweet as syrup, but I wasn't going to ask this woman to sacrifice her rations.

"Certainly," she said, dropping in a large spoonful. "Any milk?"

"No, thank you."

She handed me my tea, and then prepared herself a cup with sugar and milk. Then she took a seat across from me.

"You and Myra were close?" she asked. "I don't think she ever mentioned a cousin."

I took a sip of tea as I considered my answer. It was possible that Myra Fields had no relatives in England, and I didn't know what she would have confided in her friends. I had to tread carefully and make sure I stuck to my story.

"I am not technically a cousin," I said. "Our mothers were close when we were girls, and we took to calling each other cousins. We've stayed very close since, though I didn't get to see her as often as I would have liked to. Especially since the war started. And now . . ." I trailed off and managed to get a tear to spring to my eye.

Mrs. Paine tsked sympathetically and took a sip of her own tea. "The war has prevented so many of us from doing things we'd like to, dear. Don't be hard on yourself for not seeing her as much as you'd like to."

I nodded, wiping my eye. "Perhaps if you told me something about . . . about what she's been doing lately, I could feel close to her."

She sipped her tea. "Well, as I said, the girls do much of their own activities most of the time. I see them as they're in and out."

"Was she working somewhere? I don't think she'd mentioned that in any of her recent letters."

"I believe she was working at a factory, secretarial work, though that sort of thing is hush-hush."

"Oh, yes, of course."

There was the sound of approaching footsteps and voices, and then the major and Cindy came back into the room. Apparently, he'd been successful, for she was positively glowing.

I wondered if he'd been able to find anything of interest while Cindy was there watching his every move. Perhaps after tea we could go into the room together and do a quick search.

"I really think perhaps you should wait until John is here," Mrs. Paine said. "He was closest to her. He might be able to help you sort through her things."

I glanced at the major. "Well, perhaps. I just thought we could help with . . ."

"We'll come back, darling," the major said. "You're all in for the day."

So he wanted us to leave. Perhaps he had learned something.

I nodded. "Yes, I am feeling a bit fatigued."

"You don't want a cup of tea, Major Grey?" Cindy asked hopefully.

So that was the name he'd given her, was it? It certainly fit the nature of the work we were doing.

"Thank you, no," he said. "I need to take Elizabeth home."

I drained the rest of my tea and set the cup and saucer on the table. "Thank you so much for your kindness, Mrs. Paine."

"I'm very sorry about Myra. It will be a loss to all of us."

"What's happened to Myra?" I looked up to see a young woman standing in the doorway. She was wearing dirty coveralls, and her blond hair was tied up on top of her head with a kerchief.

"I . . . I'm afraid Myra's dead, dear," Mrs. Paine said.

The young woman's face went white, but she was made of stronger stuff than Cindy had been, and she quickly pulled herself together. "How?"

This was, I assumed, Jane, the other of Myra Fields's friends who had been mentioned by Mrs. Paine.

"She . . . she drowned," I said sadly.

Jane's eyes moved to me. "And who are you?" she asked.

"No need to be rude, Jane," Cindy said. "This is Myra's cousin. And her fiancé, Major Grey."

Jane's eyes flicked from me to the major and back. "Jane Kelley," she said. "When did it happen?"

"So far we haven't had an answer as to that," the major said. "You see, she was found in the Thames."

Miss Kelley swore beneath her breath and came into the room. "Tea isn't strong enough for this, Mrs. P. You ought to have at least broke out the sherry."

Mrs. Paine frowned at her and said nothing. Jane poured herself a cup of tea and took a seat. "So tell me what you know."

I hadn't expected an interrogation on the matter. After all, we'd come here to ask questions, not answer them.

The major didn't seem at all flummoxed by the young woman's manner. But, after all, he was used to dealing with me.

"She was found in the Thames six days ago," he said.

"We've only just arrived from Kent today," I added. "I received word last night that she was dead and was only able to come up this morning."

"Who contacted you?" she asked, turning her sharp blue eyes on me.

No doubt she was accustomed to intimidating people with this forthrightness, but Ellie McDonnell was not easy to intimidate.

"The police," I replied with a mild smile. "You ask almost as many questions as they do."

She blinked but recovered rapidly. "The police haven't been around here yet. I'm surprised you beat them to it. Six days is a long time."

"I'm sure they'll be around soon," Major Ramsey interjected smoothly. "From what I understand, she's only just been identified."

"Then she didn't have her papers," Jane Kelley said. "It must have been a robbery."

"It didn't alarm you that she'd gone missing?" the major asked.

Miss Kelley shook her head. "I wondered when she didn't come home, but I thought maybe . . ." She glanced at Mrs. Paine. "I thought maybe she was spending extra time with John."

"Did she go out with him on the last night you saw her?" the major asked.

Miss Kelley hesitated.

"It's all right," the major said. "We're not trying to get him in trouble. We just want to see if we can find out what might have happened to her."

"I'm sure it wasn't John," Cindy cut in. "He was mad about Myra."

Jane pulled a cigarette case from her pocket and put one between her lips before offering them to the major and me. We both declined, and she returned them to her pocket and lit up her own cigarette. It was all clearly a prelude to some announcement, and at last she came out with it. "I think Myra and John had a falling-out."

"No!" Cindy gasped. "She didn't say anything to me."

Jane glanced at her friend. "She was keeping rather mum about it, but I heard her talking to him in a hushed, angry way on the telephone. And then she was crying and went to her room."

"When was this?" the major asked.

She was getting wary; I could see it in her expression.

"Let's not pepper her with questions, darling," I said. "She's had a shock, too."

The major glanced at me and seemed to realize my meaning. "Yes, of course. I apologize, Miss Kelley."

She waved the hand that held her cigarette. "It's all right. I'm not a fragile type of girl. I'll miss Myra, of course, but one gets dreadfully used to people dying in wartime."

Cindy gasped. "What an awful thing to say."

Jane shrugged. "Well, it's true. Isn't it, Major? I'm sure you've seen enough to drive most men mad."

"I've seen my share of death, Miss Kelley," he answered evenly.

"To answer your question, she took the call the last night I saw her. She went crying into her room, and a bit later I was listening to the gramophone in here when I saw her pass the door. I called to her, asking where she was going, and she said she'd be out for a bit. When she didn't come home, I thought she and John must've . . . made up."

"Do you have any idea how we might contact John?" I asked. "I . . . we'd like to let him know what's happened before he finds out about it some other way."

Jane shook her head. "I don't know where he lives, and I don't suppose she wrote it down anywhere. Myra never wrote things down."

"We used to tease her about it," Cindy said sadly. "She would never make notes. Said she would remember things. And she always did." Her voice broke on the last words, and she pulled the major's commandeered handkerchief out of her own pocket and wiped her eyes with it.

"But perhaps if you looked in the directory you could find him," Mrs. Paine put in. "Though I'm sure there are several John Pritchards there."

"And is there anyone else who might know where to find him?"

Jane shook her head. "I don't think so. She didn't really talk much with the other girls. Cindy and I were her best friends here."

Major Ramsey nodded and rose from his seat. "Well, thank you, ladies, for your time. We'll just be going now."

I rose, too, and moved to his side.

"If you think of anything else, will you ring me at the Ramsgate Hotel? It's in the directory," he said. I hoped he had someone in place to answer such a call, but I had learned that the major was always prepared.

"Yes, of course," Mrs. Paine said. "Thank you for coming to let us know."

We took our leave then.

"There was a roll of film in the clock," I said when we were outside.

We were walking down the street, my arm holding the major's in case anyone was watching from the house.

"Then Myra Fields was probably using it as a drop point."

"That's what I thought," I said. "Did you search the bedroom?"

"No," he said. "I didn't get a chance with Miss Prince hovering about. I'll send Kimble back as a policeman to satisfy Miss Kelley. He may be able to get a look at her room."

"And Cindy didn't divulge any extra information while you two were alone?" I asked.

"Nothing of use," he said. "But Jane Kelley knows more than she's letting on."

I nodded. "That must be why she was asking so many questions. I bet she knows something of the activities that Myra Fields was involved in."

"Either that or she knows more about this John Pritchard than she lets on. Regardless, I imagine she'll be slipping out of the house soon to alert any confederates of the news. We'll watch the house."

I glanced down the street and didn't see many good places for us to conceal ourselves while we waited.

"We'll call attention to ourselves if we're out after dark," I said.

"Didn't Mrs. Paine say the lady across the street rented rooms to married couples?"

I looked at him, knowing already what he was going to suggest.

"I'm not wearing a ring," I reminded him.

"Then keep your hand in your pocket."

"We're already going to draw suspicion," I said. "An officer like you bringing a girl like me to a lodging house when you could clearly afford a nice hotel is definitely suspect."

"Then we'll just have to be convincing," he said, taking my arm. "Come along, Mrs. Grey."

CHAPTER FOURTEEN

We walked into Mrs. Tully's lodging house, and I looked around. It was a simple place, as such places went. The carpet was worn, the paint on the walls a bit faded. It was clean, though. Even Nacy couldn't have objected to the sheen on the bannister, worn sleek by people's hands, and the smell of lemon polish and beeswax.

I glanced at the major to see if I could guess what he was thinking. I doubted he had ever stayed in a place like this in his life. If he went on holiday, he was staying in the likes of the Savoy or the Ritz. As his uncle was an earl, he probably had whole estates to stay at, not in a public place with a bunch of commoners.

I almost made a joke to him about it, but I could see that he wasn't in a joking mood. He had a sort of grim expression and a look of determination on his face, and I wondered if it was because he was about to have to pretend that he was my husband.

A woman appeared then from one of the rooms off the entryway. She was older, but she still preened a bit when she saw Major Ramsey. He was always impressive to women, I had noticed. We were, of course, a bit short on men at the moment, but even when the men were home, he would have stood out in a crowd.

"Oh, good afternoon. I thought I'd heard the door. Can I help you?"

"Good afternoon," the major said. "I need a room for my wife and me."

As he said this, he took hold of my elbow in a very unromantic way.

I forced the smile to remain on my face just as I forced myself to keep from pulling my arm away from him.

If the woman had been perceptive, she would have seen it, but she was focused on the major, and so she merely shot me a beaming glance. *What a lucky woman you are*, the glance seemed to say. *What a grand husband you have.*

When she looked away, I rolled my eyes.

"We have two rooms available," she said. "We are rather busy right now, being close to the station. A lot of couples meet here when the husbands are on leave."

"It is very convenient," I said with a smile.

"If you'll step this way and sign the register," she said.

"Of course." The major's agreeable tone contrasted with his firm grasp on my arm.

"Both of my available rooms are at the front of the house," she said regretfully. "Not as much privacy as the rooms over the garden."

"That will be fine," Major Ramsey said.

So far things were working out perfectly. We would be able to see the lodging house from the windows of a front room.

"Yes," I said, deciding to throw a bit of a crimp into this for the major. "We haven't been alone together in so long. We'll take any privacy we can get."

I had meant to embarrass him, but he seemed to take my sass as a challenge. His hand dropped from my elbow and slid around my waist, pulling me against him. The gesture was smooth enough, but it was entirely out of character and caught me off guard. I hit his side a bit hard, and I had to keep myself from grunting.

He then looked down at me with a hot expression perfectly

suited for a husband who had been too long separated from his wife.

It was fairly startling, the way he was able to turn a look like that on at the blink of an eye. He was a much better actor than I had given him credit for being. I sometimes forgot that he had been given this job in the intelligence services because he was so competent at deception.

Mrs. Tully clucked happily, as though her heart had been warmed by our romance, and then she handed the major a key. "Room twenty-four, at the end of the hall. I hope you have a lovely evening."

"We will." He shot me a knowing glance. "Won't we, my dear?"

"Yes, darling," I said between gritted teeth.

I heard the woman sigh as we started up the stairs. "What a sweet couple."

He dropped his hand from me as soon as we rounded the corner, and I turned and glared at him before heading up the stairs ahead of him.

He didn't acknowledge me. I wasn't surprised. He always ignored me when I was annoyed with him. All hint of the amorous husband was gone from his face, and he was once again wearing the cross expression he always had when having to work with me.

We reached the first floor, walked down the faded, worn carpet, and stopped before the door to room 24. The major fitted the key in the lock. It was an old Victorian-era key. I expected the lock might give him a bit of trouble, but he did it easily enough.

He pushed open the door. "After you, darling."

I moved past him, and he followed me inside, closing the door behind him and locking it.

"You didn't have to lay it on quite so thick with that woman," I said.

"Being convincing is always important in covert operations," he replied without looking at me, as he moved to the window.

He pulled aside the blackout curtain, and I moved to his side to look out. We had a direct view of the front door of Mrs. Paine's establishment.

"Do you think Miss Kelley will leave soon?" I asked.

"I doubt it. She won't want to make it too obvious to anyone who lives in the house. I'd imagine she'll sneak out after dark."

That was at least two hours from now.

I looked around the room. It was small, but as clean as the rest of the place had been. The floors were wooden with faded rugs, and there was a large bed that dominated most of the space, along with a wardrobe and a very small desk with a chair.

For the first time, I realized that I would be spending a very long time with this man in this small room.

He turned back to me just as I was thinking this, and some of the thoughts must have been evident on my face, because he glanced at the bed.

"I'll move the desk chair here near the window and keep the first watch," he said.

I looked at the little chair. It clearly wasn't made for a man of his size. I'd barely be comfortable sitting there for more than a few minutes.

"It's going to be uncomfortable," I said. "Open the window and turn out the lights. We can both sit on the bed. We can see across the street from here."

I said this in a breezy way, and then took off my hat without looking at him. I didn't want him to think I was some sort of prude who was going to make a scene about sitting on opposite sides of a bed.

The major did as I suggested and opened the curtain. The brightness of late afternoon sunlight made the room glow yellow.

For the first time I noticed the room was quite warm. It had been another hot day, and the windows had been closed.

I pushed up the sleeves of my dress. It was going to be a warm wait. I realized it would be doubly so for the major in his uniform.

"You needn't keep your jacket on, Major," I said. "There's no one here but me, and you know I'm not a formal type of person."

He considered. "If you're sure."

"I'm sure." I moved to the other side of the bed and took a seat as he unfastened his belt.

Then he began to unbutton the jacket, and I looked away as though I was afraid he was undressing for my benefit. Then I thought it was silly and looked back at him.

He took off the jacket and set it over the back of the chair. Underneath, his shirt was the standard khaki with braces and a necktie.

He reached up to loosen his necktie and then threw it over the back of the same chair.

As he unbuttoned his collar, he came and took a seat on the opposite side of the bed. The mattress dipped noticeably as he sat down, and I held myself stiff to keep from leaning into him.

The bed felt much smaller with both of us in it.

This was all ridiculous. I didn't know why it was that I felt so aware of him all the time, though, really, it was obvious enough. He was clearly a desirable man. No sense in pretending otherwise.

But perhaps the added uneasiness came from knowing the worlds we came from could never truly collide. I'd never been one to feel inferior in the presence of—for lack of a better term—my social betters. I hadn't been raised that way. Uncle Mick and Nacy had been the sort of loving influences that convinced me we were as good as anyone in London. It wasn't that we could do no wrong. We knew, in fact, that some of what we did was wrong.

It was just that we had confidence in our own value and worth.

All the same, there was something about spending time with the major that made me feel uneasy. Some part of me wanted to earn his approval. Some part of me wanted . . . well, it was no use thinking about what I wanted.

Things are what they are, and, if they can't be changed, we just have to accept them. More wise words from Uncle Mick.

I glanced at the major. He'd settled back against the headboard, his eyes on the window, though, according to his theory, there wouldn't be anything to see before dark.

We sat there in silence for several moments, the only sound the occasional creak of the house and the distant noise of the city.

"Do you really think she's going to leave tonight?" I asked.

"She's not going to use the telephone in the hallway to make an important call. Even if she did, it would be only to set up a meeting. I'm fairly certain I'm right."

I hoped he was. If not, we'd be spending a long night together in this room.

Speaking of making telephone calls, I wished that there was a way I could have alerted Uncle Mick and Nacy that I was going to be out late. I hadn't told either of them where I was, and I knew they would be likely to worry.

It would be worth it all, of course, to see the looks on their faces when I explained I'd spent the night in a hotel with the major.

We sat quietly for perhaps thirty minutes, both of us lost in our own thoughts, I supposed. But it was getting rather tiresome sitting quietly in the stuffy room.

At last, I sighed and slid lower on the bed, settling myself against the pillow. There was no sense in sitting up uncomfortably straight against the headboard for the entire evening just because he intended to.

The major glanced at me and then looked back to the window.

"I don't suppose, when you signed up for all of this, you figured you'd be sitting in a hotel room with a safecracker all night," I said.

There was a long pause.

"No," he said at last. "I most certainly did not."

I couldn't tell if he was amused or not, so I didn't respond to that.

"Do you suppose, if Mrs. Tully makes the rounds, she'll think it strange that we've doused the lights and gone to bed at this hour?"

"I think we gave her the impression we intended to go to bed at once."

Annoyingly, I felt myself flush. He had done it on purpose, too. I could tell by the slightest spark in his eyes when I glanced over at him.

I was tempted to banter back. His stiff reserve sometimes made me want to ruffle his feathers a bit. But I already knew it wouldn't work. Probably because he was used to women flirting with him.

But that was neither here nor there. We needed to do something to pass the time, and if he wasn't in a talkative mood, then we would have to do something else.

"Let's play a game," I suggested.

He didn't look at me. "What sort of game?"

"Cards," I said.

"Do you carry cards on you?" he asked.

"No, but there's a deck on the desk. It seems it's not all re-united married couples staying here."

He turned his head to look at me. I was certain he was going to refuse, so I was surprised when he nodded. "All right."

He shifted and reached out to get the deck of cards from the desk and then handed it to me. "You deal."

"Not afraid I'll stack the deck, Major?" I asked with a raised brow.

"I've played a lot of cards, Miss McDonnell," he replied.

"Good. Then I won't beat you too easily. What shall we play? Poker? We don't have paper to keep score for rummy."

"That suits me."

"Suits? A pun, Major?" I asked. "You're getting positively giddy."

He didn't so much as crack a smile.

I sighed then shuffled and dealt. Fair and square.

The major was, as I had known he would be, a whiz at poker. There was nothing in his expression that ever gave me the slightest hint of what his hand was like. Maybe it was because I didn't know him well, because even with my cousins and Felix, who seldom lost at cards, I could sometimes read a slight tell in their expressions.

"Three of a kind," I said, laying down my cards. I was proud of my three kings.

"Full house," he replied, spreading his out on the bedspread.

I shook my head. "That's a thousand pounds I owe you," I said, as we'd agreed to gamble for exorbitant imaginary stakes to make things more interesting.

The major, however, was not satisfied with the fortune he had just won. "Shall we up the ante?"

I looked up at him.

If it had been Felix who'd suggested such a thing, I would have been prepared for something outrageous like the suggestion we shed items of clothes as we lost a hand. We would never actually do it, of course, but Felix liked to make me blush.

The major, however, would never suggest anything of the kind, and I was wondering what it was that he would consider upping the ante.

"What do you have in mind?" I asked.

"If I win this hand, you wait here while I follow Miss Kelley when she finally emerges."

I ought to have known it would be some devious way of keeping me out of things.

"I don't think so," I said.

"Afraid you'll lose?" he challenged.

Blast the man. I hated being challenged; he knew that would work.

My chin went up. "Fine," I said, picking up the cards and shuffling them. "Then, if I win, I get to come with you when you talk to John Pritchard." I had already been trying to figure out how I was going to insert myself into that conversation. He had given me the opening.

He considered. "All right."

I handed him the deck. "You deal."

He shuffled and dealt. They were not good cards.

Good thing I'd tucked two aces away before handing him the deck.

I'd played fair before this, but the stakes were higher now and I intended to win.

When he turned over the first card on the bedspread: a jack. The next card was another jack. I'd have two pairs, at least. He turned over the third card, and I was thrilled to see an ace. There was no way he was going to win this hand. Not when I had a full house.

"I'll keep my cards," I said.

He switched out one of his and seemed prepared to call.

The movement was smoothly done. I almost didn't notice it. Even more so because I definitely wasn't expecting it from the major.

Without thinking, I reached out and caught his wrist with my hand, turning it over. There was a card tucked under the cuff of his shirt. No, two of them. Both jacks.

I looked up at him, partly appalled but mostly impressed. "You cheated."

"So did you," he said.

I said nothing. Did he know for sure, or was he speculating?

"Do you deny it?" he pressed.

I arched a brow. "Certainly. I always deny allegations against me."

"Then we're at an impasse."

"I thought you always played by the rules, Major."

His eyes caught mine and held. "Not always."

I realized that I was still holding on to him. The cuff of his uniform shirt was smooth against my hand, and the backs of his fingers warmed the skin of my wrist.

There was something in his expression that gave me pause, a jolt of awareness between us.

Dusk had fallen, and shadows had draped the room, and for a moment everything was completely still.

Then his eyes flicked toward the window. "She's leaving."

CHAPTER FIFTEEN

I turned to the window. Sure enough, Jane Kelley was standing on the front stoop, looking up and down the street.

We both got up quickly from the bed, the cards forgotten. The shadows had grown so deep now that there was no way she could see us from where she stood. The moon was waning, but there was still moonlight enough to see her as she began walking down the street.

"Miss McDonnell, you should wait here," he said, but I had already moved around the bed and pulled the door open.

"We're at an impasse, Major," I said as I left the room.

"Miss McDonnell," he called. And then, realizing we might be overheard and too polite to call me out as a single woman who'd been alone in a hotel room with him for the past two hours: *"Electra."*

I ignored him and made my way toward the stairs. There was absolutely no way I was going to wait in this room while he went chasing after our quarry in the dark. I'd been in it up to this point, and I wasn't about to get left behind now.

I heard his steps after me and quickened my pace down the stairs. I wanted to be out on the street, where he couldn't afford to make a scene, by the time he caught up with me.

"Oh, leaving?" Mrs. Tully was standing there as I came down the stairs looking flushed and rumpled, no doubt.

The major came behind, pulling on his jacket. He stopped just short of running into me where I stood at the bottom of the stairs.

"We're just going to get something to eat," I said.

Her eyes sparkled. "Yes, being young and in love works up quite an appetite." She sighed. "I remember those days well."

"Yes, we'll be back shortly," the major said pleasantly enough. He took my arm, but there was nothing pleasant about his grip on it. I gave it a slight tug, but he was holding too tight for me to escape without making it obvious.

I smiled at Mrs. Tully and moved toward the door, the major still hanging on.

"You're the stubbornest individual I've ever encountered," he said in a low voice when we were outside.

"Likewise," I hissed. "But we can argue about the title later. Let's go."

His eyes flashed annoyance at me, but he dropped my arm and began walking in the direction we had seen Jane Kelley going.

I had been worried that she might turn a corner by the time we were out on the street, but I could see her up ahead of us, barely visible in the growing darkness.

We'd gotten the room at Mrs. Tully's to watch the street since there weren't many places to conceal oneself along this particular stretch, and the same was true for following after her. If she happened to look over her shoulder, we were going to have to hope the darkness would be enough to conceal us.

Fortunately, she seemed intent on her mission, and she never looked to see if anyone was behind her. The major and I followed along at a safe distance.

I didn't know Lambeth well, and most of the streets were unfamiliar to me. It wasn't long before I had lost a sense of where we were. I hoped the major had been keeping track. Perhaps his military brain was better at mapping locations than mine was.

We followed her for perhaps half an hour, winding along broader streets and narrower ones, which required us to keep to trees and doorways as much as possible. I was good in the darkness; it had been one of the tools of my trade for most of my life. The major was no slouch either, though. I had thought before that he moved like a cat in the darkness, but moving at speed through the streets clarified my evaluation. He reminded me of a panther, a big cat stalking its prey.

Not once in all our movements did he so much as glance at me to be sure I was keeping up. I decided to take this as a compliment that indicated his faith in my abilities rather than believing that he was hoping to lose me at some point.

Finally, Jane Kelley slowed her pace. The major half shoved me into a shadowed entryway so we wouldn't be seen. But it was a smaller space than he seemed to have realized, for he was forced to press very close to me in order to remain hidden. Served him right.

He glanced out of the entryway. "It looks like this is her destination," he murmured into my ear.

"Now what?" I murmured back.

"Now we wait."

Wonderful. So we'd just continue our two-person game of sardines indefinitely.

To my surprise, however, he soon shifted away and stepped back out onto the street. "Wait here," he commanded. "I mean it."

Then he disappeared. I was half-tempted to follow him, but that would have just been my desire to be contrary, and now wasn't the time for that. He wasn't one of my cousins bossing me around during some schoolyard game, after all. This was a potentially dangerous situation that could involve people who had killed before.

I had to admit that occasionally I should leave matters to the major's judgment. I would rather have died than said as much to him, of course, but I could be honest with myself.

So I stood silently in the darkened doorway, watching and waiting. There wasn't much to see. Across the street there was a brick wall that both Jane Kelley and the major had disappeared around.

A few moments later, I caught sight of shadowy movement. I thought at first it was the major returning, but then I realized it was Jane Kelley. She was moving back the way she had come, her steps seemingly less hurried now.

I hesitated. Should I follow her or wait here for the major?

My instinct was to follow her, but I realized it would be fool-hardy. Besides, if she was retracing her steps, perhaps she had already completed her mission and was on the way back.

I decided to reconnoiter with the major before making any decisions. It was, I thought, rather sporting of me.

It was only a moment later when he returned.

"She went back the way we came," I said.

He nodded. "I'm surprised you didn't follow her. I expected to have to trail you both back to the lodging house."

"I decided not to be reckless," I said, feeling a bit smug.

"You astound me, Miss McDonnell."

I frowned at him, though it was probably too dark for him to see. "If we hurry, we can probably catch up with her, if you think we need to."

"We don't need to. She wasn't coming here to meet someone. She was coming to leave a message."

"What sort of message?"

"That's the question, isn't it?"

He turned then and began walking in the direction of the brick wall Jane Kelley had approached when we'd first ducked into the entryway. I hurried after him.

I had thought it might surround a house, but as we approached, I saw a bronze plaque affixed to the wall: THE MORRIS MEMORIAL GARDEN.

"A garden?" I asked. There was a high brick wall all around the property.

"The front gate is around the other side, but as soon as she left two workmen appeared."

Just then, as if on cue, we heard voices come from around the front of the building.

"I'll be glad to get this wall repaired," a man said. "I'm all in."

"We should've gone to the pub after we finished this, not before," a second voice said. "We'll be here all night, at this rate."

"What does it matter, so long as the job is done?"

"Let's just work fast. Maybe there'll be time for another pint . . . or five."

They laughed and then their voices lowered to a murmur. Apparently, they were settling in to do some sort of maintenance work.

"Was the message for them?" I asked in a hushed voice. If so, we were too late. Whatever the message was, they would have collected it.

The major shook his head. "She would have delivered it in person, and she made no contact with them. This is just a drop point."

"So where did she leave the message?"

"Apparently in some prearranged place," he said, nodding toward the area on the other side of the fence. "I saw her slip through the front gate. It was only a moment before she came back out."

"Is there a back gate?"

"Let's find out."

We moved along the wall toward the back of the garden. It was a nice-size area, but it seemed there was no second entrance. The only way into the garden was through the front, past the workmen.

"We can do the 'lovers out for a stroll' bit," I suggested.

He shook his head. "I don't think we should be seen."

I looked up at the brick wall. The foliage here at the back of the garden was thick enough that we wouldn't be spotted by the workmen. One thing I had learned from years of locksmithing and burglary was that there was always another way in if you tried hard enough.

"You'll have to lift me over," I said.

I turned and looked at him expectantly.

"Miss McDonnell . . ."

"We can't go in the front at the moment, and I can't climb this by myself. I'm not tall enough."

"I should go first."

"No. You'll leave me out here."

He didn't deny it.

"Lift me over," I said.

He sighed and created a cradle with his hands for me to step into. I did, and he lifted me easily to the top of the little brick wall. I sat on it and eased my legs over the other side and dropped into the cool, damp grass.

Despite his size, he was able to pull himself up easily and drop down after me.

He motioned for me to stay behind him, and we began to move through the garden. It wasn't hard in the darkness. After all, the blackout made things much easier than it would have been if there were lights shining from anywhere.

It was a pretty spot, lush and well-tended. There were several large rosebushes, the fragrance wafting up on the evening air. Thankfully, we had not landed in them when scaling the wall or my clothes would have been torn to shreds.

I moved forward. A wrought iron bench sat in the shadows. In another world, it would have been the perfect place to share a romantic conversation with a handsome man beneath the moonlight. As it was, I struck my shin on it and only just managed to keep from letting out a yell.

The major shot me an unsympathetic look and moved forward. The path that wound through the garden was lined with gravel, and it would make noise if we walked on it. We would have to be stealthy.

I looked around. It seemed an unlikely spot for a spy to drop off information, but I supposed it made sense. A random garden in the middle of Lambeth was unlikely to draw much attention. This was a place that was secluded but also open to the public. Comings and goings would not be noticed here. If one came during normal hours, that is.

But where in this garden would she have left a message?

"Do you suppose it's hidden in one of the bushes?" I asked the major.

He glanced around. It didn't seem as though there were a good many other places to hide something. Where would one wishing to transfer a secret message put it?

"Split up," the major said in a low voice. "Look around and meet me back here in five minutes."

I nodded. Then the major disappeared into the shadows like some sort of phantom. I moved in the opposite direction.

The bubbling of water suddenly caught my attention. I moved around a tall bush of some sort—I was never much of one for memorizing plant names—and saw that there was a fountain at the center of the garden.

The design of it immediately caught my attention: it was a stone maiden standing in the center of a pool, holding an urn from which the water fell.

It was a close match for the design of the cameo on the bracelet Myra Fields had worn.

I walked quickly over to the fountain and looked into it. It was fairly clean, the large basin in which the maiden stood made of pale gray stone. Though some of the stone was beginning to go green and stray leaves floated on the surface, the water was clear.

I could see there were a few stones on the bottom, but nothing that drew my attention. Certainly no hidden messages.

I looked up at the stone maiden. She looked straight ahead, giving me absolutely no hint as to whether or not she was hiding something. She held the urn at an angle, perpetually pouring water into the pool in which she stood. I wondered . . .

Stepping up onto the low edge of the basin, I reached my hand into the urn. I was met only with the cool trickle of water through my fingers. Nothing there.

I had been so sure.

Then I looked more closely. Between the maiden's hand and the stone urn she held, there was a thin space. And there was something in it.

I slipped my fingers into the opening and pulled out a folded piece of paper. Triumph swelled in me.

"Have you found something?"

I'd been so consumed with victory that I hadn't heard the major come up behind me. If I hadn't been a girl with very steady nerves, I would have jumped.

"I think so," I said.

Though I wanted to open the paper myself, I handed it over to him. I hoped he appreciated that I was making an effort to be cooperative.

Before looking at the paper, he took my elbow and helped me down from the edge of the fountain. Then he unfolded the piece of paper. There was a smaller piece of paper inside. I moved close to him to peer at it.

There wasn't much light in the garden, but our eyes were accustomed to the darkness.

I looked down at the two items. The smaller one was a baggage check for the Waterloo Station baggage storage. It was stamped with the time and date. It was the day Myra Fields had been killed.

The piece of paper that had been folded around the baggage check had a note jotted on it: "Collect and deposit."

I looked up at the major. "What do you think is in the baggage storage?"

"If I had to guess, I'd say more film," he said.

"Then you think Jane Kelley is the spymaster."

He shook his head. "I think she got reeled into this along with Miss Fields. She's instructing another operative to pick things up."

"Then who was this left for?" I asked.

"That's an excellent question. I'm going to send someone here to watch the garden and see who comes and goes."

I knew firsthand that the major had several other associates who were capable of doing this kind of stealthy work. There had been the brutes who'd kidnapped me in the guise of arrest when the major had first invited us to join his little operation.

There was also Kimble, who would probably get this job. The grim-faced former copper was perfect for skulking in the shadows.

That left the question of what our next move would be.

"Now what?" I asked.

He glanced at his wristwatch. "The baggage storage will be closed at this hour. We'll have to go in the morning. If we're lucky, we can see what's being held there and, if necessary, replace this baggage ticket before anyone comes looking in the fountain for a message."

"Because it might be best, after we've seen what it is, to watch whoever goes to collect it and follow where she leads?"

"Precisely."

I was sure he could find someone to open the baggage storage for us now, but I knew he didn't want to draw any further attention to our movements.

"So we can't do anything else tonight," I said, feeling a bit disappointed. To be honest, I'd quite been enjoying our adventure.

"Now I'd better take you home. I'm sure your uncle and Mrs. Dean are worried about you."

I was surprised that he'd thought of such a thing. He wasn't generally the type of man to factor in the personal. He was right, though, of course.

"Yes, they're probably wringing their hands at this very moment. I ought to have told them I was out with you."

"That probably wouldn't reduce their worry," he said.

"It might be dangerous work, but my uncle trusts you," I said.

"He trusts me, too, but he'd be glad to know you're looking out for me, so to speak."

I hadn't really meant to say anything quite so complimentary to him, but it was out now.

He looked down at me. "I appreciate that, Miss McDonnell. And I'm glad your uncle feels that way. I certainly intend to do my best to keep you out of harm's way. Though you don't make it easy."

I flashed a smile at him. "I'm afraid we McDonnells were built for danger."

We moved back toward the garden wall. Without comment, the major hoisted me up, and I dropped back down on the other side. A moment later, he joined me.

I was right that he must have known just where in the city we were, because he began to walk purposefully in a westerly direction. I fell into step with him.

He didn't say much as he walked. I supposed he was thinking about all that had happened tonight. For once, I decided not to pester him with questions and suppositions.

At last, we reached my neighborhood and stopped on the doorstep to the big house. I wanted to drop in there before going to my flat, since I had no doubt my uncle and Nacy were sitting inside waiting for me to come home.

Before going in, I turned to look up at the major. "You'll let me come with you to Waterloo Station tomorrow?"

"There is no 'letting' you, Miss McDonnell. I know perfectly well that if I don't come and collect you in the morning, you'll be down at Waterloo hurtling about on your own."

I smiled. "I do believe you're really getting a feel for my character, Major."

"As I said before: stubborn."

That reminded me of our quick departure from the hotel. "Speaking of which, Mrs. Tully is liable to wonder where we've gone."

"She'll assume we only required the room for a couple of hours."

I managed to keep from blushing at this matter-of-fact statement. It was true enough. We were probably not the first soldier and woman to arrive at Mrs. Tully's establishment looking for a place to be alone for a few hours.

She was going to be confused when she saw the playing cards we'd left scattered on the bed.

I was about to wish him good evening when the door was suddenly pulled open.

I turned to see Felix standing in the doorway.

CHAPTER SIXTEEN

"Oh," I said. "Hello, Felix."

"Hello, Ellie," he said, his eyes flicking to my companion. "Major."

"Lacey," the major replied.

There was a moment of uncomfortable silence. Well, it was uncomfortable for me. I don't think either of the gentlemen felt uneasy. Neither of them had been built for that particular emotion.

"We've been out doing a bit of work," I said.

"I see," Felix said. "Well, I hope it was a success."

"Oh, Ellie. I'm glad you've arrived home. You ought to have told us where you were," Nacy said from behind him as she came toward the door. She stopped when she caught sight of the major. "Oh, Major Ramsey. I didn't know Ellie was with you."

"Yes," he said. "I'm sorry I've kept her so late, but we had some important matters to attend to."

I realized, as he said this, that my clothes were rumpled, and my hair was a mess. I was thoroughly tousled from climbing garden walls and crashing through foliage. Major Ramsey, meanwhile, was far from his usual pristine self and had never found the time to put on his necktie. I did hope my family and Felix would not make the wrong assumptions.

"Will you come in, Major?" Nacy asked. "I can put the kettle back on."

"Thank you, Mrs. Dean, but no. I'd better be going."

He turned to me. "Thank you for your assistance tonight, Miss McDonnell. I'll be in touch with you tomorrow."

I nodded.

The major turned back to the door, encompassing Nacy and Felix in his farewell. "Good evening."

"Good evening," Nacy replied. Felix gave a barely civil nod.

The major turned and left, and I bustled Nacy and Felix back into the house. "I'm sorry you were worried," I said. "I just ended up working a bit later than I thought."

Uncle Mick looked up as I came into the parlor. He hadn't joined the welcoming party at the door, so at least that had been one less speculative gaze.

"So you made it home, Ellie girl," he said lightly. "I'm glad you're safe and sound."

"Yes, I'm fine. You didn't have to hold a vigil for me."

"I stopped by to see you about something, and when you weren't at your flat, I came over here," Felix said. "Then, when I found out Nacy and Mick didn't know where you were, I decided to wait."

A part of me was touched by their collective concern, but a part of me was also slightly irritated. I was a grown woman, and they didn't need to act as though a baby had gone toddling off alone in the London streets.

"Well, I'm home now," I said, wanting to be done with the conversation. "What did you come to see me about, Felix?"

"It's a bit of a long story," he said. "I think maybe we should go back to your flat and let Nacy and Mick get some rest."

"I'm not so old that I have to be put to bed," Uncle Mick said jovially.

"Speak for yourself," Nacy said. "I'm all in."

"I'm sorry I kept you up," I said, brushing a kiss on her cheek.

"No harm done," she replied, winking at me. As I had known it would, any lecture she might have been inclined to give me had dissolved in the face of the major's company on my late-night escapade.

She wished us all good night and went off to bed.

"Everything all right?" Uncle Mick asked as I took a seat on the sofa. That was his way of inquiring if there was anything about the case I wished to share. It had always been his way to gently offer his support without pressing too far, and I loved him for it.

I nodded. "We found who the dead girl was," I said, knowing the major wouldn't object to my sharing this bit of information with them since we'd already involved them to a certain extent. "And we went to ask questions at her lodging house. It seems that one of the other residents must know something about what happened to her."

I was glad that I was able to give them some of the details. It always helped to clear my head to speak about it out loud. I wondered how Major Ramsey fared, always keeping all that information bottled up as he did. Surely his head must be whirling with everything he knew. Did he have anyone he could confide in?

I didn't think there was a woman in his life, at least not one who would be a confidante. I suddenly wondered if it was difficult for him to carry the weight of all that information.

But it was Felix I needed to pay attention to now. He obviously wanted to talk to me alone, and I imagined it had something to do with our own little shared secret, the search to learn something about my mother. No doubt he was wondering what I had learned from Mrs. Norris.

I had almost forgotten that conversation had taken place today. So much had occurred in the last few hours.

We talked for a while longer with Uncle Mick, and then I rose to take my leave. "Walk me back to my flat, will you, Felix?" I said.

"Of course." He ground out his cigarette in the ashtray on the table next to him.

"Good night, Uncle Mick," I said.

"Good night," Uncle Mick replied easily. "Don't stay up too late."

I shot him a look and then turned and led Felix from the house.

We stepped out into the darkness and walked silently around the house and toward my little flat. I was tired, but I also felt oddly on edge. So much had happened today, and I was still trying to make sense of everything I had learned. I was glad Felix was here, glad for his comfortable companionship.

"Come in for a while, will you?" I asked when we reached my flat.

"Of course."

I opened the door to my flat, and he followed me inside. "Do you want some tea?"

"No, thank you. I drank two cups with Nacy and Mick."

"All right. I think I'll have some. Sit down while I put the kettle on."

He moved to the sofa as I went into the little kitchen, filled the kettle, and set it on the hob. After my long evening of trailing suspects, I was going to give myself today and tomorrow's daily allotment of my sugar ration.

I went back into the sitting area while the water heated and sank onto the opposite end of the sofa from Felix.

"Now," I said. "What did you come to see me about?"

"I was worried when I didn't hear from you after you went to see Mrs. Norris."

I nodded. "I was going to ring you, but the major was waiting for me when I got home. I didn't have time."

"I'm glad you're making progress on the case," he said. There was something a bit stiff in the way he said it, and I knew he wasn't entirely happy I had spent the entire evening with the major.

Felix was not the sort of man to be jealous, but I thought he probably felt much the same way about me as I did about him. While there was nothing settled between us, we both felt a certain propriety over our long-standing relationship, over the possibilities that remained unspoken.

"I had a good chat with Mrs. Norris," I said, bringing the conversation back around to something that was no more comfortable but less unsteady, somehow.

He didn't say anything, just waited for me to continue when I was ready. That was something I loved about Felix, how he always seemed to know just the right way to encourage me, to support me when I needed it.

"She said my mother suspected who might have killed my father, but that it would just cause more harm if it was revealed."

I related to him the whole of our conversation, and Mrs. Norris's assertion that she believed in my mother's innocence.

When I had finished, he sat back on the sofa and appeared to consider everything. "What are we going to do next?" he asked.

I didn't miss the "we." He was going to move forward on this with me. I felt an overwhelming sense of relief. Whatever I discovered, Felix would be at my side.

I considered his question, and the answer seemed clear enough.

"I think the next step is to see my mother's barrister, Sir Roland Highgate," I said. "He knows the ins and outs of the case, after all. I'm sure he'll be able to give us some clear idea of what evidence was used to convict my mother."

Perhaps he would also be able to tell me how to locate Clarice Maynard, my mother's friend.

"Wasn't the evidence used against your mother listed in the papers?" Felix asked.

"Yes. Or at least a good deal of it. But there are always things that don't get put into evidence. It's that sort of thing that I am interested to know."

"It's a good idea," Felix said. Then he hesitated. "But what if you find out something you don't want to know, Ellie?"

The question had been at the back of my mind through all of this. "I want to know," I said simply. "I want to know, whatever the truth is."

He nodded. "Then we'll find out."

He made it sound so simple.

"Do you really think we can?" I asked.

"Certainly. There's got to be people who remember the events of that night. It was a big news story, after all. I'm sure there's a lot we've yet to uncover. It's only a matter of finding the right place to look."

I realized that it was going to be hard on me, but it was also going to be difficult for Uncle Mick. He had lost his brother, and my bringing all of the past up again could only cause him pain. When it all came down to it, however, I knew that he would understand. He had always encouraged me to follow my own path where life was concerned, and this was not a trail I could afford to bypass.

"Then you'll go with me to see Sir Roland?"

"Of course, love. You don't even have to ask."

"Thank you, Felix." I reached over and patted his hand.

His other hand covered mine and gave it a squeeze. My heart gave an odd little skip.

"Oh, let me get the kettle," I said.

I returned to the kitchen and prepared my tea, trying to determine what it was that I was feeling. I had felt that strange pull with the major tonight, that attraction that always lingered below the surface even though I tried to suppress it.

Now here was Felix, making my heart race. What was the matter with me?

I brought the tea-things on a little tray back into the sitting room.

Then I went over and turned on the gramophone. It had been

something Felix and I had always enjoyed together, sitting and listening to good music with little conversation required.

I felt it was what I needed right now, a distraction from everything that was going on. It was so much to think about all at once.

I put on a Glenn Miller record, and "Moonlight Serenade" came flowing into the room. It was a romantic song, a song that would be perfect for dancing cheek to cheek while the world faded away.

I settled close to Felix on the sofa and sipped my tea while the music floated through the air. These sorts of records always reminded me of lighter times, of times we had spent happily unaware of the hazards the future held. Usually, these songs were bittersweet for me, but tonight I allowed myself to simply sink into the melodies.

I was feeling suddenly light, happy. We were at war, surrounded by death and destruction, but, in this moment, I was with Felix, and it felt a bit like it had in those carefree days before we knew what was coming.

"What are you thinking about, Ellie?"

I looked over at him, realizing that my mind had been drifting.

"Oh, I don't know," I said. "Just the way that things have changed, I suppose. The way that the whole world is different than it was only a few months ago."

"Not so very different," he said.

"You think not?"

"When I got hurt in France, I thought I would never again sit on this sofa with you listening to the gramophone. And now that I am, I find that I feel as though all is right in the world."

"I'm glad," I said softly. I looked over at him and found that he was looking down at me. Our eyes caught.

There was a long moment when we simply looked at each other.

"May I kiss you, Ellie?" he asked.

"You didn't ask the last time," I said with a soft smile.

"Things are a bit different now, aren't they?"

"Not so very different," I whispered.

So he leaned down and kissed me.

A part of me had been expecting it, welcoming it. Things had been building between us ever since he had returned to London, and I was glad that at least one thing in my life was falling into place.

He pulled me a little closer, and I slid my arms around his neck.

For a few moments, I let myself be completely lost in the allure of kissing a handsome man as the music drifted around us. There was a sense of romance, of promise for the future. There were so many things that I was feeling all at once, it was impossible to sort through them all. So, instead, I just floated through the moment, enjoyed the sensations without trying to analyze them.

What started as a light kiss intensified into something a bit more as we moved closer. My head was beginning to swim, my heart pounding as I sank into him, his arms warm and strong around me.

At last, he pulled back slightly, his forehead resting against mine. "We'd better stop this. Your Uncle Mick will be mad if we stay up too late."

I gave a little laugh, but I sounded breathless to my own ears.

He kissed me again, briefly, and then released me, sitting back a little in his seat. The slight space he had created between us didn't seem to lessen whatever sort of atmosphere our kiss had created. It seemed that it still hovered around us, hung in the air like an intoxicating perfume.

My heart was still beating fast, my breathing unsteady.

When he looked at me, I could tell that he was not as calm as he appeared. There was a heat in his eyes that was impossible to misinterpret. Absurdly, I felt myself flush.

What was happening to me? This was Felix, after all. I had known him for years. He had been the companion of my cousins, a constant presence in our house since I was a teenager.

But suddenly I felt that we were on new ground.

"I should probably go, Ellie," he said.

I didn't want him to, but I knew he was right. Too many things were happening too fast, and I needed time. I nodded.

He rose and I stood with him, walking him to the door. Before he opened it, he turned to me and once more pulled me against him. It was a long, lingering kiss that set my head spinning afresh.

"I'll talk to you tomorrow," he said when he released me.

I nodded, not quite trusting my voice.

He opened the door then and stepped out into the night. I shut it behind him and breathed a deep sigh. It seemed that everything I had done today had only served to make my life more complicated. All the same, those things were moving me toward resolutions.

I was closer to catching the spymaster, closer to finding out more about my mother, and, perhaps, closer to some sort of relationship with Felix.

Uncertainty is never welcome, but none of us can escape it on our way to new beginnings. I would just have to be patient and trust that everything would come together.

CHAPTER SEVENTEEN

I was awakened at the crack of dawn by a sharp rapping on the door of my flat. I looked at my clock. It was five in the morning. After Felix had gone, I'd eaten and bathed, so I'd barely been asleep for four hours.

I got up from the bed and switched on a lamp, pulling on a robe over my satin pajamas before making my way to the sitting room.

I pulled open the front door, not sure what to expect. I certainly didn't expect Major Ramsey. He was back in spotless uniform, looking fresh as a daisy.

"Good morning," he said. His eyes moved briefly over me, and I found myself pulling my robe closed a bit tighter, though it wasn't revealing anything to begin with.

"Good morning," I repeated. "What . . . what's wrong?"

"Nothing's wrong. I'm picking you up to go to Waterloo Station. I see you're . . . running a bit behind."

"But . . . it's five o'clock in the morning."

"I said oh five hundred hours, didn't I?"

"You certainly did not."

"The baggage claim opens at six o'clock."

I ran a hand through my tangled curls, then stepped back and pulled the door open. "Come in. I'll get dressed."

He came in, removing his cap.

"Sit down," I said, gesturing toward the sofa. "I'll just be a few minutes. Do you want some tea?"

"I've already had some, thank you."

Of course, he had. Had he even slept? He looked bright-eyed to me, but what did I know?

I went to the kitchen and put the kettle on. Then I disappeared into the bedroom and changed quickly into a dark green blouse with black slacks.

I ran a brush through my hair, realized it was going to be one of those days when it wasn't going to behave, and rolled it into a chignon, viciously shoving pins into it until it realized who was boss.

When I returned to the sitting room, the major was standing right where I had left him by the door. No doubt he was impatient to get started.

Well, I needed my tea.

"I'll be just a minute more," I said, hurrying to the kitchen.

"Take your time," he said, though his voice hovered right on the edge of sarcasm.

I quickly poured the tea from the kettle into the pot, waited as long as I dared for it to steep, and poured it into a teacup. I scooped in a bit of sugar—technically tomorrow's ration since I'd used today's last night—stirred, and took a sip of the scalding beverage. It was much too hot, but I didn't suppose the major would wait much longer.

With my mouth burned, I returned to the sitting room.

"All right," I said. "Let's go."

We reached Waterloo Station in plenty of time, despite my need to drink a cup of tea first.

There were already several people at the station at this hour, men in uniform and women in smart suits on their way to jobs, everyone moving with a sense of purpose.

The newsstands held the morning's papers, headlines shouting out the latest news from the Continent. A florist sold bouquets of fragrant flowers, and the smell of coffee and warm pastries wafted from the café.

Morning light filtered down through the glass skylights high above with the promise of another warm day ahead as I made my way alone across the station.

The major had deigned to allow me to be the one to retrieve the baggage. His thinking was that, since the majority of the people involved in this particular ring seemed to be women, it would be more in keeping for me to be the one to collect it.

If there was some sort of conspiracy with the baggage handlers, I might not look so out of place.

So he was waiting for me at the opposite end of the station, sipping a cup of coffee and pretending as though he was waiting for a train.

I went to the counter with the baggage claim, some small part of me holding my breath lest the whole thing suddenly turn into some sort of gunfight from an American gangster film.

My imaginings of grand drama were all for naught, however. The girl behind the desk barely glanced at me as she took the claim and went to retrieve the parcel. I waited, wondering what we were about to discover.

A moment later, she returned, carrying a battered Gladstone bag.

"Here you are," she said, not in the least interested in me or the bag.

I took it from her and paid for the storage.

"Thank you," I said, before turning away. I walked back across the station on high alert, but no one paid me any attention. At last, I reached the major, who was seemingly engrossed in his cup of coffee. I always thought of him as an extremely unimaginative sort of person, but whenever he was required to do a bit of acting,

I found myself impressed by the easy way he seemed to adapt to the occasion.

Looking at him, one would never think he was doing anything more urgent than waiting for a morning train.

"Got it," I said as I reached his side.

He only gave a slight, disinterested nod.

I examined the bag, my hand fiddling with the clasp. "I think it's locked, but it will take me only a minute to . . ."

"Not here," the major said, his hand clamping over mine on the top of the bag. "Wait until we're outside."

I nodded, and he removed his hand from mine and took my arm. We walked casually from the station.

I understood that he didn't want to open it in the station, but I planned to open it in the car. He wasn't going to hide what was in it and keep the contents from me as he'd done when I'd opened the bracelet on Myra Fields's wrist.

Outside, we slipped into the backseat of the waiting car.

"Open it," the major said. He sometimes forgot to be polite when he was on edge, so I decided to ignore his terseness for the moment.

I took a pin from my hair, pried it into the semblance of a pick, and set it into the lock. It was quick work to unlock it. This type of bag wasn't made for high security. I supposed it had been used because someone had had it on hand. It looked like it had seen its share of wear. Had it belonged to Myra Fields?

The clasp released with an almost inaudible click, and I pulled the bag open. The major and I both leaned forward to view the contents.

It was filled with film. A lot of film. There were probably twenty rolls of it, rather than the one or two I had expected. Some were very small, the sort that probably would have fit in the bracelet Myra Fields had been wearing. A few others were larger, standard camera size.

The major swore. I took that as confirmation that it was much more than he had assumed it would be as well.

"And this is just one shipment, so to speak," I added.

"Yes," he replied. "That means there's a very large deposit of film somewhere, waiting to be delivered to the Nazis."

He didn't have to spell out the implications of this to me. If they were provided with hundreds of detailed photographs of important locations in London, it would be catastrophic.

"But where are they keeping it?" I asked.

"That's what we need to find out," he replied. "And soon."

I considered for a moment. "Can you pick up Jane Kelley?" She thought she was tough, but I had every confidence the major could break her.

"No," he replied. "I think she's just as much a pawn in all of this as Myra Fields was. She probably doesn't know the true identity of whoever is pulling the strings."

"Then what are you going to do?"

He considered for just a moment. Then he closed the bag. "Lock it, if you please."

I did as he asked.

"Wait here," he said, getting out of the car, bag in hand.

I didn't have time to say anything before he shut the door behind him. My eyes met Jakub's in the mirror, and we shared a commiserative look.

A few moments later, the major was back. He no longer had the Gladstone bag.

"Take us to Lambeth, Jakub," the major said as he shut the car door behind him.

"So you've decided to leave it as bait," I said.

He nodded. "I had word this morning before I picked you up. No one came to the garden last night. We still have time to replace the baggage claim where you found it in the fountain."

And from there we could follow whoever picked it up and see where they led once they'd collected the film.

It was a bold move, putting the bag full of film back where we'd found it. There was the risk someone—a conspirator yet unknown to us—might pick it up and disappear. But the major never did anything lightly. If he thought this was the best option, it probably was.

"I'm going to put Kimble on this," he said. I understood what he meant: I wasn't going to be involved.

"What about John Pritchard?" I asked, thinking of Myra Fields's boyfriend. He was still a lead we had yet to follow.

"There was no word from Mrs. Paine at the Ramsgate number, but I've had others working on tracking him."

That reminded me of the question I'd had during our interview with the ladies at the lodging house.

"I meant to ask you about that," I said. "What is the Ramsgate Hotel?"

"It's a direct line that I've set up to my office. It's in the directory, and Miss Brown knows to answer it under that pretense."

I couldn't help but smile. "That's very clever, Major."

"Thank you. I have my moments."

Jakub drew the car to a stop on a quiet street, and the major turned to me. I expected him to give me a stern warning to wait in the car, so his next words surprised me: "Can you remember the position of the note where you found it?"

"I think so," I said.

"Then come along."

I certainly wasn't going to argue with that.

We got out of the car and walked along a series of streets until we came to the spot I recognized from the night before. There was the little alcove where we had stood cozily pressed together while we watched Jane Kelley and, across the street, the brick wall the major had hoisted me over.

"Act casually," the major instructed, taking my arm. I pulled my arm from his grasp and took his arm instead. If we were going to look casual, he had to learn to stop guiding me around by the elbow.

The garden was lovely in the daytime, though it lacked the allure of moonlight espionage. The trees offered shade from the growing heat, and there were birds singing cheerily as they darted to and fro.

We walked along the path at a comfortable pace, though the major's arm was stiff beneath my hand. He wasn't tense so much as on alert, and I knew he would be glad to get the note and baggage claim planted before our quarry came to collect them.

We neared the fountain, and I saw Kimble sitting at the bench I had bumped my knee on. He was reading a newspaper and looking especially innocuous. He was about as nondescript a fellow as one could get, and I didn't think he would draw any attention in most circumstances. It was only when looking into the cool blankness of his dark eyes that one realized there was something formidable about him.

He nodded to us as we approached. "Morning."

"Anyone else here?" the major asked him.

"A couple in the other corner," Kimble replied. "But they're not likely to get in the way."

The major pulled the note and the new baggage claim from his pocket and handed them to me. "Go ahead."

I nodded and moved to the fountain, stepping up on the edge as I had done the night before. I slipped the paper into the little space between the maiden's hand and the urn, leaving one corner of the paper slightly visible as it had been when I noticed it.

Then I hopped back down off the edge. "Now what?"

"Now we leave," the major said. "I'll take you home, and . . ."

His voice trailed off, and he stilled. Kimble's eyes moved toward the front of the garden.

And then I heard it. Footsteps on the gravel path.

Someone was coming.

CHAPTER EIGHTEEN

The major hustled me behind a bush even as Kimble stood, tucked his newspaper beneath his arm, and disappeared noiselessly into the foliage.

It all happened so fast I'd barely had time to catch my breath.

And then I saw the figure approaching.

It was a man, which surprised me. We'd been thinking the contact for whom Jane Kelley had left the note would be a woman. He was very tall and pale, with blond hair so light it was almost white.

Perhaps this fellow was not here for the note, after all. I dismissed that thought at once, however. There was something furtive in the way this man was moving, something in the slow glances around that gave away the fact he was not here on a quiet morning stroll. He clearly wasn't a high-caliber spy, acting so obviously suspicious.

We stood quietly, the major so close I could feel the warmth of his breath on the back of my neck.

The man approached the fountain and looked up at the woman for a moment, as though contemplating a particularly interesting sculpture at an art gallery. Then he reached up and slid the paper from between her fingers.

Without reading it, he slipped it quickly into his pocket, then turned and left the way he had come, a bit more hurriedly this time.

We stood quietly for a bit longer, and then the major shifted away from me. "He's gone."

"Aren't we going to follow him?" I asked.

"Kimble will have that under control."

I pushed away the urge to argue, knowing it wouldn't do any good. Besides, I had to admit that the very capable Kimble would have the matter well in hand.

"So what do we do now?" I asked, looking up at him.

"I'm considering," he said.

I realized suddenly that he was still standing very close, his face dappled with the shadows of the leaves around us. He hadn't meant the words flirtatiously, but I felt that little frisson of awareness that always seemed to strike me at moments like these, the unwanted reminder that we were a man and a woman alone in a secluded spot.

You were kissing Felix very dedicatedly only a few hours ago, Ellie McDonnell. The thought made me flush, and I broke eye contact with the major and moved past him, back into the sunlight.

"I think I'll go and visit Miss Fields's gentleman friend, Mr. Pritchard," he said.

"You've found him?" I asked.

He nodded. "Kimble gave me his address when you were replacing the note at the fountain."

"You didn't tell me!"

"There are a lot of things I don't tell you, Miss McDonnell."

I knew this, of course, but it was galling to have him say it out loud. He didn't have to rub it in.

"I've earned the right to come with you. I did, after all, catch you cheating."

"We're going to have to play that game of cards again."

"I look forward to it, Major."

Jakub drove us to the address the major had acquired.

I had to admit, I was a bit nervous about this encounter. Whatever we were trying to discover about Myra Fields and her activities, we were going to have to tell a man that the woman he loved was dead.

There was, of course, the possibility that he already knew this and even that he had caused it. That option was no less daunting.

"Are we going to continue with our aliases?" I asked as we stepped out of the car. "The story we told them at the lodging house?"

He nodded. "Yes. Here."

Reaching into the pocket of his jacket, he pulled something out and handed it to me.

I looked down at the object in my hand. It was a diamond ring. A real one, emerald cut and very large in a gold setting. "Where did you get this?" I asked, wondering for a foolish moment if he had gone back to Monsieur LaFleur's shop and taken him up on his offer.

"I had it lying around," he said. I recalled then that he'd been rumored to be engaged to a beautiful socialite named Jocelyn Abbot before I'd known him. They had broken things off, but I'd had the impression that he still had feelings for her. Had he bought this ring for her? I wasn't going to pry, of course, but I was very curious.

I wasn't surprised, exactly, that he'd remembered to see to that detail. He was a thorough sort of fellow. But it felt a bit strange to wear an extravagant diamond he had meant for someone else.

"Do you . . . suppose we ought to get one a bit less expensive?" I asked. Heaven forbid I lose a piece of the major's valuable personal property; he would think I'd pawned it.

"I trust you'll look after it," he said.

I slipped it onto my finger. It was a good fit. For just a moment, I was like any other woman who'd been proposed to. I held up my hand, admiring the way the light glinted off the superior stone.

"All right?" he asked.

I nodded. "Grand."

We walked up to the door, and he rapped on it. A moment later it was opened by a young man. He was tall and fair, with pale blue eyes and a prominent nose.

"Mr. Pritchard?" Major Ramsey asked.

He looked surprised but not alarmed to see us. "Yes?"

"My name is Major Grey, and this is my fiancée, Miss Elizabeth Donaldson. I wonder if we might come in for a moment?"

The man looked curious, but he was too polite to refuse. "Of course."

He opened the door for us, and we followed him into a small parlor. It was sparse but clean, with comfortable, worn furniture.

"Will you sit down?" he asked, gesturing toward the sofa. I sat and the major sat beside me. Mr. Pritchard seated himself across from us in a faded embroidered chair.

"Now, what can I do for you, Major?"

"Has anyone been in touch with you about Miss Fields?"

It was the first time I saw concern cross Mr. Pritchard's face. "No," he said. "Why? What's happened?"

"I'm sorry to tell you she's dead."

I knew the major was being blunt to gauge the young man's reaction, but I still felt a stab of sympathy at the look of shock that flashed across his face. Then his eyes welled with tears.

"I'm so sorry," I said gently. "I know this is a terrible thing to hear."

"What . . . what happened?" he asked. The grief in his voice was raw. It was apparent that he was barely containing himself, and probably for the major's sake.

"She was found in the Thames last Saturday," the major said.

Mr. Pritchard could no longer keep his sorrow in check, and he put his head in his hands and began to sob.

I glanced at the major, who appeared unmoved, and then I rose and went to the young man's side. I put my hand on his shoulder. "I'm so sorry."

"Are you . . . sure . . . sure it's Myra?"

"I'm afraid so," I told him.

He shook with sobs for a moment longer, then, with visible

effort, he pulled himself together. Taking a handkerchief from his pocket, he wiped his face. "I'm sorry," he said.

"There's no need to apologize," I said softly. "I know it's horrible news, and I'm so sorry we've had to deliver it to you."

"But . . . but who are you?" he asked, looking up at me.

"I'm a sort of cousin of Myra's," I said, feeling bad about lying to the young man under the circumstances.

If he sensed my deceit, there was no sign of it. He sniffed, wiped his nose with the handkerchief. "She was such a lovely person."

"When was the last time you talked to Miss Fields?" the major asked.

I shot him a look over Mr. Pritchard's shoulder. The major was using his interrogation tone, and I didn't think it was quite the right way to go about things.

Mr. Pritchard, however, was in no condition to take notice of the subtleties. "I saw her Saturday," he said. "We . . . we had an argument. She wanted me to take her out, but I had to work late at the chemist. I'm so busy there. Usually, I only take her out on Wednesdays. She said she would go out alone or find someone else to take her. Oh, Myra."

"She knew you loved her," I said. Though I didn't exactly know if it was true, I felt I must say something to comfort him. "An argument wouldn't have changed her mind about that."

He shook his head. "It was so stupid. We'd row sometimes about simple things like that and not speak for a week, until we'd both cooled off, so I thought that was why . . . I was waiting for her to realize that she was wrong. And now . . ." He looked up at me suddenly, his face white. "She didn't . . . she didn't . . . ?"

He couldn't bear to ask it, if Myra Fields had thrown herself in the Thames.

"No," I said. "No. It was a dreadful accident."

Relief flashed across his features, and he nodded bleakly.

"We are trying to find out just how it happened," the major said. "My fiancée feels that she needs to know what occurred."

It was strange hearing him refer to me in that way, especially since his voice was absolutely devoid of any sort of affection. He wasn't putting much effort into this particular performance.

Mr. Pritchard nodded, rousing himself. "Yes. Yes, of course. I want that, too. I want to know what happened."

"It will be better for all of us," I said, giving his shoulder one more squeeze before going to resume my seat beside the major.

"How did you know to look for me?" Mr. Pritchard asked suddenly.

"We went to Myra's lodging house," I said. "Mrs. Paine gave us your name."

"Oh. Yes, I see." His tone had gone vague, and there was a faraway expression on his face, as though his grief was beginning to numb him. I thought we should leave him in peace, but the major wasn't finished.

"Do you know where she acquired this?" The major pulled the bracelet from his pocket. I hadn't expected him to ask that question, but I tried to hide my surprise.

Mr. Pritchard looked at it but didn't reach for it. "She'd taken to wearing it lately. Said she got it from a friend. It was . . . well, it was one of the things we argued about. I thought she'd gotten it from the fellow she'd been working for. He was sweet on her, though she tried to deny it."

"What fellow was this?" the major asked.

I reached over to put my hand on his arm, but he moved it at the same time and my hand fell on his leg. I decided to play it off, lightly patting his thigh. "Gabriel, you mustn't pester the poor man with questions."

His hand fell over mine and squeezed it slightly too hard, in a poor imitation of affection. "You're right, of course, darling. But

Mr. Pritchard is as eager as we are to get to the bottom of what happened."

Mr. Pritchard's gaze sharpened as he looked from the major to me. "Do you . . . do you suppose she was harmed by someone?"

"Do you have any reason to suppose so?" the major asked.

There was a slight hesitation. "I . . . I don't know. She'd seemed worried lately, distracted. There was something about that new job of hers that I didn't like."

"What new job?" the major asked.

"I don't know. She claimed it had something to do with the war effort, though I could never really get the details out of her. There was that man, her boss. I think he worked at the Metropolitan Bank. She worked in a factory, not at the bank, you know, but they were together a lot of the time, doing some sort of job, she said. We rowed because I was sure he fancied her. She was making a lot of money. Too much, I thought. She had that jewelry, and new clothes. Pricey stuff."

Was he really so naïve that he didn't know what she had been up to? Or was he involved and putting on a show? If so, he was an excellent actor. I would swear to it that he was devastated.

"Do you happen to know the man's name?" the major asked.

He shook his head. "Not all of it. Bill, she called him. But she didn't talk about him much. She knew I didn't like it."

The major was about to speak, but I pressed his leg again. We let the silence sit for just a moment, and then, just as I had expected, John Pritchard added something else.

"I . . . I followed Myra one day. She went to meet him."

"Oh?" I asked, at last pulling my fingers from the major's grasp.

"Myra went to the bank and he came out. They went to the restaurant across the street, Pietro's, I think it was called."

"And then what happened?" There was more, or he wouldn't have started the story.

"I . . . I went in, too. Pulled my hat over my eyes and slipped in so I could watch them."

"You had to know what they were doing," I said encouragingly. He nodded.

The major was still and silent beside me. He was perceptive, and he knew that anything he said now would only disrupt my comradery with Mr. Pritchard.

"I . . . I watched them. I think they went there often because there was a redheaded waitress that seemed to know them. Then, when she went away, Myra gave him a paper sack. He took it with him when he left."

Had it been film? I wondered.

"What does he look like?"

"You can't miss him," he said. "He's very tall and pale as a ghost. White hair, too."

My eyes came up to the major's. It was a perfect description of the man we'd seen in the garden.

"Well, if you hear from this Bill, will you let us know?" the major asked. "I'm at the Ramsgate Hotel. It's in the directory."

"Yes. If there's anything I can do. I . . . What's become of . . . her body?"

"I'll direct someone to contact you," the major said. "My fiancée and I live in Kent. Is there anyone in London who would see to the arrangements?"

"Oh, yes. I will. She didn't have much family." His eyes met mine, not the major's, when he said his next words. "Thank you for letting me know. Please . . . find out what happened to her."

I met his eyes and told him the truth. "I'll do my best."

We took our leave after that. I could tell Mr. Pritchard wanted some time alone to process the news. It was hard to vent one's grief in the face of strangers, especially a face as unsympathetic as the major's.

"You were a bit harsh, weren't you?" I said as we left the house.

"In what way?" He didn't bother to look at me and didn't sound as though he particularly cared what my answer was.

"Dropping the news on him like that."

"It's better to have out with it. No sense in dragging things out."

"Perhaps not, but I still felt sorry for him."

"He didn't strike you as overly demonstrative?"

I let out an irritated breath at his assumption that genuine human emotion was inherently suspicious. "He was in love, Major. Surely you can sympathize with that?"

"Perhaps."

The major wouldn't, I knew, be the type of man to weep over his losses. He'd tossed his former fiancée's ring to me like so much costume jewelry. Still, I didn't think Mr. Pritchard's sorrow was suspicious. He had seemed sincere to me.

"If he's lying, he's very good at it," I said.

"He wouldn't be the first man to rise to the occasion when confronted with someone getting close to the truth," the major said.

"No," I agreed, though I was still unsure why he seemed suspicious of Mr. Pritchard. Granted, if this was a regular murder, the boyfriend would be a likely suspect. He had admitted to jealously trailing Miss Fields, after all. But there was nothing normal about this situation.

"Besides," the major added, as we reached the car and he pulled open the door for me. "There was one other thing."

"What was that?"

"He works for a chemist. He would have access to toxins."

I still didn't believe that Mr. Pritchard had killed Myra Fields, but I wasn't going to argue the point with the major. We'd find out soon enough. I was sure of that. I could feel that we were getting closer to the answer.

"What do we do next?" I asked as the major slid into the car behind me.

"You're not tired of our adventures yet? I did get you out of bed at an early hour."

"You got less rest than I did. In fact, I'm not entirely convinced you sleep, Major. I'd think you a vampire if you didn't look so hale and hearty in the sunlight."

There was the smallest flicker of a smile. "I manage to get a bit of sleep here and there."

"So you are human, after all."

He looked at me. "All too human, Miss McDonnell."

There it was again, a moment of shared awareness.

I looked away first.

"Back to Miss McDonnell's house, please, Jakub," the major said.

"Oh, no! Jakub, will you take us to the Metropolitan Bank, please?"

Jakub looked at the major. I knew he wanted to do as I said, but it was the major he had to answer to.

"We're not likely to learn anything from that café," he said, easily following my train of thought.

"But we can try, can't we?" I asked. "It won't hurt anything to go and ask some questions."

The major sighed and looked off into the middle distance for just a moment, considering. I was fairly certain he was going to say no, so I was surprised when he nodded. "All right. Let's go."

It didn't take us long to get there. Jakub parked down the street, and the major and I went into the café.

I glanced around as we entered, trying to decide on the best place to sit. I spotted the red-haired waitress talking to a pair of customers in the corner and moved in that direction. The major followed, his cap tucked under one arm.

I slid into a booth, and he took a seat across from me. I was excited that the waitress John Pritchard had mentioned was here and that we might be able to learn something from her, but I tried to remain calm. The major appeared completely at ease, as though he really had just come here for a quick cup of coffee.

A moment later, after she'd finished with the two gentlemen, the waitress came to our table. I saw her eye the major, but, to her credit, she included me in her smile.

"What can I get for you two lovebirds?" she asked.

"I'll have a cup of tea, please," I said, deciding it was probably easiest to just let her assumption pass.

"Coffee for me," the major answered.

"Nothing to eat?"

The major looked at me. I considered. Was the government paying for this?

"I'll have a turkey sandwich," I said.

"Nothing for me, thank you," the major said.

The waitress moved off with our order, and I faced the major. "It looks like we're in luck," I said in a low voice.

"If it's the same redhead," he replied.

I hadn't thought of that, but, really, how many redheaded waitresses would be working in this little café?

There was only one way to find out.

She came toward us with a tray, and I focused on the major and raised my voice.

"I thought we might run into Bill here, but perhaps it isn't his lunchtime," I said. "The bank's always busy this time of day."

The waitress took my tea-things from the tray and set a mug of steaming coffee in front of the major. "Bill Mondale?" she asked.

"Yes," I said brightly. "Do you know him?"

She nodded. "He comes in here most days for lunch. But you're right. He doesn't usually come this time of day. Usually, he's earlier, but he didn't come today."

"He comes in with his girl sometimes, doesn't he?" I asked. "A pretty, dark-haired girl?"

"Myra? Yes, they have lunch together here sometimes, though I haven't seen her in several days. I don't think she's his girl, though."

I glanced at the major before turning my attention back to the waitress. "Oh, really? Perhaps I'm mistaken."

"I've never seen him act sweet on her, no lovey-dovey stuff. They just come in, drink a cup of tea, or have a bite to eat, and leave."

It all tallied. Bill Mondale met here with Myra Fields. He'd been seen by John Pritchard taking packages from her. They weren't having a secret romance. They were engaging in espionage.

"Perhaps they have some sort of business arrangement," I said, hoping to glean something more.

The major's foot nudged mine beneath the table, and I took the hint. Grudgingly, I had to admit that he was right. I didn't want to overdo it.

"Oh, I don't know," the girl said. "I generally don't hear much of what they talk about. I don't have time. Always leaves a good tip, I know that much."

She left to check on another table, and I took a bite of my turkey sandwich. It was very good. I only just then realized how hungry I was.

"Are you sure you don't want half of this, Major?" I asked.

"No, thank you."

I leaned across the table toward him and lowered my voice. "So it all fits, doesn't it? Bill Mondale is running this spy ring. The girls meet him here and drop off the film."

"It does seem a possibility," he said noncommittally, taking a sip of his coffee.

I took another bite of my sandwich and chewed contemplatively. "But what about the film in the Gladstone bag at Waterloo Station?" I asked. "Why didn't they meet here to drop that off?"

"Probably from a different subgroup in the ring. We know there is more than one operating."

"So spies coming and going from the boardinghouse would leave their film in the clock for Myra," I said. "And she would deliver it to Bill Mondale. But the other cells gather theirs and leave it in the baggage storage at Waterloo Station."

"Then how did Jane Kelley get the baggage claim?" he asked.

I considered. "Perhaps she leads that other ring?"

"Perhaps," he said. But he didn't sound entirely convinced.

I, however, continued on with my theory. "Everything was going fine, but then John Pritchard starting rowing with Myra about her frequent meetings with Mondale. She must have told him Mr. Pritchard was getting suspicious or that she wanted to stop taking photographs for him. So Bill Mondale killed her."

It all fit together, at least in a way. I had the unsatisfied feeling of shoving a puzzle piece into the wrong place. You can make it fit if you try hard enough, but the picture doesn't come out quite right.

"I'll speak to Kimble about Mondale," the major said. "In the meantime, I'll see you home. Nothing much is likely to happen for the next several hours."

I studied him, trying to decide if he was lying and meant to go off pursuing leads on his own. It was impossible to tell, of course.

There was no use in wheedling promises from him either, because I knew he would just ignore them if he saw fit. I would just have to trust that, since he'd let me be involved this far, he'd let me be in on the rest of it.

I finished my sandwich, and the major dropped some money on the table. I wondered if it was his money or the government's and then decided not to quibble. They both had plenty to go around.

Jakub drove us back to my flat, and, as the car drew to a stop, the major got out and came around to open my door.

"I'll just come to your office in the morning, shall I?" I asked as I stepped out of the car.

"I can't stop you," he said. I couldn't quite tell if he was joking, but, somehow, I doubted it.

"I'm glad you're beginning to realize it, Major," I said. "I'll see you first thing."

I began to walk away, but stopped and turned back toward the car.

"Wait. You've forgotten your ring," I said, moving to take it from my finger.

"Hang on to it," he said. "It probably won't be the last time you'll be called upon to be engaged to me."

He sounded less than thrilled at the prospect, and I smiled. "All the same, it's a rather valuable piece to leave with a girl known for stealing jewelry."

"Any value it had to me was lost long ago," he replied.

This bit of candor caught me off guard; I had been expecting a smart retort. I couldn't think of anything to say in response to his honesty, so I only nodded.

"Until tomorrow morning, Miss McDonnell."

CHAPTER NINETEEN

I had settled into my flat and made a pot of tea, the half a cup I'd had at the café insufficient, when there was a knock at the door.

I opened it to find Felix standing on the doorstep.

"Good afternoon, lovely," he said. He handed me a bouquet of lilies. My favorite.

"Felix, how extravagant!" I said, burying my nose in the blooms. Flowers were more of a luxury now that so much land was being allocated for growing food crops. "Thank you. They're lovely."

I turned to bring the flowers into the house, and he followed me, shutting the door behind him. I liked the comfortable way we were together, the ability we had of moving in unspoken companionship. There was, of course, the added element of what had happened between us last night, but I was glad to realize I didn't feel in the least awkward.

"Do you want some tea?" I asked, going to the kitchen to get water for the flowers.

"No, thank you."

Most of the glass objects in the house had been packed away and stored in the cellar in case of bombing, but there was an empty tin can that would do nicely. I filled it with water and placed the flowers inside.

I then carried them out to the sitting room, where Felix had already made himself comfortable on the sofa.

Placing the makeshift vase on the table before the sofa, I arranged the flowers.

"What's this?" Felix reached out and caught my hand, examining the ring.

I had meant to put the ring away for safekeeping but had forgotten as I went to make tea. For some odd reason I flushed at being caught wearing it.

"Just a part of my cover story," I replied.

His brows rose. "That's a real diamond."

I nodded. "Major Ramsey doesn't do anything by halves."

"Doesn't he?" He hadn't let go of my hand.

I smiled at him. "Don't frown so, Felix."

"Ellie . . ." He gave my hand a little tug, pulling me toward him, and I took a seat beside him on the sofa. "About what happened last night . . ."

I looked up at him, wondering what he would say. That it had been a mistake?

"Yes?"

"I . . . Was it all right?" he asked. "I mean, you didn't . . . mind?"

I had never before seen Felix at a loss for words, and I couldn't help but smile. "Of course not," I said. "I rather liked it."

His eyes caught mine, and I could tell at once that his equilibrium had been restored. There was that old flash of mischief, and of something a bit warmer. "I'm glad to hear it."

His free hand went to my waist, and he leaned to kiss me. This was a brief kiss, however, more circumspect than the lingering ones we had shared last night. There was no moonlight and Glenn Miller today.

"As much as I would like to say I came here just for that," he said, "I have to confess I have ulterior motives."

"The truth comes out," I teased. I sat back on the sofa, creating a bit of distance between us.

He made no declarations, and I was glad. I didn't want to put a name on what was between us, not yet. It wasn't that I relished the uncertainty. It was just that it was nice to have something easy and uncomplicated in my life at the moment, something that didn't have to be analyzed to death.

An older generation would have thought me a bit wanton, happy to kiss a man with whom I had no firm understanding. But a lot of girls of my generation were doing a lot more than kissing soldiers, and I didn't feel sorry for whatever bit of comfort Felix and I might find in each other's arms. Not that I intended to let things go too far too fast.

I was so caught up in analyzing my need not to analyze that it took me a moment to realize what he had said.

"I've found Sir Roland's address, and I rang him up for an appointment."

I stared at him. "You did?"

"Are you cross with me?"

"No, of course not." It was sweet of him to have done it. If there was any hesitation in me, it was that I was still not sure what I was getting into. Now that I had begun looking into my mother's case, it was a bit like starting a run downhill. I wasn't going to be able to stop, and there was no telling what would happen once I reached the bottom.

"When is the appointment?" I asked.

He glanced at his watch. "In an hour. I took a chance you'd be free."

Sir Roland Highgate lived in Kensington, a lovely redbrick town house with a small, tidy front garden and flowers in the window box.

I wondered if Sir Roland had been born wealthy or if he'd made his money in the law. He certainly hadn't made much from my mother's case, as we'd never had money to speak of.

Robbing safes isn't as lucrative as one might suppose.

For just a moment we stood looking up at the house, wondering what answers might lie waiting inside.

"Ready?" Felix asked.

Drawing in a deep breath, I nodded. "As ready as I'll ever be."

We went up the walk together, and I reached out and rapped the door with the lion's head knocker.

I had thought about this moment for a long time. Ever since I had first learned the truth about my mother as a young teenager and read every newspaper account of the case I could find, I had felt I would one day seek out Sir Roland. He had put up what the newspapers called "a spirited defense." There had been more than one snide remark about his doing more for her than she deserved, possibly because she was young and beautiful.

But he hadn't been the type of man to be swayed by a woman's charms. That had been clear to me, even then, from the stern features I encountered in grainy photographs, from the body language as he stood by my mother in the courtroom. He wasn't a man besotted. He was a man on a mission. I had always assumed that his ultimate goal was publicity and the acclaim that came with winning difficult cases, but Mrs. Norris's words had cast him in a different light. He had tried to help my mother. Perhaps he could now help me.

I felt very nervous and was immeasurably glad to have Felix at my side as we waited for the answer to my knock. He was standing close, and his support felt both physical and emotional.

A maid answered the door, her gaze flickering from me to Felix and settling on him. "Can I help you?"

"We have an appointment with Sir Roland Highgate," I said. Reluctantly, she pulled her gaze back to me. Perhaps I ought to have let Felix do this part.

It seemed to me that she gave me a looking-over as I was speaking, and I was glad that I had dressed smartly in a dark suit and hat.

"Your name?" she asked.

"Felix Lacey," Felix said. He'd made the appointment in his name.

She opened the door. "If you'll come into the parlor, I'll tell Sir Roland you're here."

We followed her into the house. It was much as one would expect a wealthy barrister's home would be, elegant and austere. There was a good deal of marble.

The parlor was a comfortable room, however. I guessed Sir Roland was a bachelor, for the room lacked the frills of a wifely hand and was decorated according to the habits of a bachelor who preferred comfort to presentation.

"I didn't get your name, miss," she said as we entered.

I hesitated. "I'd rather give it to Sir Roland, if you don't mind."

She looked as though she did mind, but she was also probably aware she wouldn't be able to boot us from the house now. Besides, I was sure Sir Roland had had his share of unexpected guests in his time.

He was retired now, of course, but there were probably still odd strangers and wealthy criminals who sought his services from time to time. Such things were one of the hazards of being a celebrated figure in criminal law.

She left the room and I looked over at Felix. "It's going to be all right, Ellie," he said, sensing my need for reassurance.

I nodded, hoping he was right. Perhaps one reason I'd always avoided looking into my mother's case, really investigating the matter, was that I was afraid of what I would find. I was nervous about what Sir Roland would have to tell me. What if Mrs. Norris had been wrong? What if, rather than believing my mother innocent, he knew for certain she was guilty, despite his best efforts to defend her?

But I knew that some part of me would not rest until I did all that I could to learn the truth. Whatever that might be.

We took a seat on the leather sofa. Felix sat near enough for me to feel him beside me but not so close as to crowd me. It occurred to me again how well he knew me.

A few moments later, the door opened, and a gentleman stepped into the room. Felix and I stood as he entered.

He had the look of a barrister, I thought. Tall, distinguished, with sharp eyes and sharp features in an aristocratic face. His hair had gone white, matching the wig he had always worn in court, but he still stood tall and erect. His bearing was almost soldierly. He cut a dashing figure, even after all these years, and I had no doubt that there were many a crown prosecutor who had dreaded facing him.

"Good morning," he said.

"Good morning, Sir Roland," I said. "My name is Ellie Mc-Donnell. I'm Margo McDonnell's daughter."

One thick, gray brow rose ever so slightly.

"Have a seat, Miss McDonnell, Mr. . . ." His gaze went to Felix.

"This is Felix Lacey," I said.

"Ah, yes. The Mr. Lacey with whom I had an appointment." There was a reprimand in the tone.

"I beg your pardon for leaving out the key detail, Sir Roland," Felix said. "But I had to check with Ellie before I gave you her name."

"Are you a solicitor, young man?"

"Good lord, no."

"He's a close friend," I put in. "One of the few people who know all the details of my past."

The man nodded, motioning us to resume our seats. He sat opposite, on one of two chairs arranged before the fireplace.

"How may I help you, Miss McDonnell?" he asked.

The question threw me a bit. When put that way, it was diffi-cult for me to articulate just why I had come. Had I come for an-swers, for confirmation that there was more to my mother's story than the papers had related?

I decided to start at the beginning. "You remember my mother's case, I assume."

His expression was unreadable. "Very well."

"I . . . I have a few questions, I suppose. Or, perhaps, I simply wonder if there is anything you can tell me. I don't know much about her, you see, or what happened the night my father died. I have wondered for a long time, and I recently received some infor-mation that seems to indicate she was innocent."

There was a sound at the door before he could reply. The maid brought in a tea tray, and there was a lapse in conversation while she poured for us. Sir Roland sucked on his pipe, smoke billowing up around his head, his shaggy brows lowering over those keen dark eyes.

I wondered what he was thinking, if he was reliving the case with my mother. It had been more than twenty-four years ago, but surely some of the details of so sensational a case would stick with a man, even one with Sir Roland's long and celebrated career.

The maid left at last, and Sir Roland took a sip of his tea before he spoke.

Felix and I waited in silence. I took a cup of tea but held it without drinking it. Felix declined a cup.

At last, Sir Roland began to speak. "Your mother's case is one I've thought about often over the years. It wasn't, contrary to pub-lic opinion, one I took on because of the notoriety. Nor, as the scandalmongers would have it, because I was deeply in love with your mother." He said this dryly, and I could find not a hint of sentimentality in his words as he said them. No, he wasn't the sort of man who would have fallen in love with his clients.

"She was undoubtedly a beautiful woman," he went on. "It

was part of the appeal of her trial. A young, beautiful woman on trial for a brutal crime has been a subject of public interest for as long as there has been press to cover it. And it's true I was not her original barrister, and I took on the case after it became well known. But the interest it attracted was simply how it came to my notice, not the motive for my taking it on. I took the case because there were a great many details which I found interesting, out of the ordinary."

He had a low, rich voice, perfectly pitched for giving long speeches. I could imagine him standing before the bench, pleading on behalf of his client. No, not pleading. He would lay out thoughtful, well-plotted arguments, lead judge and jury along a path lined with carefully cultivated facts.

An alarming thought occurred to me: if this man hadn't been able to prove my mother innocent, perhaps she had been guilty after all.

"You say you know little of the case. What do you know?" he asked me.

"Only what I've read in old newspaper accounts. That my uncle discovered my father dead in my family's kitchen, killed with a butcher knife. My mother was found a short time later, wandering the street dazed and bloody. All the lurid stuff they made a great deal of in the papers. My family doesn't speak of it."

He studied me. "You were adopted by your father's brother, the man who found his body, if I remember right?"

I nodded. "My uncle has been very kind to me. No one could have been more so. He told me the barest of details when I was young, but it hasn't been something we've talked about. I don't suppose it could have been easy for him."

"No," he answered. "I don't believe it was easy for him at all. He found it difficult to believe that your mother could have killed your father."

"But she was covered in his blood and had cuts on her hand,

as though she had wielded the knife," I said. It felt strange, hearing myself give this calm recital of the story that was my family legacy. It was like a dark fairy tale, the sort of thing that happened to other people. But it was my father who had died and my mother who had been accused of killing him.

He nodded. "That was the case against her. That and the raised voices that were heard by neighbors perhaps an hour before your father's body was found."

"But she claimed she didn't do it," I said. "That she had found my father's body on the floor herself, cut her hand pulling the knife from his body."

"Yes. That's what she said."

"And did you believe her?" It was the question I had always feared asking, but it had come from me unbidden, as though it had waited too long and could no longer be repressed.

I felt as though the air in the room was charged with meaning as I studied the man's face.

His brow creased as he considered for a moment. Then he leveled his dark eyes on me. "No," he said. "I didn't."

Before I could work my mind around what he seemed to be saying—that my mother was guilty—he continued. "Let me make myself clear: I do not believe she killed your father."

I felt instantly as though a weight had been lifted from my shoulders.

I hadn't known what Sir Roland was going to tell me, but I realized now that I had come prepared for the worst. I had come prepared to hear that he had known my mother was guilty but had defended her anyway because it was his job.

Now I felt a surge of hope, almost elation. For a moment I couldn't seem to catch my breath.

Felix reached over and silently took my hand.

"But I didn't believe her story," Sir Roland went on. "It didn't make sense to me from the start. She claimed she found your father

THE KEY TO DECEIT

dead, pulled the knife from his body, ran out in a blind terror, and remembered nothing until she was discovered. It was clear that she was hiding something."

"But what?" I asked.

"I would have given a great deal to know. Your family had certain criminal associations at that time," he said, carefully avoiding suggesting we might still have them. "It occurred to me that she might have been either afraid of someone or else protecting them. But no matter how much I urged her to tell me the full truth, she stuck doggedly to that version of events. I did what I could with it. In the end, however, the evidence was too difficult to overcome. The blood on her clothes, the cuts on her hand."

I didn't like to picture it, to think of what my mother must have felt when she saw my father lying there, covered in blood. What had it been like for her to lose her husband and then be accused of the crime? I couldn't imagine.

"Your mother was an unusual woman," he said. "She was not afraid, even to the end of the trial. I have defended the most hardened of criminals who had to be helped to their feet when the verdict was read. Not your mother. She was steady throughout; she never wavered."

I tried to consider what secret might have been worth dying for and came up short.

"And you never had any idea what she might have been hiding?" I asked.

He shook his head. "Whatever secrets she kept, she took to her grave. It was a great relief to me when she was reprieved from hanging."

"But then the flu took her," I said.

"Yes. A bad business."

"Is there anything more you can tell us?" Felix asked. "Any clues that might have pointed to another suspect?"

Sir Roland considered. "This case was a quarter of a century and many, many trials ago, and my memory's not as sharp as it used to be. I'd have to consult my notes for anything more specific."

"Ellie spoke with a fellow prisoner, a Mrs. Norris, who said a woman called Clarice Maynard might be able to tell us something," Felix pressed.

"Clarice Maynard," he said reflectively. "Yes, I remember her. She came to visit your mother often. It's possible your mother confided in her, I suppose."

"Does she live in London?"

"I believe she went to live with family after the trial. In Lincolnshire, if I remember correctly. I wish I could tell you more. If you'll leave your telephone number, I'll look over my files. If anything of interest comes to mind, I'll be sure to ring you."

"Thank you very much, Sir Roland. You've been a great help."

We said our goodbyes, and Felix took my arm as we turned toward the door.

"Miss McDonnell."

I turned at Sir Roland's voice.

"You'll forgive me for saying so," he said, his eyes on my face, "but you look very much like her."

I felt a little flush of pleasure, just as I had when Mrs. Norris had told me the same thing. "Thank you," I said softly.

"I hope you find the answers you're looking for."

Felix and I walked away from his house in silence for several moments. There was so much to think about. I felt the weight of what I had learned, but I also felt lighter than I had in a long time. Perhaps lighter than I had since I had learned what had happened to my mother.

The next step would be to locate Clarice Maynard in Lincolnshire. Perhaps she would be able to tell me something more. Perhaps she would even know what secret it was that my mother had apparently been keeping.

We didn't have answers yet, but we were getting closer to them. I could feel it.

I was convinced now beyond doubt that my mother had been innocent. I just had to find a way to prove it.

CHAPTER TWENTY

I made my way to the major's office the following morning still pondering what Sir Roland had told me.

What would Major Ramsey think of these latest revelations? I realized that I felt the odd urge to share with him what I had learned, though I didn't know where the impulse came from. It wasn't likely, after all, that the major would be inclined to offer much encouragement.

I had talked to him about my mother's case just once. He had been aware of my history even before we met, but when he finally brought up the subject of my mother it was only to tell me that he had read the trial transcripts and didn't see how the jury could come to any other conclusion than guilty.

It ought to have given me pause, I supposed. Though he could be arch and disapproving, Major Ramsey was also fair and intelligent. He was going solely on the circumstantial facts of the case, however. And there was much more to it than that.

Now that I knew Sir Roland really believed in my mother's innocence, I thought perhaps the major would like to know what I had discovered.

Constance greeted me with a warm smile when she let me into the major's office.

"I believe he's expecting me," I said.

"Yes. I'm just bringing him some documents that have been dropped off. I'll show you in."

She led the way to the major's office and knocked on the door. "Come in."

I noticed she modified her expression to something slightly less cheerful before she pushed the door open. "Miss McDonnell to see you, sir. And I have some papers that were delivered for you."

"Thank you, Miss Brown. Come in, Miss McDonnell."

He had risen from behind his desk upon my entry and motioned to the chair I was coming to think of as my "usual" seat in his office. Constance set the papers on the edge of the desk and turned to leave.

"Close the door, please, Miss Brown."

"Yes, sir."

Constance left, closing the door behind her, and I turned to look expectantly at the major. Something in his tone as he'd instructed Constance to close the door told me something was wrong.

"What is it?" I didn't stop to wonder why I could tell something was amiss, the way I was beginning to understand the subtleties of his shifts in demeanor.

He looked up at me, his expression grim. "Jane Kelley was found dead this morning in the Thames."

I'm afraid my mouth dropped open. This I had not been expecting, though, when I considered it, it seemed that it should not really have come as a surprise.

The young woman who'd seemed so confident and competent when we'd talked with her in Mrs. Paine's parlor hadn't struck me as the sort of person who would be easily led into a trap. Then again, perhaps she had been overconfident. Whoever had killed Myra Fields had clearly struck again. Had it been Bill Mondale?

"Was she killed with a toxin, too?" I asked.

"Yes."

It seemed the spymaster was eliminating his spies at a rapid rate. Perhaps, now that they had delivered the goods, there was no further use for them. Once they ceased to be useful, they were only a liability.

It was sad. It was horrible, of course, that those girls had been working for the enemy. Everything in me rebelled against such a thing. But, all the same, they had been used and cruelly murdered. I hoped we could find whoever had done this before they were able to strike again.

"I rang you yesterday evening," he said. I sensed the vague disapproval in the words and instantly bristled at them. He expected me to sit around at his beck and call. Well, I had my own life to manage.

"I was out with Felix." I wasn't sure why I said this when I knew the major didn't care for Felix. No, that wasn't true. That was exactly why I had said it.

"Perhaps you can keep your romance on hold until we catch the ring of spies we're after," he said, his tone cool.

"We went to see my mother's barrister," I said. There was no crime in seeking out my past. Even if Major Ramsey believed my mother guilty, there was no reason I had to give up learning about her.

He sat back in his chair. "Sir Roland Highgate."

It was a reminder to never underestimate that steel-trap memory of his.

"Yes."

"And what did he say?" I was a bit surprised at the question. I'd expected him to brush the matter aside.

"He told me he believed in her innocence."

He seemed to consider this. "Sir Roland was an excellent barrister. I wouldn't take his opinions lightly."

I stared at him. Was it possible he was encouraging me, after all?

"What did he advise you to do?" he asked when I didn't say anything.

"There was a friend of my mother's I learned about recently. He told me where I might seek her out. That she might know something that would help me prove her innocence." I paused, then added, "Do you think I should?"

His answer didn't matter, not really. I had already made up my mind to find Clarice Maynard. All the same, I was curious about what the major would have to say. For some reason, I had begun to value his opinion.

"I don't see there would be any harm in it," he said at last. "Unless, of course, you get your hopes up. You realize it will be very difficult to prove anything at this late date."

"I know," I said. "But I have to try."

There was a moment of silence.

Then he said, "May I ask you something?"

I looked up at him. He seldom used that sort of polite tone with me, spoke to me the way I imagined he would with a society woman, careful words that didn't press too hard.

"Of course."

"What does it matter?"

I frowned. "What do you mean?"

"What does it matter if your mother was guilty or innocent? You can't change the past, and knowing won't change anything now."

There was a brief moment when I felt a surge of anger, but then I realized that he saw things differently than I did. He was a man who viewed life in black-and-white. What he said was true enough, of course, but that was because he discounted the emotional element. He was not a man inclined to emotions, and so he overlooked them; if he had a fault amongst his list of perfections, this was it.

"You don't think the truth matters?" I asked.

He didn't reply for a long moment. "If you find out she was guilty, it will hurt you. And if you find out she was innocent, it will hurt you even more." His eyes met mine. "I shouldn't like to see you hurt, Miss McDonnell."

I blinked. I had not expected this sort of remark from him, and I was a bit at a loss for words.

"That's kind of you, Major," I said at last. "But I need to know."

He gave a short nod. "I understand that, certainly."

There was a tap on the door.

"Enter."

Constance stuck her head in the door. "Mr. Kimble is here, sir."

The major didn't have time to reply before Kimble materialized from behind Constance and came into the room.

"Mr. Kimble . . ." she began, but the major waved her away, and she closed the door behind the uninvited guest.

Kimble ambled to the open chair beside me and sank into it. He was the only one of the major's subordinates I had seen thus far who was not at all intimidated by the major's stern attitude and strict orderliness. Then again, Kimble was the most emotionless man I had ever met. I rather suspected Kimble would be unimpressed even if the king should suddenly burst into the room.

The major didn't greet Kimble but simply waited for Kimble to deliver whatever news he had come to report.

Kimble gave a slight nod in my direction. "You fill her in?"

"Not yet," the major said. "Go ahead and tell her what you found out yesterday."

"I followed the chap from the garden. He picked up the case from the train station and then went to a bank," he said. "He works there. Name's William Mondale."

"So we were right," I said.

"It would seem so," the major replied.

"He put the goods in a safe-deposit box," Kimble continued.

This bit I had not anticipated. Safe-deposit boxes were generally kept in a vault, which would, naturally, be much more difficult to access than railway station baggage storage had been. Perhaps it had been unwise to let the film out of our hands.

"Are you sure?" I asked.

"Yes. I overheard him telling one of the girls he was with on his day off to put something in his box."

I looked at the major. "Do you suppose the bank manager can be taken into our confidence? If we tell him why we need to access the vault . . ."

"Mondale is the bank manager," Kimble said.

"Oh."

There was a short moment of silence. I considered our options. "But does it really matter if he knows you're onto him?" I asked at last. "After all, if you confiscate the film, the spy ring is going to realize they've been found out."

"It's like the old adage of tossing a stone into a smooth pond," the major said. "The ripples travel. We need as few ripples as possible. Better they don't know who has taken their film or why."

"It needs to be done quietly," Kimble agreed.

And then I realized what they were saying, and I couldn't stop the grin that spread across my face. "Then, gentlemen, it seems we're going to do a bank job."

CHAPTER TWENTY-ONE

Major Ramsey and I went to case the joint together.

The bank was one of those impressive buildings with pillared chambers and echoing vaulted ceilings. People talked in whispers, as though it were a hospital. Or maybe a church was more accurate; people do tend to worship money.

I followed the major as he approached the teller. We'd agreed that he'd do the talking. This was more his world than it was mine. We McDonnells had never had much to do with banks; we knew how easily they could be breached.

He had ungraciously suggested I continue to be his fiancée.

"Leave the ring on," he'd said. "We might as well keep up this farce."

"I do love it when you sweet-talk me, darling," I'd replied.

I think he was beginning to regret that we'd started this ruse, but there was no sense in quitting while we were ahead.

"May I help you, sir?" the teller asked prettily, eyeing him and ignoring me.

"I'd like to speak to the bank manager, please," he said. The plan was to brazen it out, kill two birds with one stone. We'd get a read on Mondale and have a look at the vault at the same time. And so the major was using his imperious manner today, the one that no doubt made his subordinates snap to attention.

The woman behind the counter looked both intimidated and intrigued.

"Yes, sir. I'll tell him you're here. If you . . . What is . . . What name shall I give him?"

"Major Ramsey. He may be familiar with my uncle, the Earl of Overbrook."

"Oh, yes, Major." The woman was clearly impressed. "If you'll wait for just a moment. I'll be right back."

As the major waited, I wandered around the lobby a bit, taking in the layout of the bank. Bank robbery was not, of course, in my family's line. We had never had any links to the sort of crime that could be considered a stickup. And, as for robbing a bank by night, we'd never wanted to draw that sort of attention to ourselves. No, the McDonnells had never had any illusions of grandeur as far as a life of crime went.

But I wasn't worried about the job ahead, not even in a big bank like this one. The bigger they are, the harder they fall, as Uncle Mick always said.

My attention returned to the major as William Mondale emerged from an office and hurried toward us. I'd only glimpsed him through the bushes in the Morris Memorial Garden, but his tall, pale figure was unmistakable. He was wearing a navy-blue pin-stripe suit today with a snappy tie and a matching handkerchief in the breast pocket. He wore a pair of gold spectacles on the bridge of his nose. In contrast to his uneasy demeanor when he'd been picking up the message in the garden, he was very much in command of himself here in his own domain.

"Good morning. You wish to speak with me?" he asked. Just like the teller, he had barely spared a glance in my direction. They had good instincts in this place about who came from money and who didn't, it seemed.

"My name is Major Ramsey. My uncle, you may be aware, is the Earl of Overbrook."

"Ah . . . yes," Mondale said.

The major indicated me at his side. "This is my fiancée, Elizabeth Donaldson."

The man looked at me then. "How do you do, madam."

"How do you do," I replied, my accent a bit more posh than usual.

"Miss Donaldson and I are to be married, and I'm making her a present of some of the Overbrook jewels," the major went on. "With the safety of London in question, I'd like her to store them somewhere safe. I'll need to see your safe-deposit vault."

I could've kissed him. It was done so smoothly and so confidently that Mondale didn't so much as blink. "Of course, sir. If you'll just follow me."

I had to give it to the major. Sometimes that commanding attitude of his paid off.

William Mondale led us across the lobby to a lift. We got in and began our descent to the sublevel.

"You'll find that the premises are quite secure," he said, launching into what was no doubt his standard speech. "The vault door is composed of solid steel. It is locked at night, of course."

No wonder, then, that he felt safe storing the film there.

I let his spiel fade away after that and focused on what was before me. The lift opened onto a small vestibule. A guard stood near the steel door at the hallway's entrance. He nodded to the manager but made no comment as Mondale inserted a key into the lock, opened the door, and ushered us through.

On the other side, a short hallway led to the vault. The door was open, as it was during the day, according to Mondale. I couldn't get a great look at the door without being obvious, but it looked to be a four-tumbler lock.

"And the safe-deposit boxes are here," Mondale said, ushering us inside the vault. It wasn't a very large room. It felt cramped with the three of us inside, though, in fairness, the major always seemed to use up a great deal of space.

It was lined on three sides, floor to ceiling, with boxes. The ones toward the top were smaller, and they got progressively bigger as they moved toward the floor, the small ones being the size of a post office box and the larger ones like deep drawers or small cupboards.

"Do you know what size box you'll be needing?" Mondale asked.

"Probably one of the larger ones."

"You spoil me, darling," I purred.

The major and Mondale chatted about box sizes, and I sidled back up to the vault door to get a better look. It was fairly standard. The four-tumbler lock was a challenge, but not too much of one. I wasn't worried.

The men concluded their business with a handshake, and I returned to the major's side, tucking my arm into his.

"I think this is a lovely place to keep jewels," I said in my best imitation of a woman besotted with both her fiancé and his family's money.

Mondale smiled tightly at me. Pretty haughty for a man spying for Nazis, I thought. Then he led us back down the hallway, through the steel door, past the guard, and into the lift.

Within five minutes we were back outside.

"Can you do it?" the major asked without preamble as we made our way down the front steps.

"No," I said. "At least, probably not in the time we've got. But Uncle Mick can."

"All right. What else?"

"We'll need someone to disable the alarm."

"I assume you have someone in mind?"

"Do you think you could get Colm up here?" My cousin was stationed in Torquay, but he'd been pulled into our last adventure on short notice.

"Is he the best man for the job?"

"I wouldn't have suggested him otherwise."

"Then I'll get him."

I knew he had to ask, to make sure that I wasn't just trying to make this a family affair. But my cousin really would be the best person for it.

"What did you make of Mondale?" I asked.

"I think he's smarter than he looks."

I glanced at him, surprised. "In what way?"

"I don't know," the major said. "He tried to hide it, but he was wary."

"I think he was just putting on airs."

"Let us hope so. Is your uncle at home now?"

"I think so."

"Then let's go and talk to him."

"A bank robbery, is it?" Uncle Mick said, his eyes twinkling when we had related the details to him.

"Not exactly," the major said. "We're only taking the film."

"'Tis a pity," Uncle Mick said with a wink at me.

The major did not smile. He had no sense of humor when it came to our illegal escapades.

"We've never done anything on this scale before," I reminded my uncle, lest he get too carried away with enthusiasm.

"Ah, Ellie girl, you've got to have ambition," Uncle Mick said. There was a glimmer in his eyes that I recognized. He was ready for danger. He liked the thrill of it.

The major realized this as well, for he gave a nod of approval.

"Good man," Major Ramsey said.

I glanced between my uncle and the major. There must be few men in London who were more different, and yet there was something about both of them that was very similar. There was in both of them a sense of daring and a relish for accomplishing their goals in the face of tremendous odds. The major kept his adventurous streak under tight control, but I'd bet good money that it was there.

"When are we going to do it?" I asked.

"I'll have your cousin sent up from Torquay tomorrow. Once we get him up to speed, we'll do the job on Sunday."

The day after tomorrow. That was soon, sooner than I had expected. Men in this line of work often plotted bank jobs for months. It wasn't something to be done lightly. Of course, wartime changed everything. We didn't have time for plotting, not when the film might be picked up at any point by the spymaster and brought back to Germany where it could be used to do maximum damage.

"Quick work," Uncle Mick said, echoing my thoughts. "But I don't suppose it'll take us much longer than that to get the lay of the land."

"I'm afraid it will have to do," Major Ramsey said. "I worry we'll be cutting it close, as it is. We don't know exactly when the German operative will retrieve the cache of film."

"We'd better begin preparing tonight, then," Uncle Mick said. "Colm's a quick lad. He'll catch on soon enough."

"Stay for dinner, Major," Nacy said. "I've got a pot of Irish stew on."

I thought for certain he would refuse, but, to my surprise, he nodded. "Thank you, Mrs. Dean. That would be lovely."

We sat in the sitting room after dinner planning a bank robbery.

The major had removed his jacket and sat with a cup of coffee in one of the chairs before the unlit fireplace. Uncle Mick was smoking his pipe. Kimble, who had arrived after dinner, sat in a corner of the room, blending in with the shadows until he occasionally spoke up and reminded us he was there.

Nacy sat on the sofa beside me, knitting socks for soldiers as she often did in what little spare time she had, but she wasn't concentrating and kept dropping stitches.

Nacy wasn't normally party to the discussions of our less than legal pursuits. She knew, in the way she seemed to know everything, that we were up to things we shouldn't be. But she didn't want to know the details, and we all thought that was for the best.

With the major's official sanction of our activities, however, she could enjoy the thrill of the planning without the moral ambiguity such things usually entailed. And so she listened raptly as we discussed the layout of the bank and the type of security system.

After a dinner at which the major had held a charmed Nacy in thrall, he had telephoned Kimble, instructing him and his shadowy associates to ascertain the bank's workings at night. Kimble had apparently set his men to the task and then arrived at the house with the bank's blueprints and a copy of the security system installation documents, neither of which anyone asked how he had obtained.

"What about Mondale?" the major asked as we discussed the bank. "Have you been keeping an eye on him?"

"Went home after work same as usual," Kimble said. "My man followed him there before circling back to the bank. My man's also been monitoring the movement of the guards. There's only one at night; he patrols the perimeter."

"We'll have to get rid of him," the major said.

"Couldn't you just send him away?" I asked. It was naïve of me to think so, perhaps, but it seemed that the major's domineering presence in an officer's uniform might have an effect.

"He's not going to take my word for it that we should be allowed to enter the bank at night," the major said.

"Well, what will we do with him then?"

"Leave that to Kimble."

"We don't want to kill the man!" I said it before I could think better of it.

"We won't kill him," Kimble said. "It would be easiest in the short term, of course, but it would call too much attention after the fact."

I saw Nacy blink.

I would take his word for it, and hope the poor bank guard wouldn't suffer too grim a fate simply because he was in our way.

"The boys and I'll take care of the outside of the bank," Kimble said. "No need to worry about that, as long as you can get yourselves in and do the vault."

"Colm shouldn't have a problem with the alarm, and it will be easy enough to get in a side door," Uncle Mick said.

"Yes. Once we're inside, there's a staircase here," I said, pointing to an area on the blueprints. "It will be better than using the lift." My finger traced along the staircase and then down a short hallway to the steel door where a guard had been stationed.

"We'll have to get through this door. And then into the vault."

"It's not going to be easy," he said cheerfully. This was not meant to be bad news; Uncle Mick loved a challenge.

"Do you think you'll be able to do it in the time allotted?" the major asked.

"Well, Major, you've been a bit mum about how much time we'll have."

"We need to be in and out as quickly as possible." I knew he was right. We could disable the alarm system and silence the guard, but our risk of being caught went up exponentially the longer we were inside.

It was going to be a risky job, possibly even dangerous. I supposed the major would be able to talk our way out of legal trouble if things went wrong. But that would probably let the spy go free, and we couldn't risk that.

"Don't fret, Ellie girl," Uncle Mick said, seemingly following my train of thought. "We've always come out on top, haven't we? Or nearly always. And the time we didn't, the major here did."

"How long will you need?" the major asked.

Uncle Mick looked up at him. "I don't know. I'll work as quick as I can."

"No estimate?" the major pressed.

"You can't ask an artist to time their art," Kimble put in from the corner.

Uncle Mick grinned. "That's about the size of it. Until I've got my hands on the lock, I can't be exactly sure how long it will take me to open it."

Major Ramsey didn't look pleased; he was a man who liked order and method. "We'll only have so long inside the building."

"An hour, perhaps. Two at the outside," Uncle Mick said. "A four-tumbler lock is no joke."

Something occurred to me. "We could bring in Merriweather Hastings."

"Ah," Uncle Mick said. "There's a thought!"

"Merriweather Hastings?" the major repeated.

Merriweather Hastings was an old associate of Uncle Mick's. It was hard to describe just what he was. The phrase "jack-of-all-trades" was appropriate. If I had to estimate, I would say that a good ninety percent of those trades were illegitimate.

And the one that would work best for us was that he was a master of explosives.

"He'll be able to blow the vault," I said.

One of the major's fair brows rose ever so slightly.

Nacy made a small sound of alarm, but she didn't say anything. We'd apparently shocked her into silence, no small feat.

"It's not a bad idea," Kimble put in. "It'll be quicker in and out that way."

Uncle Mick nodded. "I'd put my skills up against any safe-cracker in the country, but dynamite is faster than my fingers."

The major, to my surprise, appeared to consider this. I'd have thought he would have dismissed the suggestion out of hand.

"Do you trust him?" he asked Uncle Mick at last.

"With my life."

"All right," the major said, shocking me further. "Let's bring him in."

CHAPTER TWENTY-TWO

Uncle Mick and I went to see Merriweather Hastings the next morning. The major had agreed that it would be best for us to talk to him alone.

"Do you think he'll help us?" I asked as we approached the door to his flat.

"I think he'll be glad to," Uncle Mick said. "He already gave an eye for Blighty and has always said he'd have been willing to give both. He's our man, all right."

The door was pulled open at our knock, and Merriweather Hastings stood before us. In another age, the man would have been a pirate. He had a long beard, wild black hair streaked with white, and he even wore a patch over one eye. Though he'd lost his eye in the Great War and not in a sword fight.

"Ah, Mick!" he said, shaking my uncle's hand. "It's been too long."

Then his gaze moved to me. "And don't ever tell me this is my little Ellie."

"Hello, Merriweather."

"Ellie, love." He came to me and pulled me into an embrace. He smelled like tobacco, rum, and, somewhat alarmingly, gunpowder.

He stepped back, his hands still gripping my arms, and looked me over. "You're prettier every time I see you. You got yourself a husband yet, lovie?"

I smiled. "No, not yet."

"Well, there's time enough for that. I've always been of a mind that a person should wait until they find the right one. No sense rushing into things. I've made that mistake often enough to know."

He grinned, and I laughed.

I wasn't sure why his boisterousness delighted me as it did. I should have been afraid of him. Any proper woman likely would have been. He was fearsome in appearance and manner.

But he had never been anything less than courteous to me. Even as I had grown to womanhood, he hadn't taken to flirting with me as many of Uncle Mick's friends had. Instead, he treated me as if he, too, were one of my uncles.

It was this quality, perhaps, that endeared him to me. Not that anyone who was nice to me was worth trusting. I had known that very well from a young age. Uncle Mick said my instinct for people was as keen as any he had ever seen, and it had guided me well over the years.

"How's the family?" he asked as he led us inside. "Has my girl found herself another man yet?"

Merriweather had always flirted mercilessly with Nacy. She huffed and grumbled about it under her breath but was secretly delighted.

"I'll tell her you asked after her," I said.

"Do that. Tell her I'll be back to sweep her off her feet one of these days. And what about the boys?"

We briefly updated him on the situation with my cousins. A frown creased his face as he heard about Toby. "You'll hear something soon," he said. "There's been a lot of confusion, and Toby's a tough lad."

I nodded. It was the thing that most people said; the hopeful optimism was the only thing they could offer in the face of my cousin's uncertain fate.

"But there is another reason we've come," Uncle Mick said, changing the subject.

Merriweather smiled, that old grin that I remembered so well. "I supposed as much. Have a seat, and we'll talk it over."

He drew me up a chair as Uncle Mick took a seat in a wooden chair nearby. Like its resident, the interior of Merriweather's flat wouldn't have been out of place in a ship's cabin. It was all dark wood, the furniture sturdy but plain.

"Care for a drink, Mick? Lovie?" he asked.

We both declined, and he shrugged. "Suit yourself." He picked up the bottle and took a long swig from it.

Then, bottle still in hand, he took a seat across from us. "What do you want me to do? Must be a big job if you're prepared to choose fire over finesse."

"We're on the side of the angels with this one," Uncle Mick said.

His bushy brows rose. "Is that so?"

The major had authorized us to tell him the full truth. "We're working with military intelligence," I said. "This is a matter of national importance."

Merriweather Hastings looked at us for a moment and then threw back his head and laughed. Then he rose from his chair. "Then what are we waiting for?"

We all made our way to the major's office together. Constance, to her credit, didn't so much as blink when presented with Merriweather Hastings in all his glory.

"I believe the major is expecting you," was all she said.

I wondered about Constance. Was she from the major's world or a world closer to mine? One day we would have to sit down and have a chat.

She led us to the major's office, and he bid us enter.

I watched Major Ramsey as Merriweather entered the room. The major's expression gave nothing away, but then he turned to look at me and one brow went up ever so slightly.

He would have something to say about this when the matter was over, I was sure.

"Merriweather, this is Major Ramsey, our commanding officer, so to speak," I said.

"Sergeant Merriweather Hastings, Nineteenth Division, London Regiment, at your service, sir," he said with a jaunty salute.

"I'm pleased to meet you, Sergeant," the major said. "Mr. Mc Donnell tells me you may be just the man for the job."

"I believe I am, sir," he said.

"It goes without saying, naturally, that we won't take anything of value from the bank, but I'm authorized to pay you for your services."

"Nothing wrong with taking an honest wage when you can't get a dishonest one," Merriweather said cheerily.

The major's gaze flicked to me, and I suppressed a smile. Poor Major Ramsey had had no idea what he was in for when he threw in his lot with us.

"And you can open the vault quickly?"

"It's a simple enough thing, the way Mick's described it. Won't take much to get it open. A bit of nitroglycerin and a couple of blasting caps. Easy stuff."

The major took this casual talk of explosives in stride. "How much noise will it make?"

"You can't create an explosion without a bit of noise, Major. But the vault is underground, so we should be able to keep from drawing too much attention."

"What supplies do you require? I can get you what you need by tomorrow."

Merriweather shook his head. "I've got my own supplies, Major. No need to worry about that."

The major considered this for a moment, but whatever he felt about Merriweather stocking his own nitroglycerin, he didn't comment on it. He merely nodded. "All right. Then welcome to the team."

Merriweather winked at me.

The major was still looking at Merriweather. "You understand, of course, that this work is, by its very nature, dangerous."

"I've always said a job's not worth doing if there isn't the chance of danger." Merriweather grinned, and I had the image of him standing on the deck of a pirate's ship, the cannons booming and swords clashing. He was a man who would enjoy the danger, who would enjoy the fight. I was not entirely sure he was not the sort of man who would enjoy killing if it came to that.

There was about him the sense of danger beneath his placid exterior. He was jovial and friendly, always good for a joke with his ready grin. But there was always the sense that he was not a man to be crossed. I didn't personally know anyone who had ever come to a bad end with Merriweather Hastings, but I had seen many a man back down from him.

There were rumors about him, too. That he had been an assassin for the government, a paid killer in various locales during the last war. Though they were both military men, he was different from Major Ramsey. He wasn't the sort of man who would be comfortable in a stiff uniform, saluting his superior officers. I could picture him in the desert, however, or wading through the muddy trenches, knife in hand. I thought of him as a man out of his time, a warrior born in the wrong era.

I think Major Ramsey recognized it, too, for, despite Merriweather's unorthodox appearance, the major treated him with the respect due a peer and a professional as we began to make our plans.

"I've laid out the maps and begun charting the best means of ingress and egress, as well as possible routes to and from the bank," Major Ramsey continued, nodding toward his desk, which had been cleared of everything, save the blueprints of the bank and a map of the surrounding area. We all gathered around to study the neat markings he'd made across the documents. "What are your opinions?"

We spent the next hour or so going over the blueprints from every angle, the men fueled by inky coffee, while I sipped from a cup of tea Constance had brought me. We studied the map, too, deciding on various routes should we encounter opposition. There were surprisingly few arguments for three men—and one woman—of decidedly strong opinions. We were united in a common purpose, and that purpose overrode any small disagreements.

It made me like the major even more, seeing him defer to Uncle Mick and Merriweather as though their opinions were as important as his. He could be rigid and imperious at times, but he recognized the value in the experience of others.

As I was thinking this about him, watching him, he looked up at me across the desk and our eyes met. I almost looked quickly away, but instead I gave him a small smile. The corner of his mouth tipped up in return, and I felt the impact of that little look in the pit of my stomach, like a flash of electricity straight through my middle. How silly I was being.

". . . right here?" Uncle Mick asked.

I realized I hadn't been paying attention to his question and returned my gaze to where he was pointing at the map on the desk.

"I'm sorry. Could you repeat that?" the major asked.

"I think this might be another option right here," Uncle Mick said, running his finger along an area of the map. "Provided there's no fences?"

"Kimble will have the answer to that," the major said. "He's doing reconnaissance today and will meet with us tomorrow."

"Any word on Colm?" I asked, having recovered my poise.

"I couldn't get him away until tomorrow," Major Ramsey replied. "He's due to arrive first thing in the morning."

"Then I think that's all we can do for tonight," Uncle Mick said. "The rest will be Colm's domain."

The major nodded. "We'll meet tomorrow at thirteen hundred hours at your house, if it's convenient, Mr. McDonnell. We can go over our plans again until it's time to go to the bank."

I felt a little thrill at his words. In a little more than twenty-four hours, we would be entering the bank.

The major walked us outside. It was already late afternoon, the sun moving its way back toward the horizon. Nacy would have dinner waiting for us when we returned home.

"It's been a pleasure to meet you, Major," Merriweather said. "I look forward to the mission."

The major nodded. "Until tomorrow, Sergeant Hastings."

"Until tomorrow, Major," Uncle Mick said with a smile. "Wait a moment, Merriweather. I'll walk with you to the end of the block."

He went after Merriweather, leaving me alone with Major Ramsey. His intention, no doubt.

I turned to look at the major.

"You do have the most interesting assortment of friends, Miss McDonnell," he said.

"You ought to come to one of Uncle Mick's poker games," I replied. "You do owe me a rematch."

I tried to picture the major at one of Uncle Mick's poker nights. He'd often hosted them throughout the years, and the participants had been some of the most successful criminals in England.

But they were more than that, too. They were complex, interesting people, each with their own reasons why they had been drawn into a life of crime. Some were purely in it for profit. Others were doing it because they liked the excitement and challenge. Others had chosen a strange method of righting the wrongs they felt had been done to them.

One thing I had come to learn over the years was that you could never judge a book by its cover. People were seldom what they seemed to be on the outside. Even the major was far more than I had taken him for in the beginning. Just because he was a stern, officious man in uniform didn't mean that there wasn't a bit of daring and thirst for adventure lurking just below the surface. Perhaps he wouldn't be so out of place at the poker games, after all.

Perhaps when all this was over.

I looked up at him. "Do you think we'll really be able to pull it off?"

"I don't think anyone has a better chance."

I nodded. That would have to be good enough. "Then I'll see you tomorrow, Major."

"Yes. Good evening, Miss McDonnell."

I caught up with Uncle Mick, and we made our way home on the Tube. We didn't talk much, both of us going over the night's events and thinking about what tomorrow might hold.

We had just reached the house when I heard it. The sound that made my blood chill.

It was the air-raid sirens. And behind it, a low buzz I only now recognized: approaching aircraft.

The Germans were coming.

CHAPTER TWENTY-THREE

For a brief moment, I stood still, incredulous. Was this really happening? In a way, I think we'd been expecting it would any day. But, at the same time, we had not wanted to believe it, had done our best to convince ourselves that the awfulness of the war on the Continent would not touch our shores.

I looked up and caught a glint in the distance. Then another. And another. They were planes, I realized. A sky full of them.

It was indeed finally happening. The moment we had waited for and dreaded for months was finally upon us. The Germans weren't coming; they were here.

It was a surreal feeling. Even as I heard the steadily approaching whine of Heinkel and Dornier engines, I stood transfixed, mesmerized by the sudden materialization of all our fears. Then there was an odd whooshing sound in the distance and a bright flash of light followed by a loud rumble.

They were dropping bombs.

"Ellie. We've got to go to the cellar," Uncle Mick said, shaking me from my fog.

He took my arm and began to lead me across the yard. There was the same steady calm in him that had guided me all my life, and it was reassuring now. Even in the face of this deadly assault, he was still the same old Uncle Mick, never rushed or frantic under pressure.

We found Nacy in front of the house, her eyes also cast southward. "So they've finally come," she said in a resigned voice.

"We're ready for them," Uncle Mick said, his tone no less chipper than usual. "To the cellar we go."

With one last glance at the sky, now lighting up repeatedly as the bombs hit below, I turned and allowed him to herd us back into the house, through to the kitchen, and down the wooden steps that led to the cellar.

While many Londoners had been issued or purchased Anderson shelters, small shedlike structures made of corrugated steel that could be buried outdoors, we'd been fortunate enough to have a brick-walled cellar. Uncle Mick had fortified it with sandbags and some extra crossbeams, though we'd all hoped it would prove unnecessary. Now it seemed the time had come.

In the cool dampness of the cellar, the sound of the bombs being dropped was not as loud, but we could hear it still and feel the distant vibration as the earth shook.

None of us said anything for a long while. Nacy muttered a prayer under her breath, but my own prayers were too jumbled to speak aloud. I thought of Felix, hoping he'd made it safely home or to someplace he could shelter. I thought of Major Ramsey. I thought of my friends, my neighbors. I thought of all the beautiful buildings in this city that I loved.

After all those months of the Phoney War when it seemed that nothing was going to happen, our homeland was under attack. We were living in a war zone now. It was almost impossible to believe. But perhaps one always wanted to think that bad things would remain distant, that it would be others who lived where the bombs fell.

Poland had been razed; Denmark, Norway, Belgium, and France had been overrun. Now it was our turn to face the enemy.

It was a sobering thought. A daunting one.

But, even as fear and uncertainty moved through me, I felt my jaw tighten and my backbone grow straighter. They could try all they wanted. But they were about to see what we were made of.

I wasn't sure how long the bombing went on. It all seemed like rather a blur. It was a strange sensation, waiting for the ceiling to come crashing in at any moment.

It was frightening, but I realized that, confusingly, I also felt resigned, almost relieved. It was the feeling that comes when you've been dreading something for ages and it finally happens and you're almost glad because the waiting is over.

There had come a brief lull in the bombing, and I thought perhaps it was finally over.

Were they gone? How much damage had they done? How many people had been killed? The thoughts flashed through my head in the space of a moment.

"Is that it?" I asked Uncle Mick.

His expression was grim. "I wouldn't think so. We'd better not go up just yet."

And then the sirens went off again. They were coming back.

We didn't sleep much. I don't suppose anyone in London slept much that first night. It had seemed that the bombing went on and on, the planes droning and dropping their deadly cargo. Hour after hour, there was the whine of aircraft, the strange, blood-chilling shriek of the bombs, and the shuddering of the earth all around us.

There had been the noise of RAF fighter planes and antiaircraft guns, too, as they did what they could to ward off the attacks. But it seemed as though the planes were everywhere above us, swarming above the city like a mass of mosquitoes.

I felt sick to my stomach, my entire body a knot of tension. I had convinced myself that I would be steely in the face of an invasion, but I had to face the fact that I was afraid.

I had felt the reality of the war when I had said goodbye to

Colm and Toby, to Felix; I had felt it during the Battle of Britain, waiting to hear what would happen; I had felt it when I had learned that Toby was missing. All of it had been reminders of what we were facing, of the dangers the future might hold.

But nothing had been like this, with the shells dropping all around us. With bombs exploding and fires tearing through our streets. The war wasn't just something happening on a far-off battle-field; it was happening here.

Uncle Mick was—outwardly, at least—as calm as ever. He sat beside me for a long while, his arm around my shoulders like he had done when I was a child. "It will be all right," he said. "It can't go on forever."

I tried very hard to believe him.

"Let's eat a bit of something," Nacy said, reverting to her need to care for people in times of crisis. True to her motherly instincts, she'd grabbed a loaf of bread and the roast chicken she'd prepared for dinner as we'd passed through the kitchen on our way to the cellar.

"I ought to have thought to bring a knife, but I suppose this will have to do," she said, tearing pieces of the bread from the loaf and deftly making sandwiches.

"We'll have to store some food here," Uncle Mick said, looking around the cellar. "Some canned goods, at least. Some water."

The cellar now was crowded with boxes and some of the more fragile furniture from the house. We'd stored a good deal of our breakable objects here, but we hadn't made much provision for ourselves. Perhaps we hadn't really believed that the time would come when we needed to sleep here.

Nacy handed me a sandwich, but I didn't feel like eating. I took a few bites to appease her, and Uncle Mick did the same. The food felt like a lump in my stomach.

"At least we have a few blankets," Nacy said, pulling out a few of the warmer winter blankets we'd stored during the hot days of summer. She brought a blanket to me and wrapped it around my shoulders. Her hands lingered on my shoulders for a moment, giving them a reassuring squeeze, and I reached up to squeeze her hand in return.

Incredibly, I think I finally dozed off for a short while an hour or so before dawn. It was actually the noise dying away that woke me up, a variation in the nearly constant rumbling that alerted my senses that something had changed.

I sat up drowsily.

"I think they're leaving," Uncle Mick said.

We sat listening until there had been only quiet for some time.

At last, the all-clear signal sounded.

I looked over at Uncle Mick.

"Are they gone?" I asked at last. My voice sounded hoarse to my own ears, and I realized suddenly how dry my throat was.

"It seems so," Uncle Mick replied. He glanced at his watch. "It's nearly morning. I suppose they've flown back toward France."

"There's only one way to find out," Nacy said, rising. She turned toward the stairs.

I wondered if I should stop her, but I knew that we would have to come out of hiding eventually.

We followed her up the stairs. I was half-afraid that the house might be gone, though my rational mind knew I would have heard it if a bomb had hit directly above my head. Despite the way it had felt, the noise and vibration of the bombs reaching us here in the cellar, I didn't think any had hit particularly near us. I didn't think there had been any of them that were loud enough to have landed in Hendon.

Still, it was a relief to see that everything was as we had left it in the house. We had been spared.

I knew, however, that many people were not so lucky. How many Londoners had died in the past few hours? How many had lost homes, automobiles, their livelihoods?

The scope of the damage was hard to imagine, and I couldn't

seem to wrap my mind around what had happened. I had been steady enough while it was happening, but now that it was over, my hands had begun to shake and my legs felt like jelly.

Without speaking, we all moved through the house toward the door. Uncle Mick opened it, and we stepped outside. The sky was a strange color, the smoky orange of a city on fire. Like fire spewing from Mount Olympus in the wake of Zeus's wrath.

I looked toward the Thames and saw the billowing smoke rising up like a wall into the sky. It looked as if half the city might be ablaze. It felt as though we were going to be swallowed up by the great gray cloud.

How many people were dead? Were my friends all right? Felix, the major? I didn't want to think about what might have happened to people I cared about as bombs rained down on the city.

For a moment, I felt rooted to the spot.

Uncle Mick put an arm around me. "We'll weather this storm yet, Ellie girl."

I nodded.

The three of us stood there for a moment, looking at the billowing smoke and trying to comprehend what had happened, trying to determine what we needed to do next.

"Ellie!" a voice called suddenly. I looked up to see Felix hurrying in my direction.

"Felix!" I hurried off the porch and ran to him.

"Ellie. Thank God." Felix reached me and pulled me into his arms. "I was so worried about you."

"We're all right," I said, clinging to him, enjoying the secure feeling of his arms around me. For just a moment, I allowed my face to rest against his shoulder, tucked into his neck. I was so glad that he was all right.

"I came as soon as I thought it was safe, but it was hard getting through."

I nodded. "There must be a great deal of damage."

"Yes. A great deal. There are buildings down everywhere, glass and debris strewn in every direction. And the East End is on fire. I've never seen anything like it. The city is in shambles."

Though I had known it must be the case, the confirmation made me feel a bit sick.

I pulled back from him as Uncle Mick and Nacy approached, though he didn't drop his arm from around me.

Together, we looked toward the East End.

Even from here, we could tell the extent of the wreckage. There were fires still burning, black smoke floating up to the morning sky.

"How many people have died?" I asked, looking at the devastation that surrounded me.

"There hasn't been an accurate count yet, but the hospitals are overflowing, and I imagine it won't be long before the mortuaries are, too . . . I'm sorry, love. I shouldn't have said that."

"But it's true." I could only imagine how many bodies would be dug from the rubble of the city over the next hours and days.

What will we do now? That was the first question that crossed my mind.

"Well," Nacy said, breaking the silence, "we'd better get moving."

I looked at her.

"Aye," Uncle Mick agreed. "There are people who need help."

And suddenly, it seemed the fog had cleared and the world came back into clarity. There was no use standing around lamenting, especially when we could be useful. There were people who needed help, and we would get out and help them as quickly as we could.

"What needs to be done?" I asked.

"I'll gather some food and a thermos of tea," Nacy said. "Ellie, go and get the bandages and my jar of homemade ointment."

"Come with me, lad," Uncle Mick said to Felix. "We'll get shovels and picks. There'll be people to dig out."

Martialed into movement, we all began to move about with renewed purpose. There was work to be done, and we were ready to do it.

My British patriotism swelled along with the Irish temper in my blood. We might have been knocked down, but we weren't going to be beaten. If anything, we would fight harder than ever.

CHAPTER TWENTY-FOUR

We started on the outskirts of the most damaged area in the East End. The streets were littered with broken glass, rubble, and debris that made it difficult to walk. Some buildings had completely collapsed, but there were also solitary walls still standing, as though too stubborn to fall. The area looked like a battlefield. And then I realized that it was.

This was war and its aftermath.

The Germans had obviously been targeting the docks and factories in that area, and the fires were still burning too brightly for us to get anywhere near them. They hadn't needed the photos Myra Fields had taken to find their mark. Walls of flame were all that existed of what had once been huge warehouses, and the smoke was thick and choking.

We weren't able to get near the worst of it, but we stopped to help some of the people that lived in the outlying areas. There were many other people out surveying the damage, some looking dazed and shell-shocked. Others with the look of steely determination. I recognized both as emotions I had felt since last night.

There were children, too, some of them crying, some still and white-faced with shock, some playing quietly while their parents sifted through the wreckage looking for anything that could be salvaged.

A man smiled at us from the rubble of what I assumed was his home. "If the Jerrys think this'll beat us, they've a surprise in store."

Another man across the street added a more strongly worded sentiment along similar lines.

All along the street, people were going about their business, doing what needed to be done with quiet acceptance. There were drawn, white faces, but there were also expressions of resilience and unshakable resolve.

I felt a sense of pride in my country and its people. The war had reached us, but we weren't going to be broken so easily.

Nacy had brought along a first aid kit, and her skills gained raising three rowdy children came in handy as she bandaged wounds and applied her homemade salve to burns.

Uncle Mick and Felix helped with moving and digging in the rubble. I helped them and Nacy in turn and even stopped to play a few games with the children who I knew could use some cheering.

It was early afternoon by the time we returned to the house in search of food. We were all of us caked with dust and dirt and even blood.

We had done what we could to help. It hadn't made even a small dent in what was needed, but it was something.

"I'll put the kettle on," I said vaguely as we entered the house.

Uncle Mick ran a hand across his jaw. "Something a bit stronger for me, I think. Felix?"

Felix nodded. "I'll take a double."

He followed Uncle Mick into the sitting room, and I went to the kitchen. Nacy came after me.

"Are you all right, dear?" she asked.

I nodded as I put the kettle on the hob. "It doesn't seem real, somehow."

"And it's likely we haven't seen the last of it," she said. "But we'll get through it like we've gotten through everything else. We're survivors."

"You're a dear, Nacy," I said, giving her a hug. "And you're right. It would take a lot more than this to beat us."

Nacy bustled about after that, fixing us something to eat, while I poured the boiling water into the pot and brought it to the sitting room.

Uncle Mick and Felix both had glasses in their hands.

"Have a drink, Ellie?" Felix asked.

I shook my head. As much as I'd have liked to dull everything I was feeling, I half feared that if I took a drink now, I wouldn't stop until I'd had too much.

There was a rap on the door.

"I'll get it," Nacy said as she came in from the kitchen. She went to the front door.

A moment later, Major Ramsey appeared in the doorway.

Though concern about his safety had been in the back of my mind all day, I hadn't expected to see him. I certainly wouldn't have thought he would have appeared here so soon after what had happened.

Somehow, the entire plan we'd formulated yesterday had slipped my mind. It was something from another world.

He took one look at us, and a frown flickered across his face. "Are all of you all right?"

I nodded, realizing we all looked a sight. Our clothes were dirty, blackened by soot and grime, and we'd all gotten rips and tears in what we were wearing. "We went out to help," I said.

His uniform, usually spotless, was dirty, too. I wondered where he had been today and what he had seen. Probably worse than we had. I still shuddered to think of all the death the night had wrought.

"Did your house survive?" I asked.

"Yes."

"Would you care for a drink, Major?" Uncle Mick asked.

"Thank you, no."

I was touched that he had come to check on us. Surely he had more important matters to attend to today. Then again, if I knew the major, there was some other reason he had come here.

He looked around the room, his eyes lighting briefly on Felix before coming back to me.

"Miss McDonnell, might I have a word with you?" he asked. "Outside?"

I was surprised by the request, but I didn't show it. "Of course."

I could feel Felix glance at me, but I didn't meet his gaze.

The major and I excused ourselves from the house and went back outside. The air was still heavy with the scent of smoke, and I couldn't help looking back in the direction of the worst of the destruction.

"I suppose it was inevitable that they'd come," I said.

"I'm surprised it took them this long."

"It was awful," I said softly. "Sitting in that cellar, wondering if the next bomb would be the one that hit us."

"Are you sure you're all right?"

I looked at him, and his eyes met mine, searching. He rarely ever used that gentle tone with me, and my emotions swelled, tears threatening to well up.

I clenched my teeth to suppress them and nodded, managing a tight smile. "I'm fine. A lot more fortunate than many people this morning."

The major turned to look appraisingly at the house. "You'll need to make sure everything in your cellar is fortified. They'll be back."

I turned to him sharply, dread creeping into me at the calm certainty in his tone. I had known in the back of my mind that it was likely, of course, but hearing it from a military officer made it worse somehow. "Soon, do you suppose?"

"Probably tonight."

I felt a thrill of horror course through me. "Do you really think so?"

"It makes strategic sense. They'll pile destruction upon destruction. They're going to try to break us." His voice was grim, but there was steel beneath it, not resignation.

My innate stubbornness surged up to bolster my spirit. We'd made it through one night; we could make it through two. We'd make it through whatever the Germans had to offer and more.

"I asked you to step outside because we need to decide what to do about Lacey," he said. "Have you told him about our plans?"

For a split second, I didn't remember what he was talking about. It seemed impossible that there was anything else that was important when our city was in shambles. But the world had to go on, and if this awful night had proven anything, it was that we had to do everything we could to stop the Germans.

"No, I haven't told him anything. You . . . you think we should still go through with it."

"I don't think we have any choice."

I nodded slowly. He was right. We needed to get that film before it could fall into the hands of the Germans. We couldn't allow them this victory. Especially not now.

"Are you sure the bank is still standing?" I asked.

"Yes. Kimble was there this morning."

Another thought occurred to me, something I ought to have thought about long before now. "What about Colm?"

"I haven't heard anything about your cousin," he said. "As I told you, he was supposed to arrive this morning, but he may have returned to Torquay if he saw the planes coming up. Or he might have been stopped at the outskirts of the city when the bombing started."

He didn't say what we were both thinking: it was also possible Colm had been caught in the bombing. But it was no use borrowing trouble, as Uncle Mick was fond of saying. We would just wait and hope that he arrived soon.

"If he doesn't show up, what will we do about the alarm system?" I asked.

"I don't think it will be surprising if the bank alarm goes off when the bombs start falling."

He was so very calm in his assurance that there would be another raid tonight. I hoped with everything in me that he was wrong.

"Then we should bring Felix in," I said. "If Colm doesn't get here in time, he'll be another pair of eyes and ears."

"All right." I was surprised at his quick agreement, but perhaps desperate times called for desperate measures.

We went back into the house. Everyone looked up from their tea and sandwiches as we came into the room. The major said nothing, and I realized it was going to be up to me to catch everyone up.

I started with Uncle Mick. "We're going ahead with the plans tonight."

He nodded. He didn't look surprised. In fact, it seemed as though he had suspected as much.

I turned my gaze to Felix, who was watching me expectantly. "We're going to rob a bank tonight."

The smallest hint of a smile flickered across his mouth. "Is that all? I thought you might be going to do something exciting."

"Will you help us?"

Felix glanced at the major before looking back to me. "I've been cleared for duty, have I?"

"It's all happened rather suddenly," I said by way of excusing my secret keeping. It was true enough that things had all fallen into place rather suddenly. "There are certain items in a safe-deposit box that we must get out."

"Then tell me what I need to do."

I smiled at him, my heart filled with affection at his unquestioning willingness to help. He smiled back at me, and for a moment it felt as if it was just the two of us in the room.

"We'll get you caught up, Lacey," Major Ramsey said, bringing me back to the present.

"Colm has been delayed," I told Uncle Mick. If there was more to it than that, we'd deal with it later.

"Then what about the alarm?"

I hesitated. "The major thinks the Germans will be back tonight. The alarm is bound to go off anyway."

Uncle Mick and Felix didn't seem as shocked as I had been by this revelation. Perhaps it had occurred to them already.

"I need another cup of tea," I said suddenly. I was going to put as much sugar as I wanted into it. I was going to be risking my life tonight, and I didn't want to die wishing I'd had a strong, sweet cup of tea while finalizing the plans that had killed me.

I had just picked up the teapot when there was another tap on the door.

Nacy disappeared from the room, and a moment later we heard a loud voice crying, "Ah! My darling. It's good to see you. I've been pining for you."

"Stop that at once, Merriweather," Nacy replied. "You're being ridiculous."

"Come on, then. Give old Merry a kiss."

"Stop it, you old rascal!"

She came into the room, flushed, with Merriweather on her heels, grinning. His black-and-gray hair was flying in every direction, and there was brightness in his eyes. He looked as though he was positively thriving after the dreadful night of bombing.

"Good afternoon, all," he said. "Big night, wasn't it? I haven't seen that much action since the Somme. Sorry I'm a bit late, but there was a bit of debris in the road. Ah, Felix, lad! It's been an age."

"Hello, Merriweather."

"Now that we're all assembled," the major said, breaking up the cheerful reunion, "we can begin to finalize our plans."

"At least we won't have to worry about the noise from blowing the safe," Merriweather said with a smile. He was not at all daunted at the prospect of another air raid. The man was quite possibly insane. But, for this plan to work, we might all have to be.

"All right, here's what we've got," Uncle Mick said, spreading the paper out on the surface of the dining room table. "We've about three hours before nightfall and, if the major's right, the arrival of the Germans. We'll get everything prepared, then, if another raid does come, we'll start over there a few hours in. We aren't bound to draw much notice when the bombs are dropping."

I felt a tension in my stomach at the words. I couldn't believe we were doing this, but, apparently, we were.

We were going to rob a bank in the middle of an air raid.

CHAPTER TWENTY-FIVE

The Germans came again, just as the major had said they would.

The sound of the siren, keening like a banshee, raised the skin on the back of my neck, but even worse was the steadily growing droning of airplanes in the distance. Airplanes filled with bombs that were about to be dropped on our city.

This was something like what men on the battlefield must feel, I realized, the threat of death constantly hanging in the air. The sure knowledge of impending destruction, of not knowing when it might come. Even if we survived tonight, would we survive tomorrow night? Would the Germans be back again?

A day at a time, Ellie girl. That's what Uncle Mick would say. The matter at hand needed my attention. It doesn't do to be distracted when robbing a bank.

Luckily, I was good at pushing things to the back of my mind. It was a trait I'd mastered when working with Uncle Mick on jobs. Focus was important, the ability to sort through all the thoughts that shot through one's head and to choose the ones that were most important. The ones that were necessary.

I could do the same thing now. Even with the sirens screaming in the background. With the distant buzz of approaching aircraft.

Even with the knowledge that we were in for another night of fire and smoke and destruction.

I could focus because I had a task that had to be accomplished. And that was all there was to it. In the darkest of times, one did what one had to do.

And we had to do this.

So we waited in the cellar as the bombing started above us, all of us quiet and alert. Nacy, prepared this time, had brought down a pot of tea and one of coffee, and we fortified ourselves with the strong, hot beverages and the biscuits she pressed on us.

At last, the major glanced at his watch and nodded. "All right," he said. "Let's go."

We split up, according to our plans, and made our way toward the bank. The streets of London were an odd mixture of quiet and chaos. In between the bombs, it was sometimes almost silent as those in their shelters waited for the next barrage to come. In other areas, there were the shouts of voices as people moved about, trying to douse fires, save possessions, and pull people from the wreckage.

How had it been that we had once sat in quiet gardens drinking tea and discussing a war we thought would probably never touch us?

All those months we had spent waiting for a real war to start, thinking that Hitler would never make good on his threats. If we had only known. If we had only appreciated that fragile peace.

Felix and I traveled together and reached the bank in good time, taking our place in the doorway of Pietro's, the diner where the major and I had discussed Bill Mondale with the red-haired waitress. We had a clear line of sight to the door we'd decided upon as a means of entry.

I looked across at Merriweather, concealed in the shadowed entryway to a darkened theater across the street. I could just make out that he was clutching something—a small ball of some sort?—squeezing it, and passing it from hand to hand.

I wondered if the bombing was affecting him and he was using it as some sort of talisman. It was worth remembering that he was a veteran of the Great War. I'd known other men who had returned home without bodily injury but with emotions that would never heal.

He'd seemed fine in the cellar, even invigorated by the chaos above us, but perhaps that, in itself, was a sign that something wasn't quite right.

Hopefully he would be able to manage. He was handling the explosives, after all.

At last, I saw the major step out from the shadows and motion Uncle Mick forward.

I could barely make out the two of them in the darkness, Uncle Mick bent over the lock, the major facing outward to keep an eye on things. Though the locks were no doubt of good quality, Uncle Mick didn't have any trouble with them.

A few moments after he'd set to work, Uncle Mick pulled the door open, and the major motioned us forward. Felix and I hurried toward the bank and Merriweather followed at a slightly more leisurely pace.

"First step complete, Ellie girl," Uncle Mick said when I reached him.

As we'd expected, the alarm went off shortly after the door was pulled open. Almost immediately, however, there was an explosion in the distance that set the windows rattling. It couldn't have been timed more perfectly.

"That explosion will buy us some time," the major said, "but we need to hurry."

He then seemed to realize that Merriweather had not yet reached the door.

He waited for him, his posture stiff with impatience.

"I'm not sure if you realize that time is of the essence, Hastings," the major snapped as Merriweather reached us.

"If the nitroglycerin in my bag gets jarred, we won't ever have to worry about being late again," Merriweather said cheerfully.

He made a rather good point.

The major closed the bank door behind us. I glanced over my shoulder and saw a shadowy movement outside. Kimble or one of his ruffians keeping the perimeter secure while we were inside. I wondered if there had been a guard and, if so, what Kimble had decided to do with him. Now wasn't the time to be asking those questions, however.

"Lacey, stay here in the lobby. Alert us if Kimble gives the alarm," the major said.

"Right," Felix said. Whatever he felt about being left upstairs in the bank while we broke into the vault, he didn't argue.

His eyes caught mine, questioning without words. Was I ready for this? I gave him a nod and a faint smile before I followed the major, Uncle Mick, and Merriweather deeper into the bank.

We moved along the path we had marked on the blueprints of the building, taking the stairs instead of the lift into the dark confines of the sublevel. Major Ramsey switched on a torch, and we moved along the hallway until we found ourselves in front of the steel door that blocked the vault room. Uncle Mick, tools still in hand, set to work.

Above us, the drone of planes and the distant sound of explosions continued.

Focus, Ellie, I told myself.

"Here we are," Uncle Mick said suddenly as the lock gave way. He pulled the handle, and the steel door opened on oiled hinges. We were inside the vault room. So far, it had taken us less than ten minutes.

"That's your cue, Merriweather," Uncle Mick said with a grin.

"Ready, Hastings?" the major asked.

"Ready and willing, sir!" Merriweather answered happily.

"Do you want to wait here?" the major asked Uncle Mick and

me. We understood what he meant. If something happened with the nitroglycerin, we'd have a better chance behind the steel door.

"No," we both said at the same time. We were all in this together. Besides, we both wanted to see Merriweather Hastings in action.

We entered the small room where the major and I had stood only two days ago, talking with William Mondale. It felt different tonight, dark and cool, almost sepulchral.

I hoped that wasn't an omen of some sort.

It was quieter here, too, the sound of the bombings more distant.

Merriweather stopped in front of the vault door. He dropped the ball that was still in his hand, and it rolled a short distance before stopping. Then he carefully took off the canvas bag that was slung across his shoulder. Reaching inside, he removed two vials of liquid, a small tin that held blasting caps, a battery, and a strip of what looked to be cellophane.

I knew about the process of blowing open a safe, of course, but I'd never witnessed it. Uncle Mick had never met a safe he couldn't open, so we'd never had any need for explosives. Besides, we'd never been the type of criminals to call attention to ourselves. In and out without notice, that was our method.

But sometimes force was necessary, and Merriweather was a master of his craft.

We watched as he took the piece of cellophane, folding it lengthwise into a V to create a little trough. He inserted this into the slight space between the vault door and the frame.

Then he picked up the ball from off the floor, and I realized what it was: a piece of soap. He'd been kneading it to make it warm and malleable. The soap would hold the nitroglycerin and keep it from leaking out of the safe.

He fashioned the soap into a little funnel around the piece of cellophane and then, toward the top of the funnel, made a small cup. Taking a tweezer from his coat pocket, he reached into the funnel and pulled out the cellophane, which had created a channel for the nitroglycerin.

Merriweather moved with the grace of a dancer and the focus of a scientist at work in his lab. Every movement was confident but measured.

Next, he picked up a blasting cap and placed it carefully into the soap cup. Then he unrolled the wires until they passed through the frame of the steel door. He placed the battery beside him.

Then he went back into the vault room and picked up the vial of nitroglycerin.

"The real art," Merriweather said to us, as he took off the lid, "is knowing just the right amount of the stuff to pour in. Too little and it won't open the door. Too much and . . . well, you can guess."

With steady hands, he held the vial over the cup he had created from soap and carefully began to pour the oily liquid into it. He watched as it flowed from the cup and down the funnel. Finally, apparently satisfied that he'd poured in just the right amount, he closed the vial of nitroglycerin and set it aside.

"All right, lady and gents. Better stand back," he said.

Major Ramsey had already taken my elbow and started moving me back through the steel door. Uncle Mick was close behind. Merriweather joined us there, swung the steel door partway shut, and then jauntily picked up the wires and connected them to the battery.

There was a brilliant flash of light and a loud bang, and the air was suddenly smoky and thick with the scent of burnt caramel.

Merriweather hurried back inside the vault, and we were just behind him. As the smoke cleared, we could see that the vault door had been blasted away just right. It hung open on one side, allowing us to see in.

"Well done, Hastings," the major said, moving forward.

"A lot more drama your way than mine," Uncle Mick said, patting him on the shoulder. "I have to say I enjoyed the show."

"Glad to have been of service," Merriweather said with a grin.

Uncle Mick, the major, and I moved inside the vault while Merriweather, his work done, began to pack up his gear. The space was small enough without his taking up more of it.

The major shined his torch around the inside of the vault, the safe-deposit boxes all completely undamaged by the blast.

It crossed my mind that, under other circumstances, my uncle and I might have felt that we'd died and gone to Heaven. Here were all these boxes, the contents ripe for the taking.

What was in them? Money. Jewelry. Gold, perhaps. There were so many tempting possibilities.

I reminded myself that we needed to focus. There were twelve of the largest boxes at the bottom toward the floor. Since we didn't know which one William Mondale had used, we would just have to start opening them and hope we got lucky.

"You start on one end, and I'll start on the other," Uncle Mick said.

I nodded. Kneeling before the first box, I pulled my lockpicking kit from my pocket and set to work.

The locks were good quality, but they weren't hard to pick. It wasn't as though they required complicated combination work. A bit of pressure, a few twists and turns in the right direction, and they opened readily.

I encountered an empty box first. It had either not been claimed or its contents had been removed for just such an eventuality as the one we were currently experiencing: German planes trying to destroy the city.

"Nothing here but a stack of documents," Uncle Mick called.

That was a common theme in the large safe-deposit boxes, it seemed. The next several boxes, too, held large stacks of documents. The one I opened had deeds, wills, and what looked to be financial paperwork.

"This one's full of photo albums," Uncle Mick said. It might seem like a strange thing to tuck away in a vault, but I couldn't blame people for wanting to keep their most precious possessions safe.

I tried to close the boxes carefully as I went. No matter what our purpose, these items mattered a great deal to their owners. I didn't want anyone to lose their documents or photo albums just because we needed to find the film.

The third box I opened contained something more interesting than paperwork. There were several heavy items wrapped in tissue paper. Curious, I pushed the paper aside and saw animal carvings made of ivory, jade, and onyx. I put them back inside, wondering at their origin but having no time to ponder it.

I had never before had free rein of safe-deposit boxes, and now it made me curious as to what other types of items people might see fit to store in them.

The fourth box was filled with jewelry boxes. I picked the one off the top and opened it. It was a Regency-era gold necklace with a large ruby that glittered even in the dim light. I ran my finger over the stone.

"We're only here for the film," the major said behind me.

I made a face at him over my shoulder and put the jewelry box back in the safe-deposit box, closing it.

Uncle Mick was a bit faster than me, and I'd been sifting through the contents of my boxes a bit, so he'd done six boxes to my four. We started on the last two at roughly the same time. His gave first, and he pulled it open. We looked into it. There was an item wrapped in cloth.

Uncle Mick took it out and pulled aside the wrapping. It was a small Rembrandt painting. He rewrapped it and gently placed it back in the box.

Then mine was the only box left. I began to have an uncomfortable feeling. What were the odds that what we were looking for was in the final box?

But it had to be there, didn't it?

"I've almost got it," I said. Even as I spoke the words, I felt the lock give.

I looked up at the major. For some reason, I didn't want to be the one to do it. Moving aside, I let him have access to the box. Reaching down, he pulled the box open.

We all looked inside.

There was no film, only a crumpled slip of paper at the bottom. The major picked it up and opened it. I leaned close to him to read it:

Location compromised. Package removed to Paddington. Be there at dawn.

CHAPTER TWENTY-SIX

The major swore savagely, slamming the box shut with a bang, his temper flashing out in a hot burst before he pulled himself back under control into something closer to a simmering rage.

I didn't blame him in the least for being angry. We'd robbed a bank for nothing.

"How did they know the box was compromised?" I asked.

"Perhaps we called too much attention to ourselves," the major said. "William Mondale must have realized what we were after and removed the film. Carried it right past Kimble's man."

"But who was the note meant for?"

"The German operative must also have a key to the safe-deposit box. No doubt the plan was for Mondale to put the film there and the operative to pick it up, posing as a bank customer. That way they'd never have to be seen together."

"But surely we can go to Paddington and look for the film?" I asked. "It's probably in the baggage storage, like the others were at Waterloo."

The major was pacing the small area of the vault. I could feel the fury radiating off him. Most of the time he kept a tight hold on that temper of his, but I knew it was there. I recognized it because I had a temper of my own that I was always trying to manage.

"The note was still here," I said. "That means the German operative hasn't been here, doesn't it? We have time to recover them before someone arrives to pick them up."

"No. The note was clearly crumpled and thrown back into the box after being read. The agent was already here and will follow instructions. We have until dawn to catch up with him." His expression darkened. "If that note didn't refer to dawn yesterday."

He turned and stalked out of the vault. Uncle Mick and I exchanged a look, then followed behind him.

"We're finished, then?" Merriweather asked as we exited the vault. He looked as chipper as a lark. I supposed it had been awhile since he'd been called upon to blow anything up.

"Not exactly finished, but done here," I said.

"Then I'd best take the rest of my nitroglycerin home."

"That would probably be best."

We turned to leave the vault room, and I cast one last look over my shoulder inside the vault. All those valuables left untouched. The Ellie of a few months ago wouldn't have dreamed of walking away from them.

But, somehow, I liked the Ellie of today a bit more.

We went back through the steel door, and Uncle Mick closed it behind us. It was force of habit for him, leaving things the way he had found them. Of course, when the bank employees saw the vault door had been blown off its hinges, it would be a bit of a giveaway that something was amiss.

We went back up the stairs and into the echoing foyer of the bank. The sound of bombing was louder now that we were aboveground, and the cavernous space seemed to magnify it. I almost wished we were back in the secure confines of the vault, but I knew we still needed to get out of the bank as soon as possible.

Felix approached me from the shadows, darting his eyes at the major and raising his brows in question. He'd clearly noticed the major was in a rage.

"The film is gone," I said in a low voice. "He's in rather a state about it."

I glanced at the major then and saw he was standing by the door talking to someone, a figure too large to be Kimble. I thought at first it was one of those hulking brutes they kept on staff, but then I recognized him. It was Colm.

I hurried to him, and he wrapped me in a tight hug. "I'm so glad you're all right."

"Had a devil of a time getting here. Missed all the fun, did I, Ellie?"

"Colm, lad. I'm glad to see you," Uncle Mick said, patting him heartily on the shoulder.

"Hello, Dad. Felix," he said, grasping Felix's outstretched hand. "Ellie's pulled you into things once again, has she?"

"I wouldn't have it any other way."

"Ah, and Merriweather's here, too," Colm said. "A right party, then."

"Hello, Colm," Merriweather said. "I'm glad to see you, though you missed the explosion."

My cousin made a wry face. "I very nearly caught a few of them on the way here. I'd just made it safely to the house and Nacy sent me back across town."

"We'll have to save the reunion for later," the major said. "We need to get out of here."

He was right. The alarm might not draw any attention. Then again, someone might feel the need to come and investigate.

We all slipped out of the bank and into the night. We'd arranged ahead of time that we would take different routes leaving and all meet back up at a square about half a mile away.

Felix came with me, and we walked quickly along deserted streets. The German planes were still buzzing, not too distant, and each thundering explosion made me flinch. An RAF fighter roared past overhead, and I said a prayer for the pilot.

At last we reached the square where we'd agreed to meet up. It wasn't the safest place in the middle of an air raid, but we wouldn't be here long. Just long enough for the major to tell us what to do next.

He'd had a bit of time to do his thinking on the way there, it seemed, because he was ready with a plan and began barking out orders as soon as we were all assembled.

"They've removed the film to Paddington Station to be picked up there," the major said.

"Risky, wasn't it?" Colm asked. "It would've been much safer in a vault than stashed in the station where a bomb's likely to hit."

"Whoever removed the film clearly wasn't in a position to know the Germans would be back tonight," the major said. "The pickup is scheduled for dawn."

"It's not far from dawn now," Uncle Mick said.

I realized suddenly that he was right. The darkness was beginning to fade ever so slightly.

It also occurred to me that the sound of the bombs had stopped and the noise of the planes was growing blessedly more distant. The Luftwaffe pilots were headed back toward their airfields in France.

"We don't have much time," the major said. "And it's likely we'll have to take the film by force from the German operative picking it up. McDonnells, Kimble, you'll come with me."

I knew my burly cousin and the vaguely sinister Kimble were better suited to this sort of work than I was. All the same, I was sure there was something I could do. At the very least, I could act as a lookout.

"What can I do?" I asked.

"Nothing," the major said brusquely. "Go home, Miss McDonnell. It's not going to be safe."

"None of this has been safe," I protested.

"He's right, Ellie," Colm said. "We all want to protect you. It's best that you stay out of the way. You'll only be a distraction."

I couldn't believe my ears. "Colm, don't you dare . . ."

"We don't have time to argue," the major interrupted, moving past me. "Go home."

"Major . . ."

"Lacey, take her home," he said to Felix as he prepared to walk away.

"Neither you nor Felix are in charge of me," I said hotly.

Major Ramsey turned to face me fully, his voice calm and cold. "If you do not do as I say, I will have you removed bodily and put under house arrest until we return. Do I make myself clear?"

I stared at him, openmouthed. Of all the audacity . . .

"You can't . . ."

"I can, and I will." His eyes glinted the color of steel to match his tone. Infuriating.

I turned to look at my uncle.

"It's for the best, love," he said.

"We'll all feel better knowing you're safe, Ellie," Felix said, though he didn't look exactly pleased that he'd been relegated to the role of nursemaid.

I realized what they were doing. All the big, strong men were protecting the helpless lady. Well, I wasn't helpless. I'd wrestled a murderous spy on the beach not three weeks ago, and now they wanted to act as though I was some fair maiden who needed to be locked in a tower. It was maddening.

I could see, however, that this was a fight I wasn't going to win. I could try to tag along, but I had not the slightest doubt that the major would follow through on his threat. He would have Kimble or one of his strong-arm men throw me over their shoulder and lock me up somewhere.

"Fine," I said between gritted teeth.

Major Ramsey gave me a curt nod and turned and stalked away.

"He means well," Uncle Mick said.

"Don't take it too hard, El," Colm chimed in before following the major.

I wanted to be angry with all of them, but I couldn't be, not when they were going into a dangerous situation. I grasped Uncle Mick's hand. "Promise me you'll be careful."

He squeezed my hand. "I always am, love."

That was a lie, but we both pretended it wasn't.

He brushed a kiss across my cheek, and then he, too, hurried after the major. Felix and I were left standing in the shadows.

Stupidly, I felt close to tears. I had worked so hard to be a part of this and now I was being sent away. It wasn't fair.

"Let's go, Ellie," Felix said gently.

I nodded. "All right."

We turned and started toward home. The pale glimmer of sunrise was just beginning to touch the edge of the horizon, the rose-colored light of dawn suffusing the smoke that hung over the city, giving everything a pink glow that was both beautiful and horrifying.

How many more lay dead after another night of bombing? How many would be dead before it was all over?

We made our way through streets littered with rubble and the scattered remnants of people's lives. We even passed a car that had crumpled completely in on itself. The scope of the damage was unimaginable.

I took Felix's arm, as much for him as for me. I knew the rubble must make things difficult with his prosthetic leg. I also knew that he would never complain or ask for help.

We didn't talk much. We were both lost in thought.

I couldn't believe how close we had come, only to be foiled again. We'd actually broken into a bank vault when the film had been stored in places as simple as a train station baggage storage and an empty clock on a mantel. Places so easy to access, surrounded by people not knowing how close they were to something so important.

Suddenly, a memory struck me nearly as forcibly as a blow. *It's rather a busy place. Myra always called it Paddington Station.* It couldn't be? Could it?

But I was convinced that it was. The note didn't mean the train station. They were talking about Mrs. Paine's boardinghouse.

CHAPTER TWENTY-SEVEN

"Felix," I said, stopping in my tracks. "I know where the film is. And it's not at Paddington Station."

He turned to look at me. "What do you mean?"

"Mrs. Paine, Myra Fields's landlady, told me that Myra always referred to the parlor as Paddington Station, as there were so many people going in and out. I think that was its code name."

"Ellie . . ."

"No, Felix, listen. They used the clock as a drop point for film until there was enough of it to collect and deliver to William Mondale. Then he put it in the safe-deposit box where the German operative was to pick it up. But, somehow, William Mondale realized he had been found out, so he moved the film. To 'Paddington Station.' It's at the boardinghouse, Felix."

He looked at me, his quick mind making all the connections as I had laid them out before him and weighing whether or not he should believe this outlandish theory. I watched him, willing him to take this seriously.

It seemed like forever before he nodded. "All right. So what do we do? Go to the station and alert Ramsey?"

I looked up at the sky. The pink-tinged gray had faded into a blue so pale it was almost white. The first hint of daylight.

"No. We don't have time. We'll have to go ourselves."

"Wait a minute, Ellie," he said. "We can't go running headlong into an encounter with a German operative. You remember what happened the last time."

I remembered very well. I'd very nearly had my throat slit. I'd risked my life once for this country, and I was prepared to do it again.

"It has to be done," I said. "And we're the only ones who can do it."

"We don't have weapons," Felix said. "We don't even know how many of them there will be."

"We can't let the Germans have that film, Felix," I said.

He looked at me for a long moment. Then he swore under his breath. "All right. Let's go. We'll figure out something on the way."

We made our way quickly in the direction of Clapham.

People were beginning to come out of their houses to survey the wreckage. Another day of cleaning up the rubble. Another day of wondering what the night would hold.

We drew little notice as we moved through the streets.

The sky was slowly brightening. I hoped that we'd get there on time. With any luck, the bombing would have slowed the operative down, too. I wondered briefly how the operative felt having been left to spy in Britain while it was being bombed. Not a very nice assignment for a German spy, to be sent to England only to be subjected to Luftwaffe bombs.

"So what's the plan, exactly?" Felix asked as we hurried along. He was limping ever so slightly but keeping pace. The one time I tried to slow down for him, he told me to go faster.

I considered. "I've been there before, as Myra's cousin," I said. "I'll go in under some pretext and you wait outside."

"No."

Just like the major, he dismissed the idea of me going in alone out of hand. But unlike the major, I knew Felix could be reasoned with.

"Felix, listen. It's the only way it's going to work. I can't show up there with a different man. They'll get suspicious."

"Absolutely not. Say I'm another cousin you've dredged up."

"No. You've got to wait outside for the operative to come. Perhaps there's some way you can distract him. Ask him for help with something."

"But what's the end goal, Ellie? You're going to snatch the suitcase and run?"

That did give me pause. What was I going to do once I was in a room with a pair of spies? It wasn't as though I could overpower both William Mondale and the German operative. And, though I hated to remind myself of it, they had proven themselves more than willing to kill to get the job done.

I slowed my pace ever so slightly and tried to work out a plan. "All right," I said. "We won't go in. We'll just watch from outside and wait for the operative to arrive. Then we'll follow him."

He glanced at me skeptically but didn't argue. We were winging it, and Felix was following gamely along. I loved him for it.

"Once we see where the operative is headed, one of us will continue to follow him and the other will go and notify the major," I said.

"You'll go and notify the major," Felix said.

"I'm not a helpless child like all you men seem to think I am."

"No, darling. You're not. But you can't blame us for wanting to look out for what we care about, can you?"

I looked at him and was caught by the sincerity of his expression.

I reached out and touched his face. "You're a dear, Felix."

He caught my hand and turned to kiss my wrist. "You can tell me all about how dear I am once we've made it through this alive."

I nodded. "Deal. Do you remember the little birdcalls we used to practice when we were younger?"

Felix did a charming and startlingly accurate warbler whistle.

"Yes, that's it. Do that if you spot him. I'll do the same. Then we'll join up and follow the operative."

He let out a disapproving groan and shook his head. "This is a horrible idea, but I can't seem to think of a better one."

It was nearly dawn as I moved behind a rosebush near Mrs. Tully's house, across from Mrs. Paine's boardinghouse. I'd let Felix take the back door since he'd seemed to think it more likely that the operative would come that way. I didn't have any more time to argue with him about the extent to which men should protect the women they cared for.

We could have that discussion another time.

I was prepared for a long wait, but it seemed that the operative had not abandoned his German efficiency, even in the time of bombing. I hadn't been there fifteen minutes before I heard the clear sound of Felix's whistle.

I moved along the closest street parallel to the house before cutting across two back gardens to reach the boardinghouse. Lambeth had not escaped the bombing unscathed. There were houses in rubble down the street, people moving to and fro, working to help their neighbors, but Mrs. Paine's boardinghouse and those around it still stood.

I skirted a bush and stopped a short distance from the house, looking for Felix.

I was just about to whistle for him when movement caught my attention. Across the garden, someone was moving toward the house. No, two people.

They came into my line of vision and I went cold as I realized what was happening. A man was leading Felix into the house at gunpoint.

CHAPTER TWENTY-EIGHT

"No, no, no, no," I whispered to myself. This was bad. This was very, very bad.

I felt myself go numb with fear, and then I forced it back. Now was not the time to succumb to fear. I would have to take action.

But what to do?

"Think, Ellie. Think."

I closed my eyes and drew in a deep breath. I'd been in sticky situations before. I was calm under pressure. But this was not like slipping into a house in the dead of night and emptying out a safe. This was Felix's life at stake.

Weigh your options. That's what Uncle Mick would say. Review the options, make a choice, and get to work.

What were my options? There weren't very many of them. I could, of course, run and try to find the major and Colm. But, deep down, I knew that in the time it took to do this, Felix would likely be dead.

I could not let him die because of me. I would not.

That left the other option: I was going to have to go into the house.

Getting up from my place behind the bush, I retraced my steps to the street and around to the front of the house. If I knocked on the door and pretended to be Elizabeth Donaldson returning, they'd have to behave themselves at least momentarily.

They couldn't shoot him with me in the house.

They could, of course, shoot us both and just have done with it, but that was not something I really wanted to contemplate at the moment.

Taking another deep breath, and brushing back a few errant curls, I went up to the front door and knocked.

It was opened by a girl I didn't recognize, her hair wild, her eyes red. She'd obviously had a bad night of it with the bombs. She certainly didn't look anything like a cold-blooded spy.

"Hello," I said, not knowing exactly what to say next.

But the girl didn't even ask who I was. She just opened the door and allowed me to enter. I saw another girl sitting on the stairs chewing on her fingernails, her face pale.

They were all suffering the effects of the bombing, it seemed.

But where was Felix? Had they pulled him into the house without anyone knowing? Who here could be trusted and who could not?

There were, of course, no answers to these questions, so I simply had to charge ahead.

I went into the parlor and found Cindy Prince sitting there with a cup of tea, knitting. "Oh!" she said, looking up. "Oh, it's you, Miss Donaldson. What are you doing here, and so early?"

Cindy was most likely in on all of this. She had been in that close-knit group of friends with Myra Fields and Jane Kelley. It was probable that they'd been involved in the spy ring together. Did she know that Felix was in the house? Did she suspect that was why I had arrived unannounced on the doorstep?

All of this passed through my head in the space of a moment, and I think I was able to keep it off my face. I hadn't been schooled at poker by my cousins for nothing.

She was surprised to see me, but she hadn't grown suspicious yet. Or perhaps she, too, was good at poker. I would just have to press forward and find out.

"I . . . I'm still staying in London. After the bombing last night, I thought I might come and see if I could retrieve a keepsake from among Myra's things before I go back to Kent."

It was an improbable lie, especially at this hour of the morning. No one made social calls at dawn after a night of bombing.

"Of course," Cindy said, setting her teacup down. "I'm sure Mrs. P won't mind if you go in there. John hasn't been yet, but . . ."

"Cindy, if you don't mind, I'd like to talk to Miss Donaldson alone."

I turned at the sound of the voice coming from the doorway. I'd been careful to keep my back close to a wall, but I still hadn't heard the approach of the landlady.

"Perhaps you can send Sally and Mae out of the house for some fresh air," she said, talking about, I assumed, the two young women I'd seen in the entryway.

"Oh, sure, Mrs. P," Cindy said, rising. She gave me a vague smile and walked from the room.

I stared at Mrs. Paine, realizing only in that moment what I should have realized before I burst into her house: she was the spymaster.

She smiled. "You're clever, Elizabeth. Is Elizabeth your name?"

"Ellie," I said. I didn't see why I should go on lying to the woman when today was going to end with either her arrest or my death.

"Let's have a seat, Ellie, shall we?" she asked, motioning toward the sofa.

I didn't see a weapon in her hands. I thought about making a run for the door, but that would mean leaving Felix to die, and I would not do that.

I moved to the sofa and took a seat. She took one in the chair opposite. There was a wooden box on the table beside her chair, and she took two cigarettes out of it.

"Smoke?" she asked.

I was on the point of refusing, but every man facing a firing squad likes his final smoke. I might as well. "Thank you."

She lit my cigarette with a lighter from her pocket and then lit her own, sitting back in her chair.

"Now," she said. "How much do you know?"

"How much do I know about what?" I asked.

"Let's not be coy with each other. You're an intelligent woman. I knew that from the moment I met you. Intelligent women recognize it in others. Much more quickly than men do, don't you think?"

She was right. I knew how many times I had been dismissed because of my gender. There was a bit of a shift in things now, with the war on, because there was no choice. Women had to do men's jobs or they wouldn't get done. But that didn't mean that women weren't still easily overlooked.

All the same, I hadn't recognized it in her. Even though I was so good with people, I had dismissed her because she was a woman of older years with hair gone gray at the roots. It had been a costly mistake. Perhaps even a fatal one.

I took a deep drag on the cigarette before blowing out a stream of smoke.

"I know you've been running a network of spies," I said. "You're working with the Germans, who are paying you in gemstones rather than currency. You send girls out to their workplaces with cameras and store up the film until you have enough for an operative to pick it up. It was in a bank vault until sometime yesterday when William Mondale realized he had been compromised and thought it would be better to bring it here."

"You are clever," she said with a smile.

"What I'm not sure of is why you killed Myra to begin with. Was she going to cross you?"

"She was getting careless, for one thing. She was told to take pictures while she was at work, not flounce around the docks in a fur coat that was going to get her noticed immediately. For another thing, that boyfriend of hers was starting to ask a lot of questions. It would only have been a matter of time before she revealed something."

"So you asked her to meet you on the docks," I said. "Or did you have someone else kill her? William Mondale, perhaps?"

Mrs. Paine shook her head. "If you want something done right, do it yourself. I told her to meet me. She was smarter than I took her for, however. She realized what I was going to do just before I did it. She tried to run."

I remembered the ladders in the knees of her stockings. "But she fell."

Mrs. Paine nodded. "Yes. She tripped and I caught up with her. A quick injection and it was all over."

"And Jane Kelley?" I thought of the sharp, assertive young woman I'd met in this very room only days ago and how she'd met the same grim fate as Myra Fields.

"Jane was getting above herself. A mite too ambitious. When I saw the way she came barging in here, challenging you and that major, I knew that she was going to be a liability. I had her deliver the message to Bill Mondale in the garden, and then she was no longer useful to me."

"Where did you get the poison?"

"Kindly supplied to me by the Germans," she said.

"The same German operative who just arrived this morning to pick up the film," I said. "I saw him come in the back door with my friend."

"Oh, is that lovely man your friend, too? You do know a good many good-looking men, Ellie."

"Where is Felix?" I asked.

"My friend, the operative, is asking him a few questions in the cellar."

The words made me cold. I knew how Germans went about asking questions.

"Bring him up here," I said.

"Not just yet." She knocked the ashes off of her cigarette in the glass ashtray on the table beside her. "If the young man currently in my cellar is your friend, what is your connection with that handsome major you came here with?"

"He's my fiancé," I said. There was no sense in grassing on the major just because my life was in danger.

"I doubt that," she said. "You didn't touch each other like people in love. If he was my fiancé, I would be touching him a great deal. No, I think it's more likely that he works in intelligence and acts as your handler. Isn't that so? He uses you when he has need of you."

It wasn't exactly a fair assessment, but for some reason it felt uncomfortably close to the truth.

"I know how it is, Ellie," she said. "I've been used by men my whole life."

"Aren't you being used by men now?" I asked.

Her gaze grew slightly harder. "I am doing this for my own benefit. I have worked hard all my life, and where has it gotten me? A cheap boardinghouse, surrounded by silly girls and their parade of boyfriends?" She let out a laugh. "I was approached by the Germans because I did a bit of similar work in the first war, easy stuff for good money. When they asked me to do it again, I thought, why not?"

There were a lot of reasons, but I suspected she wasn't really interested in a list.

"I could use a woman like you," she went on. "The girls I get here barely have a brain between them. No sense at all. But you, you're different."

I wasn't quite sure I was hearing her right.

"You're offering me a job?"

"Are you interested in one?"

"No," I said at once.

She smiled as one does at a child. "You're loyal to your country, of course. We've been brought up to be. But what has this country ever done for you?"

I considered this for a moment.

"You could be rich, Ellie," she went on. "You could have all the things you've always wanted and never been able to afford." Her voice had taken on a faintly soothing tone, as though she was trying to hypnotize me.

Even when I'd been a thief, the idea of riches wouldn't have swayed me. Not on this point. Because there was one factor I couldn't overlook, the one strong loyalty that I would never betray. My family. Anything that helped the German cause was putting my family's lives at risk. And that was something I would never do.

"What about Felix?" I asked.

She considered. "Can he be relied upon to keep his mouth shut?"

I nodded. Felix would do whatever I asked of him. I was fairly sure of that. Besides, I would tell this woman anything if it meant we could escape this place without harm.

She took another long drag on her cigarette. "I don't think, all things considered, that I'm going to be able to let him leave here."

"But . . ."

"I know it's a difficult thing to hear, but we must all make sacrifices in wartime. Isn't that what they've been telling us again and again?"

My heart had picked up the pace. She'd as good as admitted that Felix wouldn't be leaving this place alive. That meant that I was going to have to do something drastic if either one of us was to survive.

"I can see by your face that you aren't willing to sacrifice him."

"Of course, I'm not," I said coldly. "Unlike you, human lives mean something to me. Felix won't tell anyone anything."

"I can't risk it. But there's still a chance for you to save your-self."

"I'm afraid the answer is no," I said.

She gave me a small smile. "I was afraid you'd say that. You know, of course, that I can't let you leave here." She said this ca-sually, as though we were sitting in a powder room at a nightclub rather than facing off on a matter of national importance.

I eyed the door. I could probably make a run for it, but where would that leave Felix?

Cindy appeared in the doorway. "Sorry to interrupt, Mrs. P, but the . . . uh . . . plumber would like a word with you in the cellar."

"No need for that, Cindy," Mrs. Paine said. "Ellie here knows all about our little operation."

"Oh," Cindy said, her eyes darting to me before moving back to the landlady. "Well, in that case, he wants to know what he should do with that fellow he found in the back garden."

"We'll deal with that momentarily, Cindy. If you would step in here, please."

Cindy came into the room.

"Did you send Sally and Mae away?"

Cindy nodded. "I told them to go for a walk."

"Very good. Now I'll need you to keep Ellie from moving, Cindy." As she said this, she reached back into the cigarette box. It wasn't a cigarette that she took out of it, however.

I realized with a sick feeling in the pit of my stomach that there was a syringe in her hand.

CHAPTER TWENTY-NINE

Cindy moved obediently into the room. I stood up quickly, but she was faster than I expected, and she caught me, pinning my arms behind my back. She was much stronger than she looked.

I considered whether I would be able to overpower her. I had taken down men bigger than me before; my cousins had taught me how. But that included the element of surprise. And Cindy had a very tight grip on me.

What was more, we were adding a needle to the mix. One good prick and it was good night forever.

Mrs. Paine stepped forward, syringe in hand.

"Wait," I said. I was surprised at how steady my voice sounded considering the woman was about to stick me in the neck with a deadly toxin.

"Before you let her kill me, Cindy, you'd better think about what she did to Myra and Jane."

"What do you mean?" Cindy asked.

"She killed them when they became liabilities. Don't you think the same thing is likely to happen to you?"

"What's she talking about, Mrs. P?" Cindy asked. "You said . . ."

"Hush, Cindy," Mrs. Paine snapped. She turned back to me,

her eyes very cold. "I'm afraid we don't have time for any more questions." She stepped toward me, the syringe in her hand.

If there was one thing Ellie McDonnell was not going to do, it was die without a fight.

Luckily, Mrs. Paine and Cindy had both neglected to notice that I was still holding my lit cigarette. As Mrs. Paine approached, I pressed the butt of it hard into Cindy's arm.

She let out a scream and released me. I threw my head back and landed a hard blow to her face. There was a crunch as my skull made contact with her nose, and this sent her toppling to the ground. Then I dove at Mrs. Paine.

I was younger than she was and more fit, but she was taller and heavier. I aimed for low on the legs like I did when playing rugby with the neighborhood boys. It was a beautiful tackle, if I say it myself. Colm and Toby would've been proud.

Mrs. Paine landed hard on her back and the syringe fell from her hand, rattling across the floor.

"Get the syringe," Mrs. Paine screamed at Cindy, who was, I saw at a quick glance, still sitting on the floor where I'd left her, clutching her head in her hands. I'd probably broken her nose, because blood was gushing out between her fingers. She didn't appear in a hurry to move.

I'd looked away just long enough for Mrs. Paine to land me a vicious blow to the side of the face. Her fist grazed my eye, setting it watering and throwing me off-balance just enough that she was able to shove me aside and roll for the syringe.

The woman had determination. I'd give her that.

She swung at me with the syringe, but I grabbed her arm, doing my best to keep the needle from coming into contact with me.

Mrs. Paine let out an inarticulate scream of rage as she tried to turn the tip of the needle toward my neck.

From the cellar, a gunshot sounded.

Felix.

Fear and rage coursed through me like a dam had burst. If they'd killed him, I'd burn this house to the ground.

My fury gave me an added burst of strength, and I grabbed Mrs. Paine's arm, slamming it hard against the floor. She nearly dropped the syringe, but instead she rolled, bringing it with her to try to gain the upper hand.

But then I lunged at her again, and she gave out a sudden cry and fell back on the ground, no longer struggling. Then I realized why. The syringe was protruding from her stomach. She'd fallen on it.

With a gasp, she looked up at me, her face contorted, and then she gave one last, shuddering breath and fell still.

For just a moment I sat still, breathing raggedly. Then I remembered that I wasn't safe yet.

I staggered to my feet and stared down at her.

Behind me, Cindy started sobbing loudly.

There was the sound of footsteps approaching in the hallway, and I looked around for a weapon. If nothing else, I'd hit the operative with the mantel clock. It would be a nice way to bring things full circle.

But then Felix appeared in the doorway. His face was bloody, and bruises were beginning to form all across his jaw and cheekbone. He had a gun in one hand and the Gladstone bag in the other.

"Felix!" I cried. I hurried to him and flung myself into his arms.

He embraced me as best as he could with his hands occupied. "Ellie, are you all right?"

"Yes. Are you?" I reached up to gently touch his face.

"I'm fine, love. We need to leave, though. There may be more of them . . ." He let me go and moved toward Cindy, who still sat on the floor trying to quench the flow of blood from her nose. I'd walloped her a good one, and I felt almost sorry for her. Almost.

"How many more of you are there?" Felix asked her. "How many of you worked for Mrs. Paine?"

She made a blubbering sound and buried her face in her hands. Felix handed me the Gladstone bag.

"Get up," he said to Cindy, reaching down to take her by the arm and haul her to her feet.

"I . . . I didn't know she was going to kill anyone," Cindy sobbed. "I swear I didn't know."

She took to wailing again, and Felix, his expression exasperated, dug in his pocket for a handkerchief to hand to her.

"How many of you are there in this house?"

"F . . . fi . . . five," she gasped. "Well . . . three now that . . . now that Myra and Jane are . . . gone."

"Where are the other two girls?"

The words came through a steady stream of hiccupping whimpers. "They've gone out . . . out to take . . . photos."

"Sally and Mae?" I asked.

She nodded.

Mrs. Paine had sent them away to take photographs—and probably to keep them from being witnesses to my murder—assuming she and Cindy could subdue me without their help. She'd underestimated me.

"And who else?" Felix pressed.

"I don't know. There are other groups, but I don't know who. I swear I don't know."

She began sobbing hysterically into his handkerchief and sank back down onto the ground, and it seemed clear to me that we weren't going to get anything more out of her for the time being.

I opened the bag. It was full of film this time. More than 100 rolls. It would have been a lot of information to pass off to a German spy.

That reminded me.

"Felix, where's the operative?"

"He's in the cellar. I heard a scream, and I fought him for the gun."

"Did you tie him up? We should . . ."

"No," he interrupted, his eyes meeting mine. "I didn't tie him up."

I remembered the gunshot then and understood.

I didn't have time to reply to this because just then the front door burst open, and I heard footsteps in the foyer.

"Miss McDonnell!" the voice called.

It was Major Ramsey.

"In here," I called. I ought to have gone to meet him, but suddenly my legs felt rooted to the spot.

A moment later, he stood in the doorway. His gaze took in the scene: Felix and I, bruised and battered; Cindy, a bloody and tearful puddle on the floor; Mrs. Paine lying dead, a syringe protruding from her midsection.

Then his gaze came back to me, his expression dark, but a surprising softness in his eyes. "Are you all right?"

I nodded, my throat catching suddenly as the weight of all that had just happened came crashing down on me.

"I remembered her words about this room being Paddington Station," he said.

"So did I," I said. "I didn't know if I had time to come and find you, so Felix and I thought that we'd better try to stop them."

He shook his head. "Why the devil didn't you . . ." Then he let out a sigh. "Because you're the most stubborn woman in all of London, of course."

He rounded on Felix. "Of all the irresponsible things you might have done, Lacey . . ."

"Major, don't," I said, going to him and taking his arm. "Felix saved the day."

"Ellie . . ." Felix began.

I ignored him. "He retrieved the film. He . . . also killed the German operative. He's in the cellar. Besides, if he hadn't come with me, I'd have come alone."

There was very little the major could say to argue with this.

He turned. "Kimble, go with Lacey to the cellar. See if there's any information to be found on the body."

"Mondale's down there, too," Felix said. "Dead."

I gasped. It hadn't occurred to me until now to wonder what had become of the man. He must have delivered the film to Mrs. Paine. But then she had deemed him a liability, too.

I ought to have been shocked that she had killed again, but I found that I wasn't. Mrs. Paine, it seemed, had been capable of any number of cruelties.

"Two bodies are as easy to deal with as one," Kimble observed.

"Take care of it," the major told him.

Kimble nodded, and Felix, with a glance between the major and me, turned and led Kimble from the room.

"Where are Uncle Mick and Colm?" I asked.

"A bit behind us, I think. We'd already split up when I realized what had happened. I sent a man to alert them and came directly."

"Figured I'd need rescuing, did you?" I asked.

"I ought to have learned by now that you're rather keen on saving the day single-handedly."

"No such thing," I said. "It was a team effort through and through."

He stepped closer and took my chin in his hand, gently tilting my face up. "You're going to have a black eye."

I smiled, even though it hurt. "It won't be my first."

He smiled back. "That doesn't surprise me in the least, Miss McDonnell."

And so it had all come together. A dead girl in the Thames, a pouch of jewels hidden in a fur coat, a clock that didn't work, and a bank vault had combined to make the most absurd trail of clues, which we'd followed until the moment we'd once again been able to thwart a Nazi scheme.

The major seemed confident that, with Mrs. Paine and her German contact dead, the spy ring would collapse. He and his men stayed at the boardinghouse to search for documents, clean up the details, and get information from the still-whimpering Cindy, as well as Sally and Mae, who had been easily apprehended.

Uncle Mick, Colm, Felix, and I went back to the house. I was exhausted after our long night, but far too exhilarated to even think of resting.

It felt wonderful to have once again used my skills to defend my country. Already I felt a stirring in my blood, a desire to do it again. It was like an addiction, the need to chase the attainment of that feeling as soon as it had passed.

I realized it wasn't completely noble and patriotic. It was the adventure, the sense that the odds were against us. One couldn't be a successful thief without enjoying the element of danger that accompanied it. And it was the same with this spy business. Somewhat selfishly, I hoped this wouldn't be the last chance I had to foil the Germans' plans, though next time I could do without the deadly toxins bit.

Nacy made us tea and something to eat, and we sat at the table discussing everything that had happened.

"I'd like to have seen the major's face when he realized that Ellie was likely in danger," Uncle Mick said to Nacy, a gleam in his eye. "The man who came to fetch Colm and me said the major swore a blue streak and took off like a bolt of lightning to come to her rescue."

"Our Ellie doesn't need rescue," Nacy said. Then she looked at me with twinkling eyes. "Of course, I wouldn't say no to being swept off my feet by a man like that."

"I'm sure Merriweather would be happy to oblige you," Colm said, and we all laughed as Nacy feigned indignation.

"Well, I suppose I'd better go home," Felix said, rubbing a hand across the bristles of stubble on his jaw. "I'm all in."

"I'll walk you out," I said, anxious to say a private goodbye.

Felix bid the family farewell, and the two of us left the house, stopping on the front porch. The scent of smoke still hung in the air, but there was blue sky visible, and I could hear birds singing. Life went on.

"Mick and Nacy seem rather keen on having the major for an in-law," Felix observed wryly.

"They're only teasing me because they know I find it irritating," I said.

He smiled, though there was the vaguest hint of disbelief in it. "Then you promise not to run away with him when I have to leave town again next week?"

I looked up at him, surprised. "Another job?"

"Yes, and, before you ask, I'm afraid I can't tell you about it."

I had the same troubling sensation I'd had upon his return from Scotland, the one that told me he was involved in something he shouldn't be. It wasn't like him to keep secrets from me. This was something more than a simple forgery job.

"Felix . . ."

"I won't be gone long," he said. "And when I get back, we'll go up to Lincolnshire, see if we can dig up Clarice Maynard."

He was trying to distract me, but it wasn't going to work. I was eager to contact Clarice Maynard to see what she might know about my mother, yes. But that mystery had gone unsolved this long. The possibility that Felix was putting himself in danger was a more immediate concern.

He chuckled suddenly. "Don't frown so, Ellie."

"I can't help it. I'm worried about you."

"There's no reason to fret, sweet," he said, his voice warm. "If this morning taught you anything, it should be that I'm a resilient chap."

I looked up at him, the proof of his words quite literally written across his features. I reached up to gently touch his bruised face. "I'm sorry you got the worst of it."

"No permanent damage done," he said lightly.

I didn't like to think of what had gone on in that cellar. Felix had battle scars enough. But he'd charged into battle again without a second thought. For me.

"Thank you for helping me, Felix," I said softly.

His dark eyes met mine. "You're marvelous, Ellie."

"I think you're pretty marvelous yourself."

We looked at each other for a long moment, and then he leaned down to kiss me gently.

I leaned into him, relishing the comfort of his kiss. And then I heard footsteps on the walk and looked up to see Major Ramsey approaching. He looked from one to the other of us, his expression unreadable.

"I beg your pardon," he said. "I didn't mean to interrupt."

"No apologies needed, Major," Felix said. "I'm just leaving."

Felix squeezed my hand and stepped down off the porch.

"I want to thank you for what you did today, Lacey," the major said. "If that German operative had gotten away with the film, it might have done considerable damage."

"Just following my commander's orders," Felix said with a wink at me. "But I'm always glad to do my part."

Major Ramsey nodded.

"I'll see you later, Ellie," Felix said.

"All right, Felix."

He left, and I turned to Major Ramsey. "Will you come in, Major?"

"I'm afraid I don't have time. I have a great deal of business to attend to, but the phone lines are down, and I wanted to let you know we've discovered a stash of papers in the boardinghouse. It's going to prove very useful information. This particular spy ring will no longer be cause for concern."

"I'm so glad."

"And I'm confident I'll be able to get more out of Cindy and the two others."

"Cindy's lucky she survived this," I said. "Mrs. Paine would no doubt have soon found reason to eliminate her as well. I hope she realizes it and proves useful to you."

He nodded. "She's already talked quite a bit, and I haven't even set Kimble on her yet."

I grimaced. Kimble would have Cindy singing like a bird with no trouble at all. He would terrify her out of her wits.

Once again, I couldn't help but feel a hint of sympathy for her. But, after all, she was getting through all this with her life. Myra Fields, Jane Kelley, and William Mondale had not been so lucky.

"Of all of Mrs. Paine's victims, I do feel a bit sorry for Myra Fields," I said. "What she did was wrong, of course, but she didn't deserve to die in that way. I think she got caught up in something she didn't fully understand. She was, at heart, a silly girl who wanted things she couldn't have and went the wrong way trying to get them."

"We all want things we can't have in life," Major Ramsey said. "That's why restraint is key."

Our eyes met, and I realized there was more to the words than what they meant on the surface.

But, whatever he was feeling, he hadn't come here to discuss it.

"You did good work, Miss McDonnell," he said in the tone he might have used to compliment one of the soldiers under his command.

"We all did good work together," I replied.

He nodded, his expression thawing ever so slightly. "It seems that our partnership has been more successful than I thought it might be from the start. I wouldn't have known where to get someone who could blow a vault at such short notice."

"I'm glad to hear you say so," I said with a smile. "One more victory to our credit."

"We've won this battle, but it's going to be a long war."

My brows flicked upward, my natural defiance in the face of opposition roused. "And we're ready to fight it."

His lips softened at the corners, not quite a smile, but almost. "Indeed we are."

He reached out a hand, and I placed mine in it. He held it for just a moment, something a bit more than a handshake but much less than a caress.

Then he released it and stepped back. "I'm sure I'll see you again soon, Miss McDonnell."

"Yes, Major," I said. "I'm sure you will."

He left, and I watched him until he had disappeared from view. Then my eyes rose to the horizon, to the clouds of smoke that still drifted up from the wreckage of last night's attack. We'd weathered two nights of an unimaginable storm, and something told me that there were darker days still ahead. But uncertainty was always a part of life, wasn't it?

I didn't know what the future would bring, but I knew one thing: we McDonnells would face it together.

Turning, I went back into the house to join my family.

ACKNOWLEDGMENTS

Once again, I find myself indebted to the many people who have helped me—and this book—along the journey to publication. All my heartfelt thanks:

To Ann Collette, the most amazing of agents, for her guidance and friendship.

To my brilliant editor, Catherine Richards, for always knowing what will make a story better and a plot tighter.

To Nettie Finn and the wonderful people at Minotaur for their invaluable efforts.

To my fellow Happy Nappers, Angela Larson and Kallyn Lagro, for both constant support and continual silliness.

To Jolie Dubriel for her timely solution to a sticky plot point.

And to my family and friends for everything they do daily.

Words are inadequate to express how much I appreciate you all!